KILLIN
A Superh

Tony Cooper

Second Edition

To Auntie Mary,
Love from Anthony
x

Cover by Harry Corr
harrycorr.co.uk

***

<u>Also in this series:</u>
POWERLESS

Tony

ACKNOWLEDGMENTS

Thanks to Lyn for actually marrying me!

Thanks to Sharron for making my sentences
make sense

PROLOGUE

They had picked out the old woman easily and had been following her for a few days now. They had watched where she went and who she met up with, and from that had found another couple of names that weren't on the list. She always shopped for her groceries at a small corner supermarket with only four aisles, one chest freezer, a small counter by the door and a lottery machine. Even though she was now much older than in the photo they had of her, her features were still strong and she did her hair the same way. Right now she was trying to decide between custard creams or a pack of chocolate-covered biscuits on offer, just past their sell-by date. Either would be fine with a cup of tea, she thought to herself, but it would depend if she was in a chocolatey mood or not. She fiddled with a ring on her finger, set with a black stone, while she tried to decide, tugging her sleeve down to hide the faint pink scarring on the back of her arm.

They had watched her go in and waited a minute before two of them followed her. All three knew their places and their roles. The tall one in the black hooded top found the aisle she was in and stood at the end of it. He turned away from her towards the newspapers, which lay on three white, angled metal shelves in front of the long windows. The one in the dark blue top knew from where his mate was standing which aisle she was in, and moved around to the other end. The one in the grey and white top was to come in after and keep the shopkeeper busy, while the other two, "got it done".

The guy in black scanned the headlines in front of him, something about a Hero being sentenced for murder, some red-headed old guy. He snorted and opened The Sun to page three where, "Melanie from Bristol", was worried that Hero Registration alone wasn't enough to stop these dangerous people from committing serious crimes.

"Not fucking Heroes," he muttered to himself and looked down the shop to the counter. Carl, the one in grey, had just come in the door. They glanced at each other, as Carl went up to the counter. The shopkeeper, a middle-aged Indian man wearing a pale blue turban, was busy sorting boxes and ticking things off a sheet behind the counter. A small girl with big auburn hair bustled back and forth through an open doorway to the back of the shop. Carl picked his time just as she disappeared.

"Twenty Bensons mate."

The man looked flustered as he dropped his list and turned to the curtains behind him.

"Hood down please."

"You what?"

"I said hood down. No hoods up in here, there's a poster up in the bloody door that tells you this. That goes for you too son…" he called out to the tall guy in black by the papers. The shopkeeper pulled back one curtain and grabbed the packet, while shaking his head. "Damn kids can't read nowadays."

The tall guy in black squeezed the round end of the baseball bat hidden up his baggy sleeve, while the one in dark blue, now waiting at the other end of the aisle, gripped the flick-knife inside his front pouch pocket. Carl turned and nodded at his friend, who left the 'paper open on the shelf and walked down the aisle and out of sight. Carl looked up from under his hood at the small TV on a shelf behind the counter showing four black and white scenes of the inside of the shop from different angles. He could see the two figures moving in on the old lady.

"I said drop the hood OK?" The shopkeeper slapped the packet down on the counter. "I'm not going to serve you if you don't. I don't have to you know, I've got the law on my side, OK?"

"Yeah, yeah, all right mate. Another pack of Bensons please."

The man scowled at him, leaning on the counter with both arms.

"Are you taking the piss yeah? I get your sort in here all the time and I know how to deal with you. Hood down or you're out!"

"Sure. Twenty Bensons please mate."

The man jerked up straight, cheeks flushed and lips twisted in anger.

"I said get that fucking hood down!" He reached over to flick Carl's hood back, but Carl was quicker. He grabbed the arm and pulled and twisted it towards him, making the guy bend forwards, then he slammed him down on the counter. The man cried out in pain as the side of his chest hit the counter hard. As he looked up from his pinned position he saw a knife pointed at his face.

"You do nothing mate."

The other two moved towards the old lady. She had finally decided to go with the chocolate biscuits, a nice treat with her tea. The money she saved would go towards a coffee and cake at Mandy's at the weekend. It was then she noticed a tall lad in a black hoodie close to her.

"Is everything...?"

"Catherine Forbes, yeah?"

"Well... yes, how do you know..."

The guy in black let the baseball bat slip out of his sleeve, catching it by the grip.

"We know everything you've done." He nodded to somewhere behind her left shoulder. Catherine turned round to see another, shorter lad in a blue top standing behind her. He pulled out the knife and flicked it open in front of her face as the guy in black took a swing.

"What are you guys up to?" asked the shopkeeper, as he lay stretched out over his counter. He was confused and worried, shoplifters didn't usually announce themselves and this guy wasn't interested in the till.

"You'll know," said Carl.

There was a shout. He assumed it was the old lady he'd seen coming in a few minutes ago. He heard her say, "What are you...", before she screamed again. He heard voices calling her terrible names, he heard the sickening crack of bone.

"Stop it ... ah!" cried the man, as Carl twisted his arm tight, making him bring his other arm over to clutch at his shoulder. The small girl appeared through the doorway with a cardboard box full of chocolate bars and a concerned look on her face. Carl pointed the knife at her.

"You! Get back in there now and stay there!"

She hovered for a second before running away. Carl started to get nervous. This was taking too long. How long could it take to beat up an old woman?

"Come on guys, we've got to..."

There was a roar, like an angry animal, but unmistakably human. Then there was a piercing screech of rending metal as the shelves around the central aisle were torn apart, flung away from each other. Packets and jars and bags were hurled in all directions, punching holes in the polystyrene ceiling tiles which shattered above them. Jars of curry sauce and bolognese barrelled through the outer two shelves, peppering Carl in the back of his body and head. He lost his grasp on the shopkeeper's arm as cans of lager thudded into the back of his knees, making him drop. He managed to stop himself falling to the ground by grasping onto the wooden surface like it was the edge of a cliff. Bottles of wine exploded on the counter around him as he closed his eyes and waited for everything to go quiet. He looked back and saw the air full of shredded food bouncing off the windows and walls.

"Jed!"

He scrambled to his feet and ran, almost slipping on spilt beetroot and pickled onions, to where the tall guy in black had landed on the racks of papers. He was clutching his back as he bent down to pick up the baseball bat.

The middle of the shop was now clear, the two sets of shelves that had been there were compressed against the outer ones. The shelf furthest from the counter had tipped over and crashed into the vegetables in the chilled cabinet. The guy in blue was lying on the ground at the back of the store groaning, half buried in cereals. The old lady was on her back on the floor in the middle of it all, propped up on one elbow. Blood seeped through the fingers of her hand holding her stomach. Her grey hair was wild in all directions, her eyes bright and bloodshot.

"You fucking bitch! You freak!" roared Jed, as he leapt forward past Carl and swung the bat down at her head. There was a crack and a squelch and all tension left her body. Her dented head dropped away from the bat and thudded against the floor as her arms flopped outwards. "Fucking freak!" He swung again and hit her face just under her left eye, with an even louder crack.

"Jed, let's go."

Jed was about to take another swing when Carl grabbed his arm.

"We got her! Let's go already!" He stepped over her and lifted the guy in blue off the floor from where he was looking for his knife. "Leave it, come on!" Carl pulled him past Jed and out the front door. Jed looked down at his handiwork. His shoulders relaxed as he stretched up taller. Blood dripped off the end of the bat as he turned to see the shopkeeper peering horrified over the top of the counter. Jed smiled and lifted the end of the bat so it pointed at him.

"Hero freaks must die!"

CHAPTER 1
BITTERFIELD INDUSTRIAL PARK

"Got any crisps?"

"Nope."

The street below them glowed a pastel orange as the street lamps illuminated the fine mist kicked up from the pouring rain. It was quiet apart from the white noise hiss, the cacophony of thousands of raindrops spatting off every surface. Martin blinked as a fat drop fell onto his eyelashes, making him attempt to squeeze his bulky frame even further under the shallow overhang. They were huddled together, him and Hayley pressed against the boarded-up loft windows of an old empty warehouse, five floors up on the roof. Martin had cramp in his thighs and a pain in one buttock as he sat, one foot out, bracing himself on a guttering of dubious solidity. His other arm grasped a metal bar, a part of the overhang above him.

Hayley seemed to be quite comfortable sitting squat, arms wrapped round her shins. She even swayed back and forth gently now and again, seemingly oblivious to the few centimetres between her feet and the drop to the pavement below. Martin had read about so-called, "free climbers", people with no powers who have such belief in their skills that they scale cliffs and skyscrapers with their bare hands and no safety line. The very idea terrified him. It was sheer recklessness. However good you thought you were, you always had to have a backup plan. Even when he was solo, before he joined The Pulse in the 'nineties, he would plan before a mission to make sure he never boxed himself in or took on more than he could deal with. There was always an escape route. He reckoned that Hayley must be so used to being able to teleport at will that she had lost that healthy fear of danger through knowing she could be anywhere else in a split-second. It was good to have that confidence, but he would have to keep an eye on her, to make sure she didn't put herself in danger unnecessarily. Not that he had seen anything like that yet. She was very keen to get into Heroics properly, willing to do anything he asked, and she had a cool head about her most of the time.

Probably being a police Constable helped. She had told him about the training they had to go through, all the different duties they performed, (most of which Martin would never have guessed), and all the strange and sobering things she had witnessed in the three years she had been doing it. There was no room for recklessness in that job, it was all about rules and procedures, and putting the safety of others first.

But she hadn't yet been in the heat of action. Aside from giving muggers and drug dealers surprise meetings with walls, she hadn't actively gone up against a serious opponent, particularly a Hero. Martin didn't know how she would behave in such a situation, and that meant he had to train her, contrary to his own best advice to himself. Then again, he'd been out of a job since he was outed as a Hero at the end of last year and, despite his best efforts to try to return to a normal life, Hayley had been persistently insistent about what he needed to do. She had saved his life twice after all, so he owed her that much, but none of this had been in his plans for his middle years. Well, they hadn't been particularly detailed or exciting plans anyway, but then that was the point. A quiet life, a bit of security work here, a few cans of beer in his flat there, and nothing much of interest in between.

Hayley suddenly leaned forwards over the edge of the roof. Martin winced. There was a dark car coming towards them, tyres tearing through the water on the road. It was impossible to see any details at this time of night, especially through the spray. The car didn't slow down and drove on past. Hayley pulled herself back, the edge of her hood now wet and drooping onto her forehead. Her costume wasn't anything fancy or custom-made. Fancy meant too easily traceable from CCTV analysis, while custom-made took a lot of time and mistakes, and time wasn't something they had a lot of tonight. She had grabbed an old hoodie, a pair of PVC trousers and some heavy black boots that reminded him of the old Doc Martens from the 'eighties. His original costume had been so utterly ruined, that night back in September, that in the end he ripped it into pieces and burned it. The charred remains went in a black bag and were dumped in a cauldron bin round the back of a supermarket. No great ceremony for the past. No great memories from it. It was too recognisable as a signature costume anyway, useless now that his identity was public knowledge. His replacement was a black leather bikers' jacket, (bought from a charity shop years ago), a knitted balaclava, a pair of dark brown waxed workman's trousers and his old boots, the only useful item from his past. One boot was now utterly sodden.

"Any biscuits?"

"Nope."

The noise of the car blended into the hiss of the rain as Martin felt his back go stiff.

Hayley had discovered information during one of her, "unofficial", night-shifts about a group of thieves targeting office supplies. Martin initially laughed it off, cracking a joke about, "very well organised crime", that didn't seem to go down too well. He regretted his levity when Hayley said they had already stolen goods worth over forty thousand pounds in the last few months alone.

"Never underestimate the market for stuff you don't think about or you take for granted. Big companies spend thousands every year on stationery and other consumables. Trust me, it's huge."

Martin knew that Hayley was in a bit of a situation. Nobody with powers is allowed to join the police force, or any emergency service for that matter, and being a Hero and patrolling the streets means you inevitably come across information that the police would find very useful. Too worried about her voice being recognised if she called in a tip-off, or someone tracing an email or text back to her, she always had to try and deal with the situation herself. It was the larger stuff she knew she couldn't take on alone, the gangs, the drugs, the powered crime. That frustrated her. She knew stuff that her colleagues didn't, but couldn't tell them, and she was powerless to sort it out alone. She felt she was betraying her force and herself, but now that she had found Martin, "that was all going to change", apparently. Martin had smiled weakly at the time, wishing himself somewhere else, wondering how far she thought this partnership would go. Then he felt guilty for feeling exasperated with her, after all, she had saved his life. Twice.

She had told him that she knew where the group held the stolen goods before they were moved across the country in a small fleet of vans. There were six guys, no firearms she knew of, very careful people. She had laid out surveillance photos of the warehouse on her kitchen table and pointed to all the entrances, adding a rough marker pen drawing of the internal layout. As they sat drinking tea she had told him of her plan of attack. Instantly he had disagreed with her, pointing out the weaknesses, the blind-spots she hadn't thought about.

At first he was worried she would take offence at him suddenly butting in, but instead she was rapt, eyeing him intently, nodding, both hands curled round her mug. She was taking everything in like a good student. Did that make him her teacher? Her mentor? He supposed it did, and he wasn't yet sure how that made him feel. What he was worried about was how easy this came back to him. It had been nearly two decades since he had been part of a team but here he was, plotting entry and exit points, lines of sight, kill-zones, cover locations. He identified where the targets would most likely be, where they would be themselves and their path and timing through the inside, and alternate scenarios if the men were armed, ran, or stayed to fight. Within half an hour they had a detailed plan and that's when Martin realised he had just talked himself into it. He had sighed and finished his tea as Hayley stared at the photos with a huge grin on her face.

He wished he had a cup of tea now. Anything warm. They had been cooped up here for nearly fifty minutes. The vans were supposed to have arrived twenty minutes ago. The goods were being shipped up to Leeds and Manchester overnight, two big orders. It looked like the stationery business was moving! Martin kept that joke to himself. His mind had begun to wander when one of the men appeared from a small door at the front of the building, mobile phone pressed up against his ear. He pulled the hood of his jacket over his head and stood, sheltering under a corrugated iron awning.

"Here we go."

Two white unmarked Ford Transits sped up the road from where the earlier car had disappeared. Martin could see the face of the driver at the front, illuminated by the pale blue glow of a phone as he drove with one hand. The man waiting put his phone away and jogged up to the gates as the vans pulled up. After a minor struggle with the lock, he opened the gates and the vans drove through, driving down the side of the building to two large shutters. Closing the front gates, the man ran down to meet them as the drivers hopped out, clutching jackets around their chests. There was a short moment of waving hands and a loud conversation that they only caught bits of, before the gate-opener banged on the shutter near him. As they waited, one of the drivers lit up a cigarette. The gate man slapped it out of his hands, pointing at the shutters, then the van. The hand waving began again.

"At least it's not just us that's pissed off they're late." Martin observed.

"We wait until they're all inside yeah?"

"Yeah. You got the knife?" Hayley tapped her hoodie pocket. "OK. I think we're ready." There was a harsh rasping sound as the shutter opened on a chain. The three men ducked under it when it reached waist height.

"Now!"

Hayley squeezed his shoulder and in a soft huff of air they were gone from the roof.

CHAPTER 2
RANDALL FAMILY HOME

Taking a child from its family was difficult. It wasn't an easy decision to have to make in the first place and it always turned out to be emotional, and often confrontational, when it came to physically taking the child into Care. It could be especially dangerous when one or both parents were powered. Eleanor had personal experience of that in her past, an old scar on her upper left arm was evidence of it. Luckily the scar was high up enough to be hidden under short-sleeved tops, and only her close family and immediate boss knew of it. Sometimes, rarely, the scar would give a twinge and she would rub it with her palm, while remembering how her then-husband tried to stop her going back to work, "Why are you helping those weirdos when they could kill you any minute? They need putting down they do!" he would say. "I told you they're all no good", her mother would add. "I don't want you to come back from work dead, Mum!", said her son.

None of them really understood. It wasn't that she liked Heroes or thought anything in particular about them, it was always about the children, about the point of greatest need. When she started work in the Department she quickly saw that children with powers needed the most help.

Raising a child the right way was difficult enough. Eleanor had learned that the hard way too. It was even harder to raise children with an ability that could see them ostracised, isolated or end up hurting someone by accident. It was her job to prevent accidental injuries by helping the whole family to get all of the support they needed, from counselling and attending Ability Monitoring Centres, to benefits and any housing modifications or specialised equipment. Sometimes no amount of support would help, and you could often tell that the moment you walked in the door. When you saw the lack of a child's drawings on the walls or fridge, or the knee high grass threading its way through the carcasses of broken bicycles and shopping trolleys out back, or the physical distance kept between parent and child. Then there was the knotted expression of concern on their faces, hoping that their, "problem", would be taken away there and then.

Having said that, you should not pre-judge families based on an initial report, or a glance around their house. What things looked like on paper didn't always translate to the real world. She knew that from her experience too, all twenty three years of it. Whenever the Department took on a new CPO it was drummed into them that they leave their personal biases and beliefs at the door. There were set processes to follow, facts that must be discovered and recorded, there was accountability for all decisions you made and no final decision was made alone. The reason she had stayed in the job for so long, the reason she had refused promotion to management despite hitting forty eight last year, the reason she had the highest long-term success rate in the Department, was because she was good at her job. She was good at spotting the missing drawings, the long grass, the silent glances between parents during her interviews. She knew when to take a child and when to leave them, how much support was needed and when. She always followed up and always put the child's needs first.

Right now she was parked in front of a house taking one last review of the case notes before she went in. The child in question was a ten month old boy called Lewis. His parents were Jenny Crossdale and Ian Randall, a registered power. He was a PMA, a Physically Manifested Ability, or, to put it less euphemistically, his innate ability had deformed his body. Eleanor rolled in her bottom lip and bit it. The family would already be isolated from the rest of the community and would be incredibly suspicious and mistrusting of anyone, especially of her. This was going to need a gentle approach from the start.

She was glad she had declined the offer of a chaperone. Making any connection with the family was going to be hard enough without a six foot bodyguard standing in the room, "just in case". That was anticipating violence before you had even started talking. No, she was to go in alone, vulnerable. That in itself showed trust and was often enough to disarm the most defensive of families expecting a small army of faceless authority figures to barge in and kidnap their child.

She scanned down the page. The father had been an active villain in the late 1980s, many brushes with the law and other Hero teams, nine years prison time in total for a mixture of thefts, assaults, damage to public property etc. A fairly standard list of sentences from that era. All historical Hero-on-Hero attacks and deaths had, however, been expunged from the records when the Registration Act came into force, so she had no idea how violent he had been prior to that. Hero history remained classified. Eleanor was OK with that. The main point was that he had no criminal history from *after* the Act came in. He had attended the full reintegration course and was still going to regular counselling sessions. He had made a clear effort to change his ways and rejoin society, which offered some hope for the stability of the family unit and the child's future.

Over the page there was a short note on how the child came to their attention, being reported by neighbours after the baby displayed powers outside the local shops. The mother panicked and ran off with the child, screaming to be left alone.

Eleanor was the one who got the report. She contacted them by phone. She spoke to the mother first, (the father was out), and after some convincing the mother eventually agreed to a home visit. As expected, she got a call back a few hours later from the father. She then had a similar, rather more heated conversation, where she had to explain, as non-confrontationally as possible, that the alternatives to a voluntary assessment would be even less welcome. He agreed to the visit, angrier with the neighbours than her it seemed.

She grabbed the cardboard cup of tea from the holder on top of the dashboard and almost took a sip before she realised it was cold now. She opened the car door a notch and poured the drink into the gutter, before slipping the cup back in the plastic ring for recycling later. She checked her reflection in the rear view mirror, tidying some stray ends of her large auburn curls, and got out of the car with her notes in a black binder under her arm. She sniffed the crisp air, a mixture of grass and cooking smells from open windows.

The family lived in a mid-terraced house in the Mellfields area of the City. Not a bad area. It was once its own village but had been swallowed up into a suburb as the City expanded in the 'seventies. There were lots of grassy verges and pebble-dashed walls. It was now a mix of social and private housing. The Randall's Council house had new windows, but still suffered from a stubbly, dilapidated pebble-dashed exterior, despite having had a coat of paint in the last few years. The front garden was clean, not especially well looked after, but presentable. Net curtains were pulled across the windows for privacy. Eleanor could make out shadows of someone sitting inside and saw movement as she approached. The front door was old, painted over multiple times with different knocks and bangs having exposed a kaleidoscope of Council colour schemes. There was a clean oblong mark in the paint on the wall where she guessed a doorbell had been. She knocked gently under the warped glass semi-circle and waited.

Suddenly the fractured light in the glass turned dark as a large figure stepped out of the living room and into the hallway. The glass became inkier as the figure approached, only vague suggestions of a face and shoulders swirling in it. Eleanor tugged on the end of the tissue thin beige and white scarf round her neck, flattening the end out, then scrunching it up and adjusting her jacket. The door was unlocked, a safety chain undone, and the door opened.

The file hadn't detailed the father's PMA beyond, "enhanced strength and reflexes resulting from muscle and bony growth deformation". It didn't do the reality justice. Ian Randall was verging on seven feet tall and four feet wide. His bones had overgrown, but unlike the condition acromegaly, where the face, hands and feet are enlarged, the rest of his body had grown to accommodate the new structure. His heavy musculature dominated his outline, even in the loose sports top and pants he was wearing. His face looked like it had been hammered into shape from an iron block by an amateur sculptor. His large, dark eyes stared like unflinching CCTV cameras. Although he was more or less in proportion, he looked uncomfortable standing, as if his muscle mass couldn't work out the best way to keep him upright.

"My name is Eleanor Cheadham, I'm from Element City Council Child Services De…"

"I can't lie, I'm not pleased you're here." When he spoke it was deep, not overly so, and with a slight Northern twang.

"Ian!", came a sharp voice from inside the house.

"But, if this has to be done, it has to be done" he sighed. "Come in." He stepped aside and gestured to the open door on the left of the hallway. It was then that Eleanor noticed how large his hands were, even for his bulk, with walnut-sized knuckles straining to get out from under his flesh. His fingers must have been twice as long as her hands, the skin pulled tight, pale and shiny across the elongated bone underneath that tapered to pointed ends. They looked hardened. Sharp.

"Thank you." She deliberately didn't pull away from him as she walked past. A confident and controlled walk, to show she was strong yet humble in their home.

There was the smell of a flowery air freshener as she looked round the doorway and saw Jenny sitting on the sofa holding the child in her arms. She was an average, plain, round-faced girl, hair tied back in a pony-tail. Quite dumpy Eleanor thought, a couple of small tyres of fat visible under her burgundy polo-neck knitted jumper, her dark leggings tight around her thighs. Eleanor was slightly shocked that the girl was so young; there must have been at least fifteen years between her and Ian. Lewis was on her lap facing her, fingers in his mouth and staring at his mother with big brown eyes, as she flattened down thick wisps of dark hair on his head. He was wearing a romper suit and his tiny feet in little white socks poked out of the ends and twitched as they hung either side of his mother's thighs.

"Hello", she said, not standing up.

She wasn't intending to be rude. Eleanor could tell the girl just didn't know quite what to do.

She felt Ian fill the doorway behind her.

"You can sit anywhere you like, as long as it's the chair."

There was only the two-seater sofa and the chair in the room to sit on, along with a folding table opened up under the window. A small flat-screen TV sat on a white wheeled trolley. The table was covered in an old, cream coloured lacy cloth. A play mat lay against the wall adjoining the hallway, with big coloured numbers dotted around the edges and cartoon animals dancing across the middle. A handful of toys, cars and soft animals, lay scattered across it.

Eleanor walked over to the chair. Looking out the window she could already see interest from the neighbours, one lady standing at her door looking over and a couple of kids on bicycles eyeing her car as they rode in circles across the road. She sat down, tucking the sides of her skirt under her legs and placed her binder on her lap.

They were both nervous. She could see Jenny was trembling and Ian looked awkward. Actually no, they would be terrified. To them she represented the people who could take your child from you. Although that was by far the worst-case scenario, the option of last resort, it was a possibility, and that was all that mattered. With his past history and lack of work, and the fact she was a first time mum on benefits, they must have feared the worst since they got the phone call. She waited until Ian had sat down next to Jenny. He moved oddly and she could sense some pain in his face. The old white leather sofa was almost flattened at that end and surrendered to his weight easily.

"Right, thank you both for seeing me and letting me see your son. My name is Eleanor Cheadham and I'm a Senior Child Protection Officer for Element City Council. First things first, I'm not here to take Lewis away. That's not how this works. I'm here to find out about Lewis and about yourselves and about how you're both coping with him, because as I said on the phone it has come to our attention that he is displaying innate abilities." Ian's face tightened. "Now any time a child under the age of sixteen displays abilities we have to become involved. While it's most common to start manifesting abilities during adolescence and early adulthood, sometimes they appear at Lewis'ss age. In these cases we become involved in assessing the child, to ensure that they aren't a danger to themselves or anyone else, and we also want to ensure that you are properly equipped to look after them. So… how did you two meet?"

"You mean you think this is wrong? The two of us?"

"Ian!"

Lewis tilted his head backward to look up at his mum.

"Not at all, Mr Randall. If I did I would hardly have chosen this job would I?" Eleanor smiled.

Ian's eyes looked to the side while he thought about this. After a while he nodded.

"Fair enough."

"We met three years ago, not long after you got out of prison wasn't it?" said Jenny.

"Yep."

"He was going to this group for Heroes who have been to prison, you know, to give them skills to find work. Rebilitate them?" Ian gave a little smile to himself as Jenny got the word wrong, but he didn't correct her. "He wasn't living in the area then, you were in a hostel the other side of town weren't you? But the Centre is just up the road from here and I bumped into him in the supermarket while I was out shopping for my mum." They looked at each other and she smiled.

"It was love at first sight weren't it?"

"Yep."

"It was kind of a like a beauty and the beast thing you know? I know he hates me saying that but he was my secret Prince and now we've got a beautiful boy, and we couldn't be happier."

"That's lovely," said Eleanor, "so when did you move in together?"

"Not long after she got pregnant. Her mother's place was tiny so we applied to the Council for a place together and were really lucky to get one in the same area."

"Oh it's so handy for me seeing Mum."

"So that was the end of last year?" They nodded. "And you're settling in fine?"

"Yeah. Not done much to the place but can't really, not much cash you know what I mean? We've got the Child Benefit and I'm on Job Seekers... no, what's it called now? Employment Support! That's it... but I've got the chance of some work coming up. A builder who don't mind the likes of me, or my record. That's bloody hard to find I can tell you. They're just waiting on a contract to come through... haven't got enough work to take me on right now is the problem."

"Believe me, I know how hard it is for powered people to find work. I see it all the time. Unfortunately it's not something I can help with, as my main focus is Lewis, but we do take into account the difficulties and very often the discrimination involved."

"Uh-huh. You got that right."

"So how is Lewis? He looks happy there on your knee."

"Oh he's fine. Gives us a few sleepless nights, but we're lucky, he's a lovely boy."

"Do you have a health visitor?"

"Yeah, she says he's a little light and small for his age but he's been real healthy. Just a bad cold when he was four months, but he got over that. He's a little fighter, like his Dad."

Ian laughed and rubbed the top of Lewis's head with a knuckle, his claws carefully bent all the way under his forearm.

"So when did you first notice that he had abilities?" They both visibly tensed. "Don't worry, it's not some trick question to get you to incriminate yourselves. Sometimes it takes years for parents to come to us about their son or daughter and that's fine. You haven't broken the law, and there's no penalty the longer you leave it. The important thing is you are telling us now. That's all that matters."

Ian sighed.

"Well you saw it first didn't you darling?"

"Yeah."

Jenny bit her top lip and looked down.

"It were dead scary. He was, what, six months?"

"About that."

"I'd just changed him upstairs and put him down on the floor while I went to get rid of the nappy. As I was coming back I picked up his favourite toy off the floor on the landing to give to him, but when I came back in, he already had it." Eleanor was sure the girl was confused and hadn't got her words right, but Ian didn't correct her. They both sat there looking at Lewis as he tugged at the front of his romper suit. "Do you want us to show you?"

"If it's possible to? I know children, it's difficult to get them to do what you want at the best of times…"

They both smiled. They seemed more relaxed now.

Jenny nodded at Ian and he picked up a small cloth toy on the table next to him. It was some kind of off-white rabbit with blue ears, bright pink nose and a green tail. It looked like it had already had a lot of love.

"His favourite", smiled Ian, seeming to read her thoughts, and handed it to Lewis. The boy immediately grabbed it with both hands. He shook it up and down, entranced by the thin ears flapping around, then bounced up and down in happiness as he looked up at Eleanor.

"Da! Wabwa." he pointed at her.

She smiled back at him.

"Do you like your toy? What's he called?"

"Mr Bunny."

"Found it in a charity shop in town."

"Well he's lovely isn't he? Is he your favourite?" Eleanor grinned at the boy. He seemed to come over shy and hid his face behind the bunny, one eye poking round the side of its head. Then he burst into babble and the toy went flying over his head as his arms swung around. It softly hit the wall and dropped down behind the sofa.

"Here we go." said Ian.

Eleanor found herself sitting forwards.

"Oh! Where's Mr Bunny gone?" said Jenny, tilting her head round to look at him. Lewis seemed puzzled for a minute, then stared at his hands. "Where's Mr Bunny?" His eyes went wide as he became very still. Both he and Eleanor were caught in time, waiting. Then, in the palm of his hands a small ball of material started to appear out of the air. Eleanor pressed her glasses closer to her face and leant in. It was white, blue and green and was twisting around like one of those motorised ball toys that roll themselves around the floor, often with some fluffy animal attached by its nose. She tried to make out detail but it was too small, indistinct, always moving and out of focus. Lewis grunted. Suddenly it unfolded like a cloth explosion and a pair of blue ears dropped over the sides of his hands. He clutched it, smiling again, and instantly put the head in his mouth. Eleanor realised she had been holding her breath and took a large gulp in.

"So... he... teleported it?"

"Oh no, he made it!"

"Made?"

"Yeah." Ian reached one of his long arms down the back of the sofa. He pulled out the original Mr Bunny and shook it. "The other one's still here." Eleanor felt light, like a part of her had been taken away.

"He can make anything", said Jenny. "Toys mostly, of course. He gets a bit confused when you show him the original ones, or earlier ones, whatever you'd call them. He gets distressed, like he's not sure what to make of them any more."

Ian dropped the first Mr Bunny back down behind the sofa.

"So best not show him that," he said, smiling. "We've got dozens of the fuckin' things shoved in a cupboard upstairs, he just keeps making one when he needs one!"

Eleanor's throat was dry.

"And, he can do this with anything at all? Just... create it out of thin air?"

"No, he has to hold it and chew at it first, get to know it I suppose. After that, yeah. I guess as he gets older he could do bigger stuff, but it's just toys at the moment. He made a copy of my purse once! He was playing with it on the floor, and I took it off him in case he swallowed any coins you know, then the next thing, I looked back and there was another one! It opened, but it wasn't quite right inside, no pockets and it was empty."

"We haven't had him making money, if that's what you're thinking." It wasn't the first thing on Eleanor's mind, but Ian had a point. "We both know that would be wrong, and we just wouldn't do it. It would be abuse wouldn't it? Using a child like that?" He seemed to sense the atmosphere had become tense and made an awkward smile. "Anyway, if we *had* been doing that we wouldn't still be living here, would we?"

Jenny laughed.

"No, we wouldn't, eh?" and she bounced Lewis on her knees as he chewed the new toy intently, staring at Eleanor.

Eleanor tried a smile, but her mind was racing. Did these two have any idea how incredibly powerful their son was? Were they oblivious or actually very, very aware and trying to put a front on it? Did they know how much care he would need growing up, so that he wouldn't be taken advantage of? There had been no recorded Hero with the ability to create matter since The Elemental himself, the Hero who founded Element City. The Hero who could create anything he wanted through sheer will alone. Arguably the first commonly known Hero in the country, he was held up to be the ideal of how a Hero should behave, how they should use their abilities for the good of others. There had been no-one like him since. Until now. Until this small child in the arms of a girl too young to have this responsibility, fathered by a troubled ex-offender too unpredictable to give him the stability and care he would need.

No! She was thinking wrong. She had to remain objective. Think of the boy. Her mind swirled with possible future care routes, dozens of complications and considerations, guidelines for Special Powered Services involvement and more, but she couldn't focus her thoughts. She couldn't come to terms with the fact she had just seen a ten month old boy create something from nothing through sheer force of will. Her heart was twisting in her chest and her own words blurred on the cover of the binder on her lap. She had to get out of there; she just couldn't make sense of things right now. She stood up quickly and made to leave. Ian stood up too, his sudden size startling her.

"Is everything all right?"

"Yes. Yes, fine. I have everything I need to… make a decision… there is a Departmental meeting tomorrow, I'll present your case and we'll decide what… decision… he will need a formal assessment of his abilities so we know what… what we can do for you." She started to gather herself. "No need to be concerned about anything, this is all procedure and paperwork at this stage and you will both be fully involved in any decisions we make."

"About what?" Jenny looked worried.

"Support. What support we can give you. Financial, housing modifications, any training you might need to help… Look, he seems a lovely, happy boy, but surely you see yourselves that in the years to come it is going to be… challenging, bringing him up?"

Ian and Jenny looked at each other quietly.

"And that's what we're here for, to find out now how we can help you in the future. But I have to go right now..." she lied, "...I have another visit to do" she lied again. She just wanted out.

"Sure." Ian took some effort to manoeuvre out of her way. She hurried past him and into the hallway.

'Don't run, just look busy' she thought to herself as she slid the latch and turned the handle on the front door. The crisp air hit her as she stepped outside and she felt tearful with relief.

She blinked the water away and turned round to see Ian and Jenny in the hallway. Lewis sat across her hip, pulling a rabbit ear with his teeth.

"I will be in touch. Next time I may see you here or you may get an appointment to go to the Child Services Department. If you do, don't worry, it just means more paperwork is involved."

"OK."

"Lovely to see you all. Bye."

"Bye."

The door took some time to close behind her as she walked down the path, very deliberately avoided fumbling her keys and got in her car. She put the binder on the passenger seat and had to take a minute to slow down her breathing. In the quiet she was suddenly aware her heart was pounding. Checking the rear view mirror, she saw her forehead was knotted and she was flushed. She felt her arms trembling too.

"Damn!" she thought to herself, as she gripped the bottom of the steering wheel hard. As she regained her composure, the loose thoughts and procedures in her head started to settle down and knit together into a coherent plan. She knew who would need to be informed, what decisions lay ahead and what they would be. She looked back at the house, trying to discern shapes through the netting, trying to see something that would make this decision go any other way, but she couldn't. That child was going to need all the help it could get.

CHAPTER 3
BITTERFIELD INDUSTRIAL PARK

The spray mist smelt of concrete and rust. The rain itself sounded louder down here than on the rooftop, or maybe he'd just got used to the sound up there. It was like having a thick coat of noise hung over his shoulders as he hugged the brick wall next to the open shutter. Over by the two white vans Martin saw little spray clouds suddenly appear and disappear at each of their four corners. Then Hayley was back next to him, knife in hand.

"Tyres done," she whispered, "they're not going anywhere tonight" and she folded the knife up and put it back in her pocket.

"OK, quick scan."

Hayley nodded and was gone, teleporting to the position on the internal walkway she had found earlier.

Martin could just make out voices from inside, but only because they seemed to be having an argument. He took a quick peek around the corner. Some lights were on that illuminated rows of empty metal shelving and beyond them, darkness. Nearer to him there were some large cardboard boxes, a utility knife sat on one of them, a pile of scrunched up cling-film on the floor. He squinted and peered up towards the roof where a faint silver glow barely penetrated through the few small windows dotted across it. He couldn't see Hayley, but knew she'd be up there.

"I got two.."

"JEE!... sus..." No, she was back here.

"Oh sorry, thought you heard me."

"Can't hear a damn thing in this rain... you were saying?"

"Yeah, two drivers and another guy having a major argument, about twenty metres inside and to the right. There are another two standing on a walkway ten metres beyond them, watching the argument. One more on the top walkway looking down at all five of them, and the light's on in the office, top floor. I can't see in, but I heard a voice, so at least one more I reckon."

"Good. Get that guy up top while I sort the nearest three and we'll meet in the middle for the other two before we..."

"What the fuck?"

Martin and Hayley turned to see one of the drivers standing next to them holding a cigarette with a look of astonishment on his face. Their three brains spent the next one-and-a-half seconds trying to unwind and reconstruct the situation before Martin cut his short and quickly back-fisted the guy in the side of the head. He disappeared sideways into the warehouse.

"GO!"

Hayley jumped as Martin swung around the corner into the building. Inside smelt of warmth and cardboard, and Martin could clearly see the steps and walkways up towards the offices behind the four confused men, one of whom was now halfway to the open shutters, looking at the unconscious body of his partner still sliding across the floor. Martin went for the boxes, grabbed one and flung it at the nearest guy; it hit him edge on in the chest and face. As the man crumpled to the ground there was a distant yelp from somewhere above him. Martin felt a shiver of panic before he registered it was a male voice. Now there was more confusion for the robbers. The third guy nearest to him, the other one of the drivers, almost tripped over his own feet as he ran away towards the steps up to the other two men. Martin was about to chase after him until he spotted one of them, in a black jacket, pick up a crowbar and vault over the railing down to the warehouse floor. His head was almost clean shaven apart from a thin coating of hair bristle and a short goatee. He tossed the crowbar in his hand, as if gauging the weight of it and walked towards Martin, knees slightly bent.

He was probably not going to be a problem thought Martin, as he squared up to him, but you just never could tell. There was some yelling and fighting noise to his right, but he had to ignore that for now. The guy broke into a sprint and swung the crowbar down onto Martin's head. Seconds later a slightly bent crowbar clattered across the floor, his attacker clutching his stinging forearms in surprise. Martin tapped his balaclava.

"I'm not wearing this because I've got dandruff you know." Martin took a large lunge forward and planted a palm into the guy's face. He landed sideways into the end of a shelf and ended up spread out on his back. Now Martin turned his head and saw Hayley delivering an elbow to the face of the guy's mate. He dropped to his knees and slid onto his side against the railing. They both heard frantic footsteps pattering above them. The other driver was crying as he ran up to the office. Hayley suddenly jumped up to him.

"Hayl...", Martin bit his tongue, "Hey! Wait." He ran up the few steps to the first walkway then to the set of stairs that led up to the office. He could hear fighting and a man groaning and shouting in pain. When he got to the top Hayley had already dispatched him and he lay against the wall under one of the office windows.

"What did I say? Don't go off on your own towards the point of lowest visibility. At the start, separate, at the end, together, yes?"

Hayley looked sheepish.

"Sorry."

"Don't be. Be sensible and keep yourself safe. Now, one way in...", Martin pointed to the faded turquoise door next to the window. All the windows, one on the side by the steps, two at the front overlooking the racks of storage and one on the other side, were blocked by thin horizontal blinds that only let a filtered orange light bleed out. Hayley ran to the door and waited as Martin crept round the front. He gave a thumbs up signal to her and tried to peer round the sides of the blinds. He could make out a guy standing near the window, behind a desk.

"Time to give yourselves up to the Justice Squad before you end up like your friends!"

Martin looked back round the corner at Hayley, mouthing, "Justice Squad?"

Hayley shrugged.

"Shit!"

Gunshots. Wood splinters exploded from the door as Hayley instinctively jumped somewhere safe. Martin moved round to the window again and could see the back of the shooter, he was focused on the door. This had to end quickly. Martin punched through the window, splitting the blinds, and grabbed the guy round his neck. He tried to turn his arm round, firing a couple of wild shots into the wall and ceiling, but Martin quickly threw him forwards. The edge of the desk buried itself in his stomach and he folded in half, his face bouncing off a computer keyboard before he slid down onto the ground. Martin punched out the rest of the window with his forearm and stepped through, ripping the blinds away from their fixings so that they fell noisily into a heap amid the broken glass. Hayley had already jumped back in and was the other side of the desk holding a handgun by one finger under the trigger guard.

"Weapon secured."

Martin nodded and looked down at the shooter. He was out cold, "K" and "[" computer keys stuck in his forehead.

"Time to call the police, but not before we've had a chat with Mr K here."

"I'll find some rope or something."

"Doesn't have to be…"

She was already gone.

***

"You still seem to be failing to understand your situation Mr K. You're not in much of a position to argue right now." The man was tied to his chair in the middle of the office with rope around his wrists and ankles. He occasionally struggled to free his hands but had such a head and stomach ache he could barely muster the effort, so he sat doubled over, head dropped, keyboard shapes firmly imprinted on his forehead. Martin and Hayley stood side-by-side in front of him, arms crossed, serious faces.

"But I don't know any more. I promise. This is all there is apart from Isaac, the other driver in London. I don't know about any other gangs or criminals. I didn't even want to do this." He shook his head until his swaying brain hurt too much.

"Look, we don't take kindly to your kind of well-organised crime. If there is anything you know it will help you in the long run if you tell us."

Martin looked at Hayley.

"Oh, so… I get the evils when I make that joke but it's OK for you to use it?"

"Female privilege. And besides, one of us has actually got to be funny."

"Who the hell are you guys anyway, I thought Hero teams were illegal?"

"Yeah, what was that with, 'Justice Squad'?"

Hayley turned to face Martin, sweeping her arms open.

"I had to think of something."

"You haven't got a name?"

"We're... er, new on the scene."

"Oh great, just my luck to be done over by a couple of new Heroes."

"Excuse me, I've been doing this for years. She's the new one."

"A daddy and daughter team? Christ. Even better."

"He's not my dad, he's just very old. And very cranky. You've seen what he can do when he's cranky, so best not upset him even more and just tell us what you know Mr K?"

"Why do you keep calling me that? My name's Malcolm. I swear, this whole thing wasn't even my idea. My wife works for an estate agents and kept telling me about the amount of paper and supplies they go through and kept asking me if I could get stuff on the cheap, because I used to run a market stall, you know? Anyway I ask around and get her some and then I've met a guy who knows a guy who has some stock but they need more and before I know it I'm organising a whole team and shipping stolen goods around the country! All I wanted was some folders and a few boxes of photocopier paper. It just... got out of hand."

"It certainly did when you started shooting at us."

Malcolm sat up with a jolt, then winced as his stomach rippled angrily.

"I panicked! I'm sorry. Are you all right? I don't want to hurt anyone. I've never even fired the thing before! It was given to me as a 'gift' by that guy I mentioned, for the work I'd done."

"I would have swapped it for a lava lamp personally," advised Hayley. "Does this 'guy' have a name?"

Malcolm bent his head down as the pounding tried to squeeze his eyeballs out of their sockets.

"Aah… damn it. OK. Please, just don't tell him it was me who told you."

"Mum's the word."

"They call him Fitz. Well, his buddies do, everyone else calls him Mr Fitzpatrick. You only get to see him if he wants you to. He doesn't seem to have an office or anything, you always meet him in his car. You drive around while you talk then he drops you off. Always on the phone. Always business."

"What kind of car?"

"A black one."

"That… doesn't help much."

"Ah a… a limo or something? It's got those seats in the back that face each other. Really expensive. I don't know the reg."

"OK, that's something to go on." Hayley bent forward to level her face with Malcolm's, resting her hands on her knees. "On behalf of Element City, we would like to thank you for your cooperation. But for the moment Mr K, you, like your stationery business, are going nowhere."

"Because it's stationary."

"Yep, that was the joke you just explained Dad. Well done."

"Well I don't know when I am allowed to use jokes or not, so I thought I might as well chip in."

"Yeah, but you don't do that. That's like just saying, 'Paper trail!', or, 'In a bind!', out loud and expecting it to be funny."

Martin thought for a moment.

"In the sheet?"

Hayley looked at him blankly then started to smile.

"Heh, that one's actually quite good."

Malcolm studied them intently, eyebrows raised.

"You guys are insane. Certifiably insane. I want the police now please."

CHAPTER 4
THE CHURCH OF THE NEW GODS

It was a bright, but cold Sunday. The last few hurried towards the narrow door, buzzing with excitement. Some nodded to each other in recognition, but there was little talk as they fell into single file to get inside. On entering, one of two people either side of the doorway handed them a small home-printed pamphlet. Most people took one from the smiling girl on the right. Her thick, dyed black hair was pulled back from her forehead and was tied, with a dark purple band on the top of her scalp, into a short spray of a ponytail. Two strands of hair hung free by her temples. Other than a nose ring she was plain-faced, with rounded out cheeks and a pointed chin, slightly scarred by acne that had never left her since her school days. She wore grey and blue flowery patterned leggings and a close fitting black jumper that stretched out over the shelf of her bosom. Periodically, and self-consciously, she tugged the front of the jumper back up towards her neck. She smiled with her mouth closed, the corners tightening together, lips buckling into an irregular shape, and said, "hello", to everyone who came in.

The black guy on the left of the door was well over six feet tall, even with his shaven head. He was thin to the point of unsettling gauntness and wore a baggy knitted jumper and trousers that gave no indication of his actual body shape. He had a sombre expression, gazed into the middle distance and held the pamphlets tightly in his hands hanging down by his crotch, as if they all belonged to him. When one woman, who hadn't spotted the girl, held her hand out to him he slowly looked down at her, at the pamphlets, back at her, at the pamphlets, then again at her. His eye movements quickened each time until he understood what was required of him. Then, with the barest of movements, he placed the topmost one onto her palm, staring into her eyes until she walked off.

After the last three filtered into the hall he closed the door behind them. The girl held out her hand to him. Only because he knew her, and because he had done so before, he handed her the remaining pamphlets without any fuss. She took them away and left them in a pile on a small pine table in a corner. The table had a piece of hardboard secured to the back of it, shiny side forward, to provide a board onto which were affixed posters, flyers and photos. Along the top was a banner, printed in yellow ink with a black drop shadow: "CHURCH OF THE NEW GODS".

The hall used to belong to the workers at the old steel mill in this part of the City. They would come here for the cheap café in the day, the cheap bar at night and the regular functions held for them weekly. "They knew how to look after their workers back then!", would say any old local if they caught your ear. At the end of their days it was the place of angry union meetings and sombre lunches, before it was finally closed up along with the whole business. The steel mill sat and rusted and sagged for over fifteen years before finally being demolished. Modern luxury flats were built over the remains and they stood above the hall and the old houses next to it like oddly stacked Jenga towers, waiting to topple and rub out the last remnants of the previous century altogether. Then, early last year, an anonymous third party purchased the whole building for cash. The place was a hive of builders and electricians for weeks, none of whom knew the identity of their employer, despite many questions from the few remaining original locals and their families. Only when the work was completed did the brass plaque go up on the wall outside and the war of words between the residents and the Council began. For the Church's part, the hall was opened up for free use on certain days for the local community and, by the time a dance group joined the local residents association in taking advantage of the space, it had become tolerated amongst most people.

The tall, thin guy was already at the far end of the hall, having taken very few, yet precise long strides past the rows of reclaimed benches to get there. The girl looked around at the backs of the heads of the congregation, and counted seventeen, before making her way forward too.

Inside it was lit sharp morning orange through the large windows by the front door. The sunlight glared off everyone's hair like freshly struck matches, and the benches glowed golden brown where it touched them. Only one set of internal lights was on, and it was above the small stage at the far end of the room, silhouetting an old battered lectern that stood centre and front. As the girl passed the rows, she saw a man with blonde hair appear from a room behind the stage, down a side corridor that the sunlight couldn't reach. Only she could see him. As he looked at her she smiled and nodded. He smiled back and, taking a deep breath, went up four wooden steps to emerge at the side of the stage, now visible to everyone. As he stepped up to the lectern there was a small ripple of applause, which he politely waited to dissipate before speaking in a light Australian accent.

"Welcome all to the Church Of The New Gods. We have seen some of you before, and as always there are some new faces. But Heroes or not, all are welcome here in this place of worship. My name is Clifford Gaines, and we are here today to give our prayers to, and remember The Elemental. The Creator, the Hero you know as The Elemental, accomplished many great things in his life. He first emerged from the shadows in 1854 at the height of the Crimean War. It was a different time back then of course, innate abilities were not recognised as such, and Heroes either had to hide them or join a travelling freak show to have some semblance of a life. And The Elemental had been part of one such show until, still only a child, he enlisted for military service, and spent the next three years fighting alongside other men and boys in some of the most horrific conditions imaginable. But he proved himself as a soldier and as a Hero. Although initially taken aback by what he could do, the generals could see he was so committed to their cause, his country, that they put him to best use and he helped them win that war. When he came back home, this country victorious in war, he was hailed as a Hero. His abilities were strengths not to be feared or reviled, but simply accepted as a part of him, that made him the great man he was. And he was incredibly modest with it.

If you will let me read for you an extract of his journal. This is from 1858, three years after he had returned from war." Clifford picked up an A4 piece of paper that had been sitting on the lectern. "'I know I could have done more on the battlefield if I were trained as Cavalry, I had spent time around horses in the travelling show, but they didn't seem interested in me for that. I had a musket shoved in my hands and was sent out to Crimea. I did my best where I had to fight. But after they found out what I could do they would not allow me to fight. I spent my time watching my fellow Englishmen die in these distant lands, lying groaning for help or begging for death in cholera and rat-infested field hospitals. I knew I could be of more use if I were allowed to fight again! I pleaded with the senior officers daily, yet they were adamant I was of more use where I found myself, in the supplies tents making shot and muskets and horseshoes far behind the lines of battle. I helped replenish our stocks of weapons and armour, keeping us ready to defeat our enemies, so why did I feel so useless? Even now I feel like I failed all my fallen countrymen.'" Clifford smiled. "There he is in the midst of one of the most violent and bloody conflicts of its time, creating armour and weapons to help his side win the fight, and he believes he isn't doing enough! That is the spirit of a true Hero, shining through with the truth straight from his heart. He is doing all he can, yet he feels he has to do more, *must* be able to do more. Of course, in time, he would do much more. He would help found this City, create wondrous things, save many more lives. In his time, for much of his life, he was the one true Hero of this country. Everybody knew of him and what he could do. How things have changed..."

Clifford looked across the faces in the hall, all staring at him. "How things have changed. Those of you here with abilities, how many people have you told? How many people know about this intrinsic part of your being, your character? And of those that know, how many still talk to you? How many treat you like The Elemental when he was part of the travelling show, a freak of nature, instead of treating you like a Hero, somebody blessed with abilities, placed on this earth to help the less fortunate? The Creator showed the world what it meant to be a Hero. It was to not be afraid to go to places of danger where others need your help. It was to use your innate abilities to the best, selfless advantage. It was to be bold and be true to yourself. Now, since the Innate Abilities Registration Act, we are not allowed to be ourselves. They cannot take away our innate power, so they seek to take away our powers of freedom of movement, of expression."

"We are assessed and classified like scientific curiosities at best, terrorist threats at worst. We have to register such that we can be monitored and tracked. The law of self-defence, 'with reasonable force', does not count if we use our abilities to save our own, let alone other people's, lives. We cannot be trusted to wield our abilities with the innate knowledge we have of them. Our powers are to us like breathing, but in their eyes we are weapons. We are guilty without even having committed any crime. They hate us because they fear us. And this makes us angry. This is unfair. We have to hide so they can feel comfortable in their own skins. They believe in their freedom of speech to allow them to try and strip us of ours. But they fail to recognise the fundamental principle of freedom of speech, that you do not have freedom from the consequences of your speech. And that is the freedom of others to question their opinions as invalid, outdated, innatist. But they think they can freely crush us without ever expecting any response in return. And what should that response be? Well, we could attack them back, but that would be just another form of hate. That is not what the actions of The Elemental have taught us. They hope, oh yes they hope we will get angry. That we will retaliate with force, with our abilities. But we don't. We won't. We will not rise to their bait and prove to them that their misconceptions are correct."

"Those of you here without abilities, you are here because you understand what those people do not. You are here because you share the pain of Heroes across this country. The Creator knows your intent is good and you stand with us against this tide of hatred. They can hold us down, but we breathe underwater. They can trap us in chains, but we can break free. They can try to kill us, but their weapons bounce off us just as their words do, because we know how to respond to their speech. The Elemental showed us what justice is, what sacrifice is and how Heroes are meant to behave. Because we are Heroes. And just like The Elemental, the Creator himself, our day will come when we can prove ourselves, when we will once again be recognised as the Gods on earth we are. Peaceful. Benevolent. Loving. Heroic. For those qualities are as innate to our very souls as our powers. And I recognise that there will be a day, soon, when fear and hate will disappear. A day when a child will be born, another Creator as He was. And just as The Elemental changed the course of history for Heroes when they were living in their dark times, so too will this child lift us from the depths of darkness we find ourselves living in today. And yes, I have been waiting a long time for such a person to appear, but when He, or She, does, we will be waiting for them. They will have believers from day one. We here in the Church have been preparing for years to be His guardians and guides. All we need now are your words of worship to strengthen Him and help bring Him to us. And with your prayers, we wish that this world will be ready to accept Him as our saviour and to aid Him in any way we can in creating a new world for us to live in, openly, as the Heroes we are. And this day, will be glorious. Praise to The Creator."

"Praise Him," the congregation chorused.

CHAPTER 5
MARTIN'S NEW APARTMENT

Martin and Hayley had retreated to the rooftop opposite the warehouse just before the police arrived. They watched long enough to make sure all of the men were arrested and taken away. The last one to go was Malcolm, who went in an ambulance with one of the officers. Martin felt guilty about that. Instinct had just taken hold: 'guy with a gun, take him down quick!' Not just that but: 'guy with a gun, shooting at Hayley, take him down, the bastard!' A protective instinct kicked in and he did what he had to do. He hoped he would be OK.

"I think we're done boss?" Hayley was smirking. Martin sighed and nodded, glad to be getting out of the rain.

"Yep, I think we can safely say…" They appeared in the middle of his new apartment.

Every jump he did with her still made him feel slightly sick at the back of his head, although he could brush it off quicker each time. Hayley got up from crouching, said, "Another job well done for the Justice Squad!" and started peeling her wet clothes off and dropping them on the floor on the way to retrieve her dry ones from the bedroom. She had done a lot of jumping tonight and had tapped herself out. She would need plenty of food and rest before she could jump again.

As Martin stretched himself up, accompanied by a creak in his knees, he wondered why she never said out loud when she could no longer jump. Maybe she didn't like to admit it so she wouldn't appear weak, or was just uncomfortable with having a physiologically-limited power. He didn't know, and he wasn't sure how to broach the subject. As she disappeared down the hallway into the bedroom Martin took off his balaclava. It would have made a satisfyingly wet, "thud", had he dropped it on the floor, but he couldn't bring himself to do it. Instead he pulled his boots off, put them under a radiator by the door, hung his jacket on the pegs just above it, then picked up all of Hayley's discarded clothes. He dropped the lot, including his, "mask", into a plastic basket he pulled out from the airing cupboard next to the bathroom.

Hayley was singing something as he walked back down the corridor in a pair of loose, but nicely tingly, warm jogging bottoms. As he came back into the open plan kitchen and living area he had to stop for a minute. It had taken him a long while to get used to this new arrangement, having only ever lived in places with separate rooms. Coming out of the bedroom hallway felt like stepping into a small warehouse to him. Sometimes he had to take a step back for a moment before he could enter. Only the sideboard and bedroom furniture survived from his old apartment. The rest was new, as was the apartment itself, purchased outright thanks to the unprompted appearance of three hundred thousand pounds in his bank account two months after the events inside Pullman Tower.

He had slept on Hayley's sofa for just over a week, before his back and neck couldn't take any more of the odd twisting positions he found himself lying in when he woke. He felt ungrateful telling her he was leaving, but he needn't have worried. She had wondered how long he would survive her music playing until two in the morning and having to avoid tripping over clothes scattered over the floor. It was usually about one to two weeks. The longest was seven, and that was her last boyfriend. To be fair, she had splashed out on a pair of wireless headphones she'd had her eye on for some time, but that meant he had to keep dodging her as she wandered around her flat dancing, eyes closed, hands drumming the air. He made the excuse that he needed a bit more space to himself, given his bulk. "Man space," Hayley had called it, nodding sagely, before helping him look for nearby Bed and Breakfasts. He found a cheap B&B and settled in for a week or so, until his face turned up on the news along with details of Charles'ss crimes and the owners tersely asked him to leave. He didn't complain, just grabbed his stuff and went. The next B&B was more accommodating. Either that, or they didn't watch the news. It was while he was there that he finally heard from the Council.

After his old flat had been destroyed the insurance company took a close look at his details and, since he hadn't revealed on the application forms that he was powered, they very quickly decided not to pay out. So he had to apply to the Council for somewhere to live. They had found a flat for him on the outskirts of the City, which he accepted over the phone before even seeing it. It was small, with cheap fittings, smelt of fresh paint, rotten underlay and air freshener, but he was glad of his own space. Curtains, a mug and a new kettle were his first purchases. Carpets could wait. In any case, he had been spending most of his time at the hospital, waiting for Maria to wake up, which she eventually had. He had then made sure she was comfortable, was being looked after and, most importantly, wasn't alone.

When the money arrived, he bought this place, mostly because it was within walking distance of the hospital. He still remembered the estate agent's eyes lighting up when he said he would buy it outright for cash, having just seen the photos in the window. He did wonder if he could have pushed for a deal, but at the time he was just desperate to get it over and done with. He didn't much care for the tedious bargaining dance you were expected to do, he just offered the listed price and wanted it sorted. It still took seven weeks, which for Martin was far too long. There were far too many documents to sign, copy and send back. When he finally moved in, it was the first time he had been inside the apartment. Maria was going through physiotherapy sessions and he had hardly left the hospital, only going straight back to the council flat to sleep. He never did get carpets for that place.

Once his few pieces of furniture were sorted, and the rest arrived following an Argos catalogue spending spree, he had put up a folding screen on one side between the dining table and sofa/TV area and a double-sided set of shelves on the other in an effort to create separate living and kitchen spaces. Despite this, he still didn't feel completely comfortable. It felt too open. He even bounced the idea of building a temporary wall, until he forced himself to stop thinking about it. He would get used to it. He would have to get used to it. He was damn well going to get used to it, no matter how bad the dull pain in his chest felt, however many times it wanted to make him run for the bathroom and stay in there with the light off until his breathing returned to normal. This wouldn't beat him. Not after all that he'd gone through.

"So, we did good work tonight, right boss?" Said a voice from behind him, making him jump slightly.

"Good? Well apart from almost getting yourself shot and me nearly cracking some guy's skull open, I'd say this one ranked 'OK' on the scale of 'We lost' to 'We saved the world'." He walked into the kitchen area, filled the kettle half full and switched it on, while Hayley rummaged in the cupboards for cups and tea bags.

"Yeah, I get it, we need to stick closer together, so we can both be shot at the same time. Makes much more sense." Hayley's comment really irked Martin and he was about to say something until he noticed she was smiling.

"Sarcasm yes?"

"Yeah, sarcasm. Well done, you're almost starting to get it. Talking about guns, have you ever been shot? Do they bounce off you like in the cartoons?"

"Three times I've been shot at. Got a bad one in the leg in 'eighty-five, but that healed up nicely in the end. That was before I joined The Pulse. The other two were when I was with them. One got stuck just under the skin on my back and another bounced off my arm. I was lucky though, none of them were high-velocity rounds, all handguns from a distance. Not something I want to test out to be honest." The kettle gave a quiet, "click", and Martin poured the steaming water into the mugs Hayley had laid out.

"Aww, and here I was going to nick an MP5 from work and spray you with bullets in your sleep, you know, just to see what happened," she said with her head stuck halfway into the fridge. She came out with a carton of milk and finished off making the teas.

"Err, death... arrest... and prison most likely."

"Heh." She took a gulp from her mug, tightening her neck as the too hot tea roasted the inside of her throat.

They went over and sat on the sofa. Both of them were weak, Hayley from the repeated teleporting and Martin from spending too long in an awkward position in the cold.

"But we did good, yeah? The plan worked and we got them? And we now know about 'Fitz'! He sounds like a slippery one…"

She gazed at Martin waiting for her mentor's reply. Martin knew by now that she could be funny like that, one minute super-confident and sarcastic to the point of insolence, next minute the obedient student, eager for feedback, for approval. He put most of it down to anxiety and inexperience at Heroics, after all, she wouldn't have got far in the police force if she acted like that at work. How she coped putting up a professional front for a full shift he would never know.

"Yeah, we got them. Plan worked and, despite your little detour, we worked."

Hayley beamed. Martin wished he hadn't said that. It almost confirmed their pairing as a Hero duo, even though he was still in as many minds about it all. He couldn't deny a certain satisfaction though. Yes, the plan worked. His plan worked. A hasty plan with not much intel, and they pulled it off with a little bit of luck and improvisation. He had accomplished something tonight and he felt the satisfaction of a good job well done. But what now? Another job? Tracking down and taking out Fitz? Was this going to be a regular event, teaming up to take on the bad guys? Was he going to join up with Hayley on her nightly rounds as she had been bugging him to for weeks? Start pro-actively looking for crime? That was a different thing altogether, an escalation of Heroics beyond his current comfort zone.

He was trying to get back to a normal life after what happened to Vincent, and to Jack and Maria. Trying to find some work he could do, a sympathetic security company with a Hero Exemption Licence, construction, removals, anything. But he was either too recognisable from the news reports or they declined an interview the moment his name came back as flagged on the Register. That was one of the reasons he had kept quiet about his abilities and history over the years, it killed your job prospects. Then there were the intrusions and the restrictions on your movement. He had to notify the Department of Innate Ability Registration about his change of address and his reasons for moving. He had to give the Council seven days warning that he would need to enter a government building, to tell them he wouldn't need the flat any longer. If he hadn't he would have been arrested on sight. Apparently, applying for a passport was a year-long nightmare that wasn't guaranteed to have you waking up at the end. Then again, he hadn't left the City since he was a child, so that was one hassle he could easily avoid. So it looked like his options were limited at the moment. Even so, he wasn't ready to start wearing the costume every night. At least not yet.

"Great! Now, what's for dinner? I'm famished."

CHAPTER 6
ROOMS UNDER THE OAK AND
ARCHER PUB

The room smelt of slowly crumbling wood and the air had a metallic taste to it, but for the purposes of the meeting it was ideal, hidden away underground and little remembered. The Pub above had been boarded shut for nearly two years, missed only by the few regulars who used to rest their elbows on the bar sorting the world's problems, until the landlord genially ushered them out into the night. Of course, that didn't mean it was impossible to get the keys for the place, especially if one of your relatives knew the previous landlord. What did he care anyway? While the place had been a millstone round his neck in the end, it still grated with him that it had not been put to good use for so long. His only condition was, "nothing illegal", and he was satisfied enough with the explanation given.

The basement room had been done up to accommodate cheap wedding parties and discos, but the hoped for extra trade never materialised and the tenant landlord eventually quit. The pub firm that owned it couldn't find another landlord during the financial crisis, couldn't sell it on, and it had been left to fall derelict ever since. The room had been used for storage in the end. Broken chairs and tables, empty kegs, boxes of surplus glasses, a pile of dusty table cloths in the corner with a plastic gem chandelier on top. A row of four, thin windows lined the top of the wall parallel to the street. The metal wire-laced, mottled security glass let in a fuzzy light, only the top of an outside wall and the bases of old black metal railings were visible from inside. Under the windows hung old posters advertising musical events, fixed grins and cheap clothes, for one night only. The centre of the room had been cleared and was filled with an array of poorly arranged chairs, no two of which exactly matched.

A couple of young guys came through the door at the back of the room as Bobby stood at the front, preparing himself. They were new. They found seats next to each other in the middle row, nodding at him and smiling at some of the other attendees. There was a real mix of people today, nine so far not including himself and Rebecca. It was the third meeting, but he still couldn't predict who would come through the door. The anonymity of the internet meant that none of them knew who the real people were behind the user names, and that was part of the beauty of it; the net could trawl wider and catch all those who hid their true feelings behind a more respectable façade. Unfortunately the net also trawled deeper, and would occasionally drag up some full-on crazy who would disturb the forum for a few days until he/she was banned, but it was a worthwhile trade-off for the numbers of subscribers they were getting. Unfortunately, a lot of their members were in America or too far away from Element City to attend the meetings. One of them on the forum mentioned something about live-streaming it, but that was technically beyond what Bobby or the others could do. Another forum member offered help, but would need the train fare from Scotland, so that was a non-starter.

Bobby looked up as the room went quiet. That was everyone then. Less than last time. He gave a little shake of his head and cursed under his breath, but remembered to smile. He waited until Rebecca closed the door before he started.

"What about us. That's my question. What. About. Us. The ordinary person. You and me. The news is always filled with shit about these 'Heroes'. Always has been. I remember it from when I was a kid, 'The Pulse save the City again!', 'Captain England puts out oil refinery blaze,' and the first one, The Elemental, the one they named the City after, he single-handedly won some war for us according to the news. Noticed anything missing from all of these? Eh? The ordinary person. You and me. The Pulse save the City - yeah along with the several hundred emergency services without powers who, you know, did some less important shit like save lives too. Captain England puts out a fire, him and the fire fighters who risked their lives to help get it under control. And The Elemental?

Not like thousands of other ordinary blokes went to war was it? No, no. No-one else risked their lives, died, took terrible injuries for their country, just him, the 'Hero'." He looked around at their faces. They were all on him. "For a while, as a kid, yeah - I was swept up in it too. Had a few of those little picture books they did of the biggest Hero teams in the country. My mum even got me a Pulse sticker book, did swaps in the playground. Never did get Sunlight. Then again, from what I've heard, neither did anyone else." There were snorts from the small crowd. Rebecca, standing at the back of the room, gave him a sharp look.

"Anyway... one day I finally got the last part of a four-sticker photo of them in action. As I stuck it down, that was when I spotted something. There, in the background, was a policeman. Blurry, out of focus, arm round some injured woman, helping her get to safety. Now I remember staring at that completed photo for ages. There in the foreground was Pulse himself, carrying this kid, and The Black Witch next to him, just looking around. Just behind them it was Roadblock and Swift. I think it was a shot from after The Red Strike attacked a bank or something, but that's not important. Despite having four of the biggest Heroes in the country in one shot, the only thing I looked at was that policeman, and I didn't know why."

"Now I think I was only nine at the time, so nothing clicked suddenly or anything, I was only a kid after all. But I remember thinking about that photo for days afterwards. I couldn't get it out of my mind. Then finally I asked my mum, 'If a policeman is helping someone to safety from somewhere dangerous, does that mean he's a Hero like Pulse, or Roadblock?' She turned to me and you know what she said? She says, 'Of course he is Bobby. Anyone who risks their lives to help others is a Hero, not just people with special powers.' He paused, hand on his chest, pressing his palm into his breastbone. "Having grown up surrounded by a culture, news, toys, books, that revere these people as our only saviours, to find out that anyone can be a Hero blew this tiny nine-year old's mind. And then I asked her, 'Where's the policeman's sticker book?' She couldn't answer that one." He shook his head, smiling. "Anyone can be a Hero?" He put the rhetorical question to his audience, looking at a skinny black girl in a jumper. "It's not about having powers?" He looked at a larger, older man sitting with his head tilted back slightly. "The word 'Hero' has been corrupted. We are the Heroes, us ordinary people, when we do something extraordinary, when we save lives by putting our own at risk. We are the Heroes, and we need to take that word back so it means something again."

"I never bought any more stickers for that album. It held no meaning for me any more, this definition of 'Hero' that I'd grown up with. I began to see them for what they truly were, dangerous. Dangerous people, taking the law into their own hands. Turns out the Government eventually agreed with me. Nineteen-ninety six, the Restriction of Innate Powers Act came into force. Best thing any Government has ever done for this country." He saw nodding and heard at least one, "yeah". "That told them no-one was above the law.

That told them, 'You're not special, you're dangerous, and we're going to make sure you don't keep going around killing people and destroying lives with no threat of consequences'. The months after that Law came into force were some of best I can remember. Every day in the papers was news of another Hero team disbanding, or leaving the country. And if they weren't whining about it on the news, they were trying to pretend the new Law didn't exist and getting arrested on the street. Oh that was fun, remember the, 'Heroes in handcuffs!', headline in the Mail? Yeah? The grid of pictures of all the arrests?" He laughed to himself. The faces smiled back. "That front page went up on my wall. Framed it. Brilliant."

"But yeah, some didn't get the message. Some got angry and took it out on each other. Some thought they could take advantage of the lack of 'Heroes' and go on killing sprees. Sure there was a spike in crime after the Law came in, sure policemen and women and innocent civilians got killed in the violence, sure it was very ugly and dark for a while. But the law finally helped us see that the solution wasn't some mythical Hero flying down from the skies to save us all, it was ourselves. Eventually balance was restored and it was the police that dealt with crime, of all kinds, as it always should have been to begin with."

"If you had powers, you went on a database with your real name, no hiding behind masks like a, 'get out of jail free', card. If you committed a crime with your powers you went to jail, for a long time, they didn't make you immune to prosecution. And they started to get it. Well, some of them..." He sighed, looking down at the floor. "You'd have thought after all these years, they would understand what they were, what their place was. But no. They're still on the news every fuckin' week." He flung his arms wide open, leaning forwards to the front row. "'I was saved by a Hero!' says mugging victim, 'Secret Hero breaks up paedo ring.' That one's fair dos I guess, apart from the fact that if he'd let the police handle it they would have got the ones abroad. By the time he decided to let the cops in on his information, the other sick fucks had done a runner. Yeah, well done 'Hero'; how many kids are gonna keep getting abused because of you?"

"And that's what gets me the most. That attitude they have, that they still have, these... genetic freaks, that they're above us. Above the police, above the law. They're 'Heroes' because they do what the fuck they like whatever the consequences, and despite the new Law, despite their behaviour being criminal behaviour, the press and the people still gush over them when they do a good deed. Fuckin' hypocrisy isn't it? One week there's a headline about someone with powers killing someone and going to jail, 'bad guy', the next week a headline about how some guy in a costume smashed in some guy's face to stop him from stabbing someone else, 'good guy'. Er, no?" His face twisted in confusion as he paced back and forth along the front row, quickly scanning the faces before him. "Same thing, yeah? Both broken the law. You deal with them equally because if you don't you perpetuate this myth of Heroes with powers doing good deeds being *beyond* the law. You play to them, giving them confidence, making them think what they're doing is 'right'. And in the end they go mad with that power and think that only they can solve the world's problems because they can, literally, shine a light out of their arses!"

There was a ripple of laughter. Even Rebecca twisted a smile. He let the silence hang in the air as he turned side-on to them, slowly turning to look across them. "So, how do we fix it?" He left the question hanging for a while. He half hoped someone would say something, but the other half of him was on a roll and didn't want the interruption. "I'll tell you how. The only way they will realise they are not special is by reminding them of what they are, normal people with a medical condition that makes them dangerous to others. Someone with a mental illness that makes them think they can kill people as they like? They get locked up, treated if they can be. Someone with a genetic condition that allows them set people on fire based on their own random ideas of who deserves it? Nah, you're all right. Yeah, you can walk around in busy shopping centres, look after kids and we won't do anything to stop your power from happening. You, you have delusions that you can control people's thoughts and get them to do your bidding? Here, you need medication and support to make sure you don't harm yourself or others. You, you've actually *got* mind-control powers? Don't see a problem there mate, here have a driving licence and a passport, go anywhere and do anything you like. We'll just pick up the pieces after you've caused another headline disaster." His lips twisted with the words he spoke.

"You want to know what I think we should do about these people, these weapons who walk our streets thinking they have a right to save us?" He suddenly frowned. "They need to be taught just how human they are. They need to be taught, to be shown, that they are just flesh and blood and human like the rest of us. Affirmative action. Out them. Let people know who they are and what they can do. That Register of Powers? That needs to be public and searchable on the internet, with addresses, updated so you can see when one has moved into your neighbourhood and so you can see what they've done. And the ones that committed crimes before the Act came into force, that got amnesty and immunity from prosecution? They need justice." A few people cheered. "Proper justice, you know what I mean?" said Bobby through gritted teeth. "They have no right to be swanning around as normal, getting away with the deaths and injuries they caused when they were flying around and blowing shit up. No right!" Someone repeated, 'No right!', and there was a murmur of approval. "And those 'Heroes' who go out today and still use their powers for their own personal version of 'justice'? They need to be taught the exact same lesson, otherwise…" There was a short ripple of applause. "… otherwise the more headlines they grab and the more arrests they magically avoid, they'll think they can get away with it. Well I'm not having it. Not any more. Enough!"

There was a longer applause. Someone whooped. Bobby smiled as he skipped his eyes over the small crowd. Everyone was with him. "Having said that, there is one 'Hero' who is going to get justice soon. Mr Charles Heathcote, or 'Ignite' as he was back in the day, is coming up to his murder hearing in a couple of weeks." Someone shouted, "hooray". "Was never that bothered when I got a sticker of him, always thought he was a twat. He's pleaded guilty, so it's only going to be a short one for sentencing, but I want as many of us here as possible to turn up outside the court to protest at the lack of prosecutions against powered people who commit crimes. If you don't want to appear on TV that's fine, there's plenty you can do to help behind the scenes. We need banners and posters and T-shirts printed and things. We got our blog covered ourselves, but we need people to call the TV stations and papers to let them know we'll be there. We want as much coverage as possible to help get our message out there. We need to kill this 'Heroism' myth that allows them to get away with breaking the law, and you can help."

"If you can help, stop at the back to see Becca on your way out. Don't forget to check the blog for the next face-to-face meeting. Got loads of links on there to e-petitions you can sign, contact details of your MPs with a form letter to send them about tougher implementation of the Restriction of Innate Powers Act, links to other blogs and sites you may find interesting, shit like that. Got some posters at the back too, help yourself to them, pin them up at work, at Uni, get as many eyes on them as possible. We need to get numbers up, we need to get people energised about this issue yeah? Because we are The Real Heroes. Thanks for coming guys." Everyone stood up and started to make their way to the door at the back. A quick glance showed a couple of people had stopped and were deep in conversation by the door. One young guy came straight up to Bobby.

"I want to help."

"Great stuff mate! What's your name?"

"Michael."

"OK Michael, if you have a word with the others on the way out we can get you putting some flyers up or something yeah?"

"No, I mean I really want to help, you know? Proper justice, like you said. My Uncle got killed by these bastards in 'eighty-seven. Some fight down by the river and none of them gave a shit who got caught up in it. We know, the whole family knows which fucker it was that took him out, but yeah, he's immune. Moved to Canada years ago. Having a lovely life with his family apparently. It's fucked up." He took a small shuffle closer to Bobby. "I want to teach them how human they really are, you get me?"

Bobby looked the young man up and down. Scrawny, probably only sixteen or seventeen, angular face and long nose, light brown hair brushed forwards over his eyes. His eyes were locked with Bobby's, determined, focused. Bobby smiled and put an arm round him as they walked towards a side room.

"Yeah, I'm sure there's something we can get you doing."

KILLING GODS

CHAPTER 7
OUTSIDE MARTIN'S APARTMENT

"Are you sure he can help us?"

"I don't know."

"Then what are we…"

"Wait!"

They had been standing opposite the apartment block for almost an hour, Ian holding a small pocket umbrella over Jenny and Lewis while the rain ran off his hair and soaked into the oversized puffy jacket that only just stretched over his frame. They had been watching the entrance for someone to enter or leave, but it had been incredibly quiet. The rain had everyone huddled indoors at home or elsewhere. Now they saw a middle-aged woman slowing down as she approached the front of the building.

"Come on, come on, "muttered Ian under his breath.

"Look, it's OK. We don't have to do this. I mean, he might not even be…"

"Here we go!" Ian gripped her shoulder, pushing her forwards with him across the road as the woman had a minor struggle folding down her umbrella before shaking it out on the doorstep.

She pulled a set of keys from her coat pocket and pressed a red, circular plastic fob against the bottom of the number panel. It buzzed in recognition and the lock clicked open.

"Here, let me get that for you."

"Oh thank... thanks." Ian already had his huge long arm inside, holding the door open, his claw fingers wrapped round the edge to try and hide them from sight. But it was the size of his frame that startled her and made her hesitate for a split second.

"Nasty day isn't it?" he ventured. The woman looked at Jenny, who smiled, then back at Ian before giving her umbrella a couple of small shakes and stepping inside. She didn't answer, and warily stepped to the side. Ian knew they had to look confident, like they belonged here. He strode up to the lift door, hand round Jenny's back and pressed the call button.

"Floor five he's on isn't it darling?"

"Y...yes. That's right." Jenny was too nervous, glancing back at the woman who was now standing just behind and to the side of them. She was going to remember every detail of them being here, so there was no need to be sneaky any more. Ian turned to look at her.

"Just visiting a friend of ours, not long moved in. Martin. You know him? Big guy? Well, not as big as me you know?" Realisation spread across the woman's face as she nodded slowly, mouth slightly open.

"Yes. Yes, I've… seen him. In the papers."

"We're here to see his new apartment. It's nice here." Jenny had relaxed, and Ian squeezed her shoulder gently as the lift doors opened. He ushered the woman in first but she shook her head.

"It's OK, I think you'll need the whole lift for yourselves."

Ian patted the top of his head, a good five inches above the door height.

"Oh, yeah. Sorry. My mother always told me to eat my greens, and look where it got me. Ha!"

Ian and Jenny went in the lift. She reached across him, hit the button for floor five and smiled at the woman as the door closed. It wasn't a huge lift and Ian had to bend his knees slightly to keep his head straight.

"Yeah. She wouldn't have fitted in here. You got enough room love?"

Jenny looked up at him and Lewis's face appeared from between the folds of his lilac blanket.

"You know I'm always fine when I'm close to you. I feel safe." She rested her head onto his chest.

"You're doing great darling. We're almost there."

The door opened up onto a small, pale green carpeted landing with two apartment doors on each side and a window overlooking the street at the end. Jenny went out first, looking for the numbers as Ian tried not to catch his thick dreadlocks on the door mechanism.

"It's this one." She pointed to the door on the left at the end. "Do you think he'll be OK with this?"

"Well, I suppose he's got every reason not to be, but we haven't much choice."

Jenny peered into the bundle cradled in her arms. Lewis was fast asleep, pouting.

"I'm scared."

Ian felt his heart squash down in size and cupped his hands round the back of her head before bending down and kissing her gently on the forehead.

"Me too darling." He knocked on the door and waited.

***

There was a knock on the front door, which was odd, since no-one had buzzed up. It was probably the manager of the building again. Since the chap had recognised him from the television reports into Charles's murder charge he had been up once a week on various thin excuses to drop unsubtle reminders about property damage.

"Don't worry, I'll try not to blow up this apartment." Martin had told him. The man nearly jumped out of his skin and ran off. Looking at the video display next to the door he saw a young girl holding a baby.

"Great, another crazy who thinks I'm the father of their child. That'll be the third one so far."

Martin pressed the "speak" button on the pad under the screen.

"How can I help you?"

"Um… Roadblock, is it? From The Pulse?"

"Nope."

"I mean, Martin? Martin Molloy? We need your help."

Martin stared hard at the blue-tinged image on the display, carefully considering if he should bother saying anything more. She looked like she was trembling, tearful. She gently brushed her thumb across the child's face and he heard her whisper,

"It's OK Lewis, we'll be safe now."

Was that a genuine whisper or deliberately loud enough for him to overhear? Or was he over-thinking things again? What harm would it do just to hear her out? Then he could pass her on to the police or someone else who could properly help. What else was he doing anyway? Hayley was on night shifts for the next four days, so things were going to be quiet for a bit. He let out a sigh.

"OK."

He disabled the electronic lock and opened the door. The girl was even smaller than she appeared on the top-down camera view, and she was cold and wet, but he sensed something was off. He could feel the corridor outside was filled with more than the girl. Something shifted to the right, just out of sight, and then The Savage stepped in to view. He put his arm round the girl, who pulled herself towards him, and smiled.

"We need your help." he growled.

***

Martin didn't know what he found most terrifying, the fact that one of the most violent powered adversaries he had fought was standing in his apartment, (the building manager would have a seizure if he knew), or that he had just seen him smile and hug someone while being generally calm and civil. He and the girl were standing on the inside of the door, his head almost scraping the ceiling. Martin had backed off to the sofa, a good five metres away. Not far enough, he knew how fast the guy was, or had been. Maybe he had grown slow, or maybe, from what it initially looked like, he had settled down and wasn't here for revenge? He would keep his distance anyway, just to be sure.

"How did you even find me, Ian isn't it?"

"It was in the papers weren't it?" said the girl.

"You were snapped coming in here by the paparazzi a few weeks back, it was in 'My Hero!'. Didn't you see it?"

"I guess my subscription ran out." Martin was the opposite of bothered by those magazines.

"And then we just had to look for apartments in here that were for sale but weren't any longer."

"That easy? Great."

"Look, you're a well-known face now. Can't hide off the list any longer. Unfortunately, I never could do that." Ian held up his arms. "This, and the fact I spent nine years inside because of you."

Martin's muscles tightened.

"Or, more accurately, because of me. Anyway, things are different now. Not just because of the Hero law either. I've got a family now." He put his arm very gently around the girl as they looked at each other. He smiled again.

Martin felt odd. The only times he had met Ian before, the guy had been so pumped up on drugs and adrenaline that he could barely form a word as he leapt across the City Centre at him, claws first. The Red Strike would wind him up and let him loose as a weapon to keep The Pulse occupied while the rest of them carried out their plans. More than once he had been left behind to take the fall, only to later escape and go back to them like an abused dog. Now here he was, his pock-marked, lined face showing the struggles of drugs and jail, but most definitely contorted into a loving smile.

"This is Jenny."

"Hi." The girl seemed very young, early twenties perhaps, and stood very close to Ian.

"And this is Lewis. Our son."

They all looked at the bundle of cotton blankets in Jenny's arms. Ian nudged her forward, nodding. She stepped forward towards Martin hesitantly, turning her arms so that he could see through the gap in the bundle. Nestling deep inside, Lewis was fast asleep, whistling as he breathed through tiny nostrils, a blue-eared rabbit toy tucked in next to him. Martin smiled and looked up at Jenny.

"He's a beautiful boy. I'm happy for you guys."

The girl suddenly relaxed, smiling, and gently took the boy bundle back towards her bosom, rocking him.

"Yeah, he gets his looks from his mum, thank Christ," said Ian firmly.

Martin had encountered several Heroes with physical mutations before, but had never given much time to thinking about their lives beyond the obvious discrimination they faced. To have to worry about whether your children would turn out physically the same as you, or worse. To decide if you should even have children in case they suffered the same deformities. He had no idea how difficult those decisions must be to make, but he could see the relief on Ian's face even now.

"I can't imagine. You must have been really happy when he was born."

Ian raised his eyebrows, made a deep "Uh-huh." noise and nodded deeply.

"But it wouldn't have mattered if he had looked like Ian," said Jenny. "We would have loved him just as much."

Ian smiled at her lovingly. Martin felt more relaxed now that he was certain he wasn't going to be attacked, but he wasn't quite ready to boil the kettle to make them coffee.

"Look, I mean, it's a… surprise, to see you again Ian, and it's great to hear you're getting on OK, but why are you guys here?"

"They want to take him from us." Jenny nodded towards the bundle.

"Who?"

"Child Services."

"Why?"

"Because they can," growled Ian.

"But surely you can convince them you've changed from back then? I mean you convinced me in minutes! They can see that can't they?"

"That's not the problem." Ian could see Martin was puzzled. He took a deep breath in. "He's powered. He can create stuff. He's only ten months, he... just does it."

"What do you mean 'create stuff'?"

"As in The Elemental, 'create stuff'. Out of nothing"

"That's... wow, that's really powerful." Martin sat back on the arm of the sofa. "There's been no-one with that ability since The Elemental himself. I can see why Child Services want to get involved."

Maybe Ian would surprise everyone, thought Martin. By rights he should have destroyed this entire apartment in a blind rage by now, but here he was, loving and protective, calm and rational. He knew nothing about the girl Jenny however, but she seemed nice enough, good-natured. Maybe that's all the boy would need?

"Look, I know you don't owe me anything. You barely know who I am, and what you remember of me isn't good. If I remember right the last time we saw each other you'd just pounded my head in again, and seen me hauled off to prison. But I'm not The Savage any more, that's just... not who I am now. I've tried so hard to change, and I have, mostly thanks to Jenny. I could have gone back to my old team mates for help, the ones who are still alive and not in jail that is, but I don't want to be associated with that sort of shit any more. That would make everything more difficult, and it wouldn't work with Jenny." She shook her head solemnly. "And I know this yeah?" He nodded back at her, before turning to Martin again. "I came to you because you're the only person I can trust, because I know the kind of guy you are." He stepped closer to Jenny. "We need your help... to disappear."

"To what?"

Jenny butted in.

"We can't let them take Lewis. Ian is sure they will because of what he can do."

"And my past. And the fact we're first time parents, unemployed, they'll find any excuse, that's what they're like. The woman who saw us..." Ian made circles with his hand, trying to wind up his memory, before Jenny stepped in.

"Eleanor... something."

"Yeah, her, she practically ran off when she saw him make a copy of his toy. There's probably already an armed response team waiting to take him away. We've got to disappear before they come back."

Martin pushed himself off the sofa and walked towards them.

"But where would you go? After all, you're not the most inconspicuous of people, and then when they run your photos on TV... how long do you really think you could hide for? And when they do find you and put you both in prison, because they would, they'd take Lewis and neither of you would ever see him again in your lifetimes. That's not a good outcome for anyone is it?"

"We thought you'd know places... somewhere we'd be safe?" Jenny held Lewis tight to her.

"Or someone else who could help hide us?"

"I don't." They were desperate, but Martin knew that every option other than following the procedure to the letter would lose them their son for good.

"I really don't. I know this must be terrifying for you guys. I can't begin to imagine how scared you must be, but the last thing you want to do now is run. It feels right, but it isn't. Believe me."

It took Ian a long time to say anything.

"OK. I hear you. And I trust you." He pulled Jenny closer to him. "Like I said, you're the only person I do trust, so we're going with you on this."

"Good. Just do everything they say, follow every instruction. Show them all the reasons you can look after him and none of the reasons to give them any excuse to say you can't." They seemed reassured but hovered inside the doorway, holding on to each other. After a while it became awkward and Martin offered them a coffee. They declined, but that seemed to work and, not saying anything else other than, 'Thanks', they left his apartment. He saw them standing outside his door for a while, talking to each other. He wasn't one to listen in so he didn't know if they were discussing taking his advice or not. Eventually they left the view of the camera and he could hear the lift door opening.

Martin turned the TV on to BBC News 24 and sat on the sofa not really watching it, distracted by his fights with Ian replaying in his head. That was one hell of a blast from the past. He wasn't sure how many more of those he could take, given everything that had happened this past year, but it seemed as if this one could have a happy ending, just as long as neither of them went and did anything stupid.

CHAPTER 8
MORRELL RESIDENCE

It is a Tuesday and you are going to work again today. Tuesday is the Team meeting day. Monday is when the Heads of Departments meet and today is when they tell us what came out of that meeting. You like to be prepared for this meeting, even if it is just a small notebook and pen in front of you. You don't recall ever writing anything down... no, that's incorrect, you once wrote down the name of a new manager in the Bristol office. They were only tangentially related to your Department and your area of work, but you thought it best to make a note, just in case you or anyone else needed to know in the future. Other than that you've never written anything down. You always like to arrive early for work on Tuesday, to grab a coffee and a biscuit before the meeting, and to get your usual seat between the radiator and the old whiteboard that faces the window across the car park, to the engineering firm offices opposite. You like to watch the tiny people sitting at their desks, moving around between rooms. You chuckle to yourself, (before anyone else arrives), that you could reach out and squish them between your fingers. Then you dunk a biscuit in your coffee and suck the wet end into your mouth.

You brush your hair across your bald patch. It seems to take longer each day to make it look natural. The front and crown started to fall out in your twenties and what hair remained went grey years ago, with white patches around the temples. Stress you think, but your wife tells you it's because your father went grey very young. You don't believe her because she doesn't understand the stress you have at work and isn't interested in hearing about it. You finally get your hair to look just so as the wife shouts not to forget that the Thomsons are coming round tonight. "Yes dear," you say. You did mention it to her once that it would be a better idea to invite people over at the weekend instead of during the week, but there was an argument where she made the point that other couples had family and not everyone was free at the weekends so we had to accommodate them. Then she said we had to invite people around as they were our neighbours. You did mention that we don't really get on, or have anything in common, with the Thomsons, but then there was an argument where she made the point that you would be happy if nobody ever came round and we didn't have any friends at all and that you were selfish because of this and then she slammed a door as she walked away and then we didn't talk about it again. So the Thomsons are coming round tonight.

With the naked scalp covered successfully, you pick your round-rimmed glasses off the side of the sink and slip them on. Yes, that's you in the mirror. You still recognise parts of your face from when you were at school, university, started work, but the rest is new and unwanted. You wish you could turn back time to when things were always happy, when no-one bothered you, when you still looked like you. You go into the bedroom and take your suit jacket from the back of the bedroom door, carefully putting it on so that you don't tear the stitching under the armpit again. The wife was terribly angry when you did that before. You did mention it was an accident but she still told you off for not being careful with your clothes and that it was a good thing we didn't have children because if we did we wouldn't have the money to keep buying clothes to replace the ones you'd damaged. You did mention you had only torn two pieces of clothing in recent memory, the suit jacket and a shirt button that had unwound its stitching and dropped off somewhere, but she said you were putting on too much weight because you just didn't care any more and should be ashamed of yourself and that she would fix the suit tear herself anyway because we needed to save money. You didn't mention she had contradicted herself.

You pick up your briefcase from the chair in the bedroom and go downstairs. You take your coat off the hook in the hallway, while looking through into the kitchen where the wife is tidying drawers or something.

All the dishes were done last night and she is always cleaning and tidying. You're not sure what chores are left to do, but she seems busy with something, emptying all the contents of one drawer onto the work surface and soaking a cloth in hot soapy water from a plastic bowl in the sink. You stare at her mop of curled, brown-dyed hair, gently bouncing around as she moves. Her thin pink, flowery top under her grey cardigan, of which she had dozens stuffed in wardrobes and drawers and large plastic store bags piled in corners of the upstairs rooms. Her face is puffy and starting to wrinkle, old-looking, not a patch on how beautiful she was when you married her. You didn't think she would turn out this way. Sometimes, in your darker moments, and you do have dark moments occasionally, you imagine taking one of the kitchen knives from the block and plunging it into her back. Sometimes she dies straight away, slumping to the floor, a pool of oily blood appearing around her, but sometimes she stays alive for a while, in shock, a look of pain and disbelief on her face. Disbelief that you could do something like this, that you had the self-awareness to decide and act on your own wishes. As she crawls through the house dragging a smear of her own fluids behind her, you follow her and you tell her everything you have been through for the past quarter century and just before she dies she finally, finally, understands you.

It's just a moment though, it doesn't mean anything. You suppose everyone has those sorts of thoughts now and again, and that's all they are, thoughts in your mind, never acted upon, that don't mean anything. You are safe as long as they don't start recruiting psychics into the Company. You chuckle at the thought. "Goodbye dear." you say. As usual she doesn't reply, her face just tightens as she ignores you, and you make your way out of the house to the car, a 2007 Volvo Estate. You can't go wrong with those, very reliable and cheap insurance, especially with your twenty-eight year no-claims. You put your briefcase on the passenger seat and make sure you're securely fastened in before starting the engine. You think it's going to be an alright day. You have to think that, otherwise what's the point?

CHAPTER 9
ELEMENT CITY COUNCIL CHILD SERVICES DEPARTMENT

It had been less than a week since the woman from Child Services had visited them. They got an appointment card through the door two days after she left and had the weekend to worry over what would happen to them after Martin sent them away. They understood what he told them, but the part of themselves bound to little Lewis reflexively twitched at the possibility of separation. Ian had proposed they go to his aunt's place up near Glasgow. She wasn't an aunt by relation, rather a friend of the family since he was little, but he knew he could trust her and that it would be hard to link her to them. Jenny had almost agreed for a while, but the certainty of losing Lewis if they were caught eventually made her decide against it. Ian reluctantly went with her decision. He couldn't be angry at her for being so fearful, after all he could barely hide his own terror.

All the times he fought other Heroes back in the day was nothing compared to this process. Here he felt like a non-powered going up against The Pulse, completely naked and vulnerable. The outcome of this battle had nothing to do with his abilities and everything to do with what a group of officials decided for them. For Lewis. That was the hardest part of it all for him to fathom, how could people who hadn't gone through the pregnancy, the birth and raised Lewis for the last year know whether he and Jenny could bring him up right? About whether they could cope with his abilities? How could they be given the power to rip a child from a family based on what, numbers? Whether more of something matched up to something else on a spreadsheet? It was bullshit. All of it. Ian scraped his claw fingers together as they hung between his knees. They had been waiting for nearly fifteen minutes past their appointment time and he was feeling increasingly anxious, making up daft plans for an escape through the fire exit.

"Don't do that, you'll irritate your skin again." Jenny smiled at him tensely. He attempted a smile back as he unmeshed his fingers and rested his palms on his knees instead. He couldn't help that his instinct was to fight for his son. It was how he was raised and all he knew how to do for many years. A voice came over some speakers they couldn't see.

"Lewis Randall, interview room three please."

They left the waiting room into the corridor outside. Jenny pointed at a sign on the wall and they walked down to the interview room, knocked on the door and went in.

In the room Eleanor sat behind a desk. Behind her sat another woman, taller and larger with dark hair. Also in the room, at the back, was a young man in a dark blue suit and tie, clutching an open folder on his lap like it was a life preserver. Everyone stood up as they entered.

"Mr Randall, Miss Crossdale, and Lewis of course. Lovely to see you again, thanks for coming, please take a seat." Eleanor motioned to two chairs opposite the desk.

"Sure. You'll excuse me if I don't shake your hands." An old ice-breaker. He wasn't sure if it worked at first, but Eleanor smiled as they all sat down.

"I just want to introduce everyone here before we start. I'm Eleanor Cheadham, I'm a Senior Child Protection Officer and we've met before of course. This is Jane McGowan, my line manager and Team Leader for Element City South."

Ian and Jenny said hello as the woman gave a brisk smile.

"And behind us is Matt, a trainee protection officer who will be sitting in on this meeting, that is if it's fine by you? If you would like him to leave that's not a problem, we totally understand."

"No no, that's... yeah, that's OK." The only problem was being here thought Ian, not how many people were in the room.

"Yeah, that's fine." Jenny tried to smile. Matt smiled back weakly, eyes flitting between Ian's huge face and hair and the claws curled up under his wrists.

"OK, good. Now, when I came to your house last week to introduce myself and meet Lewis and you both for the first time you may remember I said that this was all part of a process to assess your son and yourselves to see what degree of help we could give you."

They nodded. Eleanor blinked faster than usual and had to clasp her hands together on the desk to stop the small tremble she could feel starting. She knew this wasn't going to go well. Matt shouldn't be here, but Jane insisted it would be good training. It should be just her and the family, there were too many extra variables messing things up. She just had to breathe and use her training and experience.

"Well, we have discussed your case at some length and, given the facts, we have decided that it is best that we assess Lewis away from the family environment, as much for your safety as well as his."

They both looked at her puzzled.

"The main facts that led us to this decision are the specific classification of his ability, the level of his abilities, and the fact that they are developing at such an incredibly young age, meaning he does not have full understanding or awareness of them. Now it isn't that we think you aren't good parents, not at all. I could tell from our first meeting that you clearly love him very much and have already taken strides to accommodate what he can do. But we don't think you quite understand the full extent of his abilities. To give you some frame of reference, this is the most extreme example of power manifestation in such a young child I have seen in over thirty years working here. He is very special, but dangerously so. And he will have no idea how special or dangerous he is for some time. He is going to need highly specialised and dedicated care that, as we have so far assessed, you would be unable to provide him, however much support we were to offer you."

Jenny and Ian were frowning. She could see him flexing his wrists as it started to dawn on him.

"Because of this I have to inform you that we have decided that we wish to apply to Element City Court for a Care Order under Section 31 of the Children's Act 1989 for the reason of an innate power requiring special risk assessment."

Jenny still looked puzzled and was looking at all the faces in front of her for an explanation. Ian however had worked it out and was pressing his lips tightly together. When he spoke he spat the words out.

"You mean you're taking him from us."

"What?" said Jenny, horrified.

"What it means is that until we know the extent of his abilities and the risk he poses we can't allow him to be brought up in your house. He is too dangerous. Now if you agree to the Care Order, we will submit it to the Court where it can take up to eight weeks before they see it and act on it."

"What, and that's it? You take him away from us and we never see him again?"

"No, not at all..."

"And if we don't agree to this?"

"Then… given what I've already said about his abilities and the level of care skills he requires, we would apply for an Emergency Protection Order. We wouldn't need your agreement for that and, unfortunately, that would give us the right to forcibly take your son from you. But nobody here wants that."

Ian hadn't heard the last sentence as he had already jumped up from his chair. His huge thighs accidentally bumped and lifted Eleanor's desk so that it crashed back down, scattering pens and almost tipping the monitor over. Matt sat upright and pulled the folder to his chest.

"You bastards! I KNEW you'd try this. This is because of me isn't it? Because of what I used to do?"

"No. Not at all Mr Randall, the truth is the fact you are Physically Manifested came out in your favour. We knew from what you went through as a child, your active phase and your subsequent rehabilitation that you would not wish the same for Lewis, that you would be a caring and protective parent. And you still will be. A Care Order doesn't mean you won't see your child again. That's not how they work. It means that we, and you, both recognise the challenges involved in raising him and agree that at the present time the best place for him to live and be educated to cope with his abilities is in a Powered Child Care Facility. We *absolutely* want you to be involved in his care plan, in bringing him up and raising him properly. You will not be excluded from that."

"How can we not be excluded from that when he's not with us? None of this makes sense! You say we need to be involved as his parents then you give him to someone else. You say it's not because of me, but one of the reasons we're here is because of me. You say he's powerful, well so am I!" Ian opened his hands. His claws nearly reached out over the desk to Eleanor, who pulled her head back slightly. She had a flashback to her attack and felt her scar twitch. Matt jumped up in terror and stepped away towards the window, pulling the chair with him like a shield. Eleanor's manager, Jane, stood up.

"Now Mr Randall, please put those weapons away!"

"Those aren't weapons Mrs... whoever the fuck you are, they are me! I grew up with these and despite every piece of shit that was thrown in front of me I have managed to make something of my life. I have a family, I have a job coming up soon, and I want to bring up my son in our house so he grows up happy and strong and doesn't have to be afraid of anyone taking *his* kids away one day."

Jenny clutched Lewis to her and tried to reach out to Ian with her other arm as he started to prowl the room, shaking his head.

"Ian, it's OK. Please sit down. Let's hear them out."

Jane stood her ground.

"We are not 'taking him away' Mr Randall. As Eleanor has said, this is a temporary measure so that both he and you can be properly assessed. Our goal is always for the biological family to bring up their own child with all the support they need."

"Then he stays with US, and you can assess him in OUR HOUSE!"

"Mr Randall, we can't do that because…"

"Which means you're taking him from us!"

Eleanor's line manager was growing red with frustration as Ian was flexing his claw fingers in and out, in and out.

"Only for assessment, we fully intend to give him back to you once…"

"Fully intend? You fully fucking intend to make sure a freak like me never has a fucking chance of a normal life!"

Ian swung a fist at the wall by the door. He punched out one of the hinges and the momentum tore the other from the frame as the door toppled out into the corridor, narrowly missing a secretary who fell backwards in shock.

"IAN!"

Everyone was standing now, except for the secretary who had to be helped to her feet by a colleague who came running. Ian stood still, breathing heavily and staring at his hand, covered in plaster dust. It had been years since he last lashed out. It turned out he hadn't missed the adrenaline rush. It used to be his fuel, used to power him for hours at a time, but now he just felt sick. He swallowed against the blood pressure rising in his neck. Slowly, he bent his long thumb across his palm and one-by-one curled each of his claws over it so that they all rested across the lower end of his sleeves. He looked at the secretary who was being helped down the corridor by her colleague.

"I'm sorry."

She looked back.

"I'm sorry, I didn't think anyone would be there." He turned to face the room. They were all staring at him. Jenny looked in pain, almost crying. Matt was pressed so hard into the window frame he looked as if he would slip through. Jane looked angry, but was shaking her head at the same time, like a disappointed teacher. Eleanor herself had no expression at all. There was nothing in it that Ian could pick out, despite looking at her for some time. "I'm sorry," he said to her in the end. Her face didn't change. "I'm sorry.", he said to all of them. "I love my son. I never thought I would ever have one, what with... everything. I just can't face anyone taking him from me. I can't lose him."

"Then you need to let us do our job Mr Randall," said Jane. "Which, I'm sorry to say, involves calling the police to inform them of this incident. I need you to go with Security and wait in a secure room until they arrive. Can you both do that for me?"

"Yes, yes." Jenny nodded vigorously, rubbing one hand on Ian's shoulder as he dipped his head. Lewis had been dozing throughout the meeting but had woken on the door collapsing and was now looking around at all the strange faces, very alert indeed. Eleanor looked at him and felt her heart sink. He was completely innocent in all of this. Totally unaware.

As Security arrived and Jane explained to them what they needed to do, Eleanor took off her glasses and had to rub her eyes to hide her welling tears. Jenny and Ian went with Security, stepping over the fallen door. Ian made a gesture to pick it up but Jane snapped at him to leave it where it was as she followed them. Eleanor had to excuse herself to go to the bathroom, leaving Matt sitting on the windowsill. He didn't move from there for a very long time.

CHAPTER 10
LENNOX MARKET SHOPPING CENTRE

Martin sat back and rubbed his stomach with the ball of his hand. It was nicely filled with a steak and ale pie in suet pastry with creamy mashed potatoes and garden peas. All courtesy of Pam's Pies in Lennox Market. You couldn't beat good old British food. A large mug of coffee washed it down nicely. They always made it nice and hot, so much so that he could actually feel it trickling down his throat. An amazing sensation when you could barely feel anything. He was glad that the only branch wasn't in the New Merlin Centre, otherwise he would never be able to feel this full ever again. Ever since the Centre management, and the security company he worked for discovered he had lied to them about being a Hero he had been barred, with the threat of being arrested if he tried to go in. Unable to find another decent job he had been a man of leisure ever since the payment from Jack came through. And until Hayley had co-opted him into her Hero routine he had been bored senseless.

He had no interests or hobbies. TV and beer, that was pretty much it. He had never been academic enough to find anything that fired his imagination and once he got into Heroics his life existed only for that. After the team disbanded and he finally, painfully worked his way out of his years of solitude, it was the security work. Long, unsociable hours to fill the time between sleeps. To keep him occupied. There had been job offers since he had been, "outed", just not the legit sort. There were jobs that had seemed OK, until he met the people involved. He had quickly sussed out what they were after, but there had only been a couple of those. He was too recognisable to be of much use to anyone within the law or otherwise. He wouldn't employ *himself* for goodness sake.

So now he filled his time hiding in his apartment from the intermittent paparazzi, (ironically at a time when he felt the freest he had in decades), or wandering the City whenever he got the chance to slip out, trying to look inconspicuous in a wool hat and generic coat and jeans. It didn't always work. He had been clocked on the street several times, getting thumbs up and abuse in equal measures. Going inside shops was the worst. Close quarters. It looked odd keeping his hat on indoors, which drew attention, but if he took it off then he was spotted in minutes. Some assistants had refused to serve him and one firm but very cautious security guard had quietly asked him to leave a clothes store. He politely complied each time. If he kept things happy and simple then that's how his life would be. Well, that was the plan.

A waiter came to take away his plate and he dropped a Euro on it. The young lad gave him a barely concealed look of disdain and sloped off.

He started people-watching as he sat there. It was now late Friday afternoon and the place was surprisingly busy. A group of three scrawny young guys caught his eye as they came up the escalator and towards the food court. They were out of place. He could tell by the way they walked in a different step to the other shoppers, in the hesitant way they looked around at other people, in the way one of them kept touching his cheek in a little nervous scratch and another kept one hand on the back of his neck. They were also not moving in the right direction. Martin had been a security guard long enough to see how people walked around a shopping centre, all the paths of movement. From clothes store to clothes store, a determined route to the toilets, from videogame shop to fast-food outlet, from entrance to exit as a shortcut, idly window shopping and properly lost. There were patterns to it all that the eye picked out the longer you observed it. It made it very easy to spot the suspicious ones, as they did everything wrong. Those trying hard to, "act normal", stood out as particularly odd. As he watched he noticed a pair of shopping centre security guards on the other side of the atrium looking across. One was speaking into his over-ear microphone and the other was slowly matching the boys' position on the other walkway, keeping a close eye on them. Martin relaxed. It was all under control.

Hayley would be sleeping right now, recovering from her string of night shifts, ready for two days off. Meaning they would be out again tonight. The night prowls were quiet affairs. The odd mugging, or low-level power trying to be threatening to a passer-by. He was surprised how many of them openly used their powers. They were lucky it was the two of them that knocked their lights out instead of the police, otherwise they would be facing years in prison. Martin found it quite contemplative to be sitting on rooftops and watching from alleyways. He remembered doing the same when he was solo. After a time you slowly began to feel like a part of the City. You got used to the ebb and flow of people and cars, discovered the shortcuts and drops criminals used, got the, "feel", of the buildings by sitting in amongst it all. You knew when something was up, because there was a change from normality. Mostly it was subtle, like a delivery van changing route, the closing up of a shop taking just a bit longer than usual, or a street or building quieter than normal. But you could definitely feel it.

In The Pulse they had three small video-drones that did the scouting for them, a wall of monitors in the Communications Room and a computer system that even back in those days could identify and track criminals from camera footage. All they had to do was decide whether an incident needed their intervention or if the police could handle it themselves.

Yes, it was probably more efficient than having the whole team hiding down the side of takeaways every night on the off-chance they spotted a crime, but when you automated something like that, you lost a sense of the place you were protecting. They all became discreet incidents to be dealt with by the book. You lost the context, and often the context would determine the best course of action. He wondered if that was the start of the public mistrust of Heroes. They turned into heavy-handed policemen, diving in to save the day, seemingly oblivious to the events on the ground, just ticking off good deeds before buggering off, leaving people safer but annoyed at their distant smugness.

Martin remembered Mr Justice, (the 'sixties version, not the original wartime Hero he inherited the title from), being interviewed by the BBC about his exploits. When asked about his most famous villain take-downs he went quiet for a moment before saying that the best Hero was one who saved the day without anyone knowing, other than the criminal involved. Quite an incredible thing to say for such a high profile power. It was something that had stuck with Martin from when he saw that part of the interview on a documentary on Britain's Biggest Heroes. That was how he had operated on his own, keeping things just between himself and the bad guys and now he was doing the same all over again with Hayley who, he had to admit, was a master at it.

Knowing she couldn't risk being identified, she had memorised the location of every CCTV camera in the City. She had dozens of "safe spots" that she could teleport to if needed, which were always clear of people and objects, one of which was inside Martin's apartment. She kept to the shadows as he once did, although more out of necessity than design. The more time he spent with her, the more he began to feel the flow of the City again, like it had been waiting for him to rediscover it.

A waitress carrying two cups of coffee, her arms trembling, bumped into the back of his chair. A family of four came in and the two kids ran to the table next to him, loudly scraping the chairs back and clambering on while shouting their food demands at their parents. A girl's phone rang loudly while she stared at it as if the display was written in Russian. His table started shaking. No, it was his arm resting on it. He pulled it down between his thighs, clasped his hands together and squeezed tightly while breathing in deeply. It's fine. They are all normal people and have every right to be here. One child hit the other and it started crying as the mother sighed, wearily, and proceeded to tell them both off for playing up. The girl finally answered the phone and started talking loudly in a Cockney accent. The waitress, coming back from her coffee delivery, bumped his chair again, saying nothing.

He silently swore at himself. Deep breaths. Deep breaths. He willed himself to do this, to be able to leave of his own accord, not when his brain made him. He was a 120kg sack of (mostly) muscle that ran from crowds and hardly left his apartment. Christ. He felt weak. It was all over. Charles was going to prison, Jack was free, and he had begun to forgive himself for his failures, so why did his anxiety persist? He felt hemmed in. The shoppers didn't seem to be moving with any rhythm now, they were zig-zagging about, loud and far too close to him. He couldn't see their patterns any more. He felt sweat on his forehead.

"Shit." He got up quickly, hop-skipped out the entrance and made for the nearest set of stairs. He had no choice but to force his way through people. He dropped his head and ploughed through, well aware that he would now stand out as suspicious to the security staff, but caring only to reach the exit.

Most people curved their paths around him, although he did end up separating a young couple holding hands and had a brief dance-off with a woman with a child in a pushchair. She laughed it off, but he wasn't in any mood for a convivial shared joke and quickly went sideways. He collided with several people who called, "Watch it," and, "Careful," as he mumbled an apology and pushed onward. He could see the top of the stairs ahead. The escalator was nearer but was heaving with bodies. He shoulder-slammed a guy as he sped up his pace.

"Hey, you fuckin'... ah...yeah..."

It was one of the three guys he had spotted earlier. The change to his tone of voice coincided with him noting that Martin's arm was as thick as his own waist. Martin made the steps. It was quieter here. He ran down, pulled a sharp left at the bottom and hugged the line of the shop windows. At the sides he had a mostly clear route to the doors and finally emerged into the early afternoon with rain hissing in his face. He kept the same pace up until he was on a side street a block away, when he slowed.

The sun had gone in and the wind was now chilly. He felt it against his flushed face as a sharp prickle. He was glad of it, and the rain. It helped cool him down, calm him down. Some deep breaths later and the feeling returned to his hands. He took out his phone, turned the screen on and stopped the timer. It read twenty-three minutes, fourteen seconds. A record. As he slipped the phone back into his pocket, the rain spittle started to get thicker, like fine cold sand blowing at him. He zipped up his jacket and started to walk home with a smile on his face.

CHAPTER 11
OUTSIDE ELEMENT CITY
MAGISTRATES COURT

"I am speaking to you from Element City Magistrates Court where the sentencing hearing of Charles Heathcote, AKA 'Ignite' of the 'nineties Hero team, 'The Pulse', will be taking place next week. He is charged with the murder of Vincent Hayden-Phillips, AKA 'The Seeker', and the attempted murders of both Professor Maria Gionchetta and Martin Molloy, 'The Black Witch' and 'Roadblock' respectively, all old team members of his. Mr Heathcote has pleaded guilty to all charges, maintaining that he killed Mr Hayden-Phillips after making a pass at him, being rebuffed and striking out at him in a panic, worried that the details of his sexuality might be made public. He similarly tried to kill Professor Gionchetta and Mr Molloy after discovering that they both knew of his sexual orientation, while still in a state of shock from having committed the earlier murder. Questions have been raised recently about whether it is possible for him to receive a fair hearing and sentencing, due to the amount of media attention his case has had over the last few months."

"With me now to discuss this are David Astell, of the powered rights campaign group INNATE, and Dr Clifford Gaines, head of the Church of the New Gods, based here in Element City. If I can come to you first, David Astell. Charles Heathcote has admitted all charges against him, so this hearing is pretty much a formality for sentencing, yet you don't believe it will be fair?"

"No, not at all. How can it be? This is the very definition of trial by media, his face, the details of the crimes, private details and borderline homophobic editorials about his sexuality have been spread across the tabloids and television news for months now. Now this would be bad enough for any ordinary person, but the fact he is powered has fuelled the media speculation and intrusion into his private life. This has been done under the guise of, 'the public interest', and because powered individuals have so many restrictions placed upon them, the press feel it's their duty to dig as deep as they can to try and, 'catch them out', somehow. I mean, the Mail had a whole series of articles around the fact he used to light cigars on the set of his TV show with a flame from his thumb, crying out for him to be charged under the Restriction of Innate Powers Act, and calling on readers to email them with instances of other famous Heroes using their powers on private property, which IS legal by the way, just so they can run one of their, 'crusades', to have them all retrospectively charged under the Act. I mean, if that's not a witch-hunt I don't know what is!"

"Dr Gaines, do you believe that the tabloid media have gone too far in intruding into Mr Heathcote's private life, or is it justified given the seriousness of his crimes?"

"Hello Kirsty. Now first of all I do agree that I very much doubt this Hero will have a fair trial, but not just because of the media attention on him, but also for the simple fact he is gifted. Us powered individuals have been alternately worshipped and now vilified by the people they seek to guide and protect. This isn't just limited to this trial, but I see it across the whole of society. At the Church of the New Gods I speak to new members of my congregation every day and the stories of the harassment and hate crimes committed against them saddens me greatly. What saddens me more, is that under UK law these are not considered as such. Apparently there is no such thing as a, 'hate crime', against a powered person, it doesn't exist, and it's against this backdrop of tacitly permitted discrimination that we have this show trial."

"Do you agree, David Astell, that even if there had been no media coverage of his private life that his trial would be unfair?"

"Yes. I completely agree with Dr Gaines, there is a long-standing complicity between the legal establishment, the Government and the right-wing media in this country that people born with innate powers are open targets. You can see the change in tone of any news item as soon as it's discovered that somebody involved is on the Innate Powers Register. Even innately powered people as successful in their fields as Professor Gionchetta, Jack Pullman and Mr Brilliant have an uphill battle from the start to gain any positive press coverage."

"Now Mr Heathcote pleaded guilty to all charges from the moment of his arrest, surely this will count in his favour when it comes to sentencing?"

"Only in as much as the judge will assume that this is what he should have done anyway. With any non-powered person a judge would praise them for admitting guilt straight away, but like I say, for Heroes there is a different set of rules. Admitting guilt does you no favours, and we have seen this across other cases where the sentencing tariff doesn't tally with that of non-powered people committing similar crimes."

"Dr Gaines, there has been a lot of speculation around his sexuality for many years, in fact it was pretty much an open secret within the showbiz world, so why do you think Mr Heathcote resorted to murder to cover it up?"

"Well I don't know if can answer that one Kirsty. Mr Heathcote himself has alluded to his reasons in press interviews, but his true reasons lie only with him. I have not experienced myself the life situation of having to conceal my sexuality like that, but I, like many other Heroes, did have to conceal my abilities as a child back home in my native Australia, where even until the early two-thousands any child found by mandatory DNA test to have powers was taken from their parents into State

Care by default. I remember living with that fear of discovery, the strange shame of being different, wishing I was, 'normal', so my parents and I wouldn't have to keep moving around the country, and eventually leaving the country just to stay together. I suppose the pressure for him was the same, albeit for different reasons. I guess that fear made him react to protect himself. Part of the reason I set up the Church of the New Gods was because, after being free to use my abilities after coming to England, I was suddenly made to feel afraid again when the law changed. After it did, the Creator made it clear to me that He would return to set society right, to let all powered people walk openly in this country and allow us guide everyone into a great new era of freedom and knowledge."

"Can I just add that it won't be his sexuality that will prejudice him in this trial, thanks to the advances in LGBT equality over the last few decades, but it will be his powered status, which has shown no similar movement towards acceptance and in fact, further suppression and discrimination by the State and the Courts since the Restriction of Innate Powers Act came into force."

"Thanks to the both of you for being here. Mr Heathcote's hearing is dated for next Tuesday. We will of course be here throughout to keep you updated. Back to the studio."

CHAPTER 12
ARNOLD DRIVE, ELEMENT CITY

It was just before lunchtime as Hayley and her Police Community Support Officer beat partner emerged onto Arnold Drive, the main road through the middle of the south side of Element City. David was finishing off a breakfast baguette, wiping the brown sauce from the corners of his mouth with a cheap paper napkin. One way the road went straight towards South Bridge and into the City Centre, the other way it curved like a restless snake before splitting away into clusters of houses and small shops. They were heading towards the City, back to the station to complete their morning beat. It was busy with traffic, clustered around red lights and side road junctions waiting, or sometimes, forcing their turn into the flow. Most of the pavement edges were lined with cheap, dull grey metal railings, the odd flower basket hung over them to try and add some colour. Squat shops with flats above them lined both sides of the road. It was a typical mix of newsagents, "pound" shops, letting agents, cheap eateries and charity shops, with the occasional small branch of a bank or pharmacy separating them. Three boys in navy blazers and black trousers leaned against the railings next to a pedestrian crossing.

David walked over to a rubbish bin near the boys and dropped the food wrappings inside before moving over and chatting with them. Hayley joined him and they tried to find out why they weren't at school. The group lied, one of them failing to hide his amusement, saying school was starting later today because the first period teacher was off ill. Hayley said they had better get moving then, as the second period was almost starting. They seemed taken aback that she knew this and reluctantly picked up their backpacks and hurried up the road away from them.

David was a good partner for this part of town. He lived here himself and knew a lot of the shopkeepers and locals by name. He had good rapport with people, especially the kids, which meant they usually gave him at least some grudging respect.

"Just need a bit of a nudge sometimes," he said to Hayley as they walked on.

"As long as we don't see them again. If we do then I'm calling their school. Seriously, no first period? They never seem to think we've been to school too."

"I'll give them one point for coming up with a decent excuse though, but I'll dock it off again for the snickering."

Hayley watched them further up the road. They were looking back, trying to see where the officers were. One of them tapped another on the arm and disappeared into a newsagents. The others quickly followed.

"Oh dear. Looks like someone's getting a written warning."

"Oh come on, don't be too harsh on them. They're probably just getting some drinks before they head back to school."

"Somehow I doubt that's their plan. We've got a visit along here anyway. If they're still in there by the time we go in, it's trouble."

They called in to a small, narrow jewellers with a single window display and one long counter inside. The shop had been robbed a couple of months ago and Hayley liked to pop in whenever she was assigned this beat, just to give a bit of reassurance to the nice couple who ran it, as well as making themselves visible to any more would-be thieves. Of course, David knew the couple well and started chatting to the wife as soon as they went in. Hayley smiled and let him do most of the talking. She looked into the new toughened glass counter and found herself staring at engagement rings.

"You know, we're getting lots more women proposing to men than we used to." The husband had spotted her. "Society changes all the time you know, so don't hold back if there's a special man in your life!" he smiled.

Hayley shook her head.

"Nobody special. Not in that way, at least."

"Ah, one day there will be. Don't give up hope."

Hayley didn't think she had been hopeless in the first place, so it was nice of him to plant that thought in her head. It was then they heard screaming.

Hayley raced out of the shop onto the pavement to see a tall bald man collapsing onto the concrete clutching his neck. Bright red blood sprayed in dozens of fine spurts between his fingers and round the side of his palm as he fell on to his back. Two boys were running away. She picked out their details in seconds. She heard one of them shouting something about, "freaks", as she ran up to the man who was shaking on the ground, no longer able to hold his hand to his neck.

She grabbed her gloves and pressed them to the wound. She jumped back as an electric shock twisted her arm away.

The man's eyes were wide as he made grunting noises and tendrils of visible electricity started coursing over his face and neck. David was running up to her and stopped in his tracks as he saw this.

"Damn it." Hayley pressed the gloves into the wound with her fingers again, gritting her teeth against the pain, but had to let go for a second time as her arm convulsed itself towards her chest.

"Sir? Can you hear me? I'm a police officer. I need to put pressure on this wound. Please don't use your powers, otherwise I can't touch you. Do you understand?"

He slowly rolled his eyes towards her as he took sharp breaths in, the blood gushing out into a small stream that trickled away from his body towards the gutter. She wasn't sure he understood or if there was anything he could do. Sometimes Heroes gave one last burst of their powers just before death, some kind of unconscious physiological reaction, like they had been holding back a low-level manifestation of it all their lives and only now was it let out in one final expression of power. She pressed the wet, sticky gloves back against the wound. This time she only got a small shock, like static, small sparks going off in her hair.

Then she remembered the kids getting away. She was faster than David and he knew it.

"David take this."

"What?"

"Take this, put pressure on the wound and wait for the ambulance. I'll call it in."

"What? Look at him, there's no way I'm going to…"

"You will put pressure on that wound to save his life you hear me? Here…" She dragged his hands onto the gushing cut, forcing him to kneel, and pressed them down as sparks buzzed off their uniforms. "Like that, and keep them there!"

She got to her feet and ran round the corner that the attackers had disappeared behind.

"I337, State 14. Ambulance required Arnold drive and Mansfield Crescent, IPV neck stabbing bleeding heavily, E14 State 6."

They had already gone far, but weren't bright enough to have scattered and taken side routes. Hayley powered down the pavement, head cocked to her radio.

"In pursuit of suspects, Mansfield Crescent heading…" she took deep breaths "..away from Arnold drive. Suspects one IC1 male red top, blue jeans, blue trainers, careful sir!" she hop-skipped around a man in the middle of the pavement, "second IC3 male black hoodie, black jeans, white trainers."

She dropped her hand from the radio and pumped her arms to pick up speed. The wind rushing past caught her hat and blew it off. She ran past a side street, causing a van driver to hit his brakes.

The one in the dark hoodie turned round at the noise and spotted her. It was then the boys split up, the white lad took advantage of a break in the traffic to bound across the road. Hayley followed the taller black lad, trying not to disrupt her running pace.

"IC1 male heading up... Bower Park Road. In pursuit of other suspect."

Dispatch confirmed just as the runner suddenly dived into a grocers, scattering slim metal funnels of flowers across the pavement. Hayley leapt over them and followed him in. She saw his jacket disappearing into the back of the store and heard the shopkeeper yelling at him as she ran past and pushed through the swing door herself into a cramped stockroom. A stack of boxes was slowly tipping over at the end of a row of shelves, but there was no immediate sign of him. Hayley hopped on the spot.

"Shit." Then there was a scrape from the far corner and outside light burst in around the edges of the metal rails and boxes.

She kicked at the floor and scampered round the tight corner as the door slammed shut in front of her. She slid to a stop, pulled it open with a step back and threw herself out into the delivery alleyway. There were a surprising number of vehicles here, some deliveries, some belonging to the shop owners, some trying to avoid the parking charges on the main street.

Hayley looked left and right down the line of cars parked close up to the back of the shops, but saw nothing. She squeezed her way between a van and a black BMW to the other side of the alley. In front of her was a brick wall, just above her head height, that stretched from beginning to end of the road. She looked both ways again, barely enough room to squeeze a car through, no sign of the lad.

"Damn it." She started jogging up the alley, checking between the parked vehicles in case he was hiding there, checking behind her in case he had gone the other way instead. There was a percussion-like sound of a railing shaking from a collision. It came from the other side of the wall.

Hayley put her hands on the top of the wall and lifted herself up to look over. The land at the back was disused with old, two-storey warehouses in differing states of collapse. They bore notices of planned demolition and the building of new apartments dated to before the financial crisis, but now the work was on-hold. There was a strip of land about thirty metres wide between the wall and the back of the buildings. It was mostly tall grass and weeds, boxes and cooking oil drums dumped by the shopkeepers and scattered breeze blocks, huge wooden spindles used to hold piping and metal fencing left there by the original owners.

There was no sign of the lad, but she knew he must be in there. She could teleport over there in a split-second! She nervously glanced left and right. There was nobody there, but she still couldn't take the risk. If someone suddenly came out from behind the cars, or someone in a window with a view of the alley, or some hidden security camera, or someone sitting in one of the cars waiting, if anybody happened to spot her, it was all over. She grunted under her breath and stepped back as far as she could. She ran up and pulled herself on to the top of the wall, cursing her bulky stab-vest as it got in the way. She had to walk along the top of the wall for a few metres to avoid a pile of bricks on the other side and jumped down into the long grasses, slightly twisting an ankle on a hidden plank of wood. Guessing he would have gone the most direct route, (but with a sinking feeling that he knew all the rat runs in this area far better than she did), she ran into the building ahead of her.

The door was open, but it looked like it had been open for some time, debris blown into a small pile against it. She was in a series of corridors around the back offices, panels of plaster falling off the walls. There was nothing left, even the door handles and light switches had been scavenged and spirited away. She heard laughing.

"You want me copper?", echoed a voice from somewhere distant. She jogged through the corridors, checking corners carefully and soon emerged into a large empty storage room. She couldn't see him anywhere. She took a guess on a doorway on the far side of the room and moments later ended up pushing open a stuck door back onto Arnold Drive, a good mile back down the curving section away from town. The slow, nudging traffic forced its way along the road as pedestrians gave her a wide berth, eyes wide. The lad was nowhere to be seen.

Hayley bent over, resting her hands on her knees to regain her breath. It was only then she saw her hands. They were covered in blood, the ends of her right sleeve soaking in dark crimson halfway up her forearm. Bright red sprays patterned her reflective jacket and cut across her face.

She looked up to see a man in a car staring at her horrified. He said something to his children in the back seat, who looked anyway. She shook herself into the present, called in his last known location and ran back up the street to check on the victim.

CHAPTER 13
RANDALL FAMILY HOME

"I saw them on the TV, the Church of the New Gods. The guy who runs it understands what we're going through. He knows how Heroes are... prosecuted against by people. He must be able to help us."

"No, we're not going there."

"Well where then? There's nowhere else to go! No-one else is going to help us. We're going to lose him Ian! We're going to lose Lewis!" Jenny shook with tears, wiping her cheeks on the sleeve of her cardigan. Lewis was on the play mat, babbling to himself and driving plastic trucks over plastic cars, the latest of his self-made doggies lying on its side as wheels ran over it. Both of them were standing up, Jenny by the sofa, the back of her calves resting against the bulging edge of the seat pad, Ian in the middle of the room with his back to the windows, uncomfortably straight. She had shouted at him that he didn't care about Lewis because he wasn't doing anything, which she knew wasn't true as she said it. He had said she was stupid to think anyone else had more interest in helping Lewis than him, especially some creepy Australian guy running a Hero church. She had said she knew he thought she was just a stupid girl, she'd always known it and why the hell did he hook up with her anyway. He had said he knew she wasn't stupid at all, just worried. She had said that if he knew that why wouldn't he listen to her and get help. The exchange had been going on for the last twenty minutes and now they had reached that part of the argument where neither of them could get their point of view across any more clearly and both were exhausted from trying. Jenny dropped herself onto the sofa, red faced and hugging her ribs, sore from sobbing.

Ian knew she wasn't stupid, just naive, a bit gullible and a bit desperate. She didn't know much about the world of Heroics except what she'd seen on the news. He knew nothing about that Clifford guy, but his type were all the same, only in it to further their own goals, whether it was lining their pockets or getting famous. There was a whole range of powered and non-powered individuals who built their careers around scamming Heroes one way or another. Publicity agents, Registration guides, drug dealers, exponents of power suppression techniques, dodgy security companies looking for powered bodyguards for, "under-the-radar", clients, peddlers of fake DNA test results for job applications, specialist insurance brokers, blackmailers and, religious foundations on both sides of the divide who could help get you work, clear your record or cleanse your tainted soul for a fee. They were everywhere, especially if you were as obvious as he was.

The moment he got out of prison he was hassled by one or other of them at least a couple of times a week. Most got the message when his anger surfaced, after all, his history was public record, and they weren't that much in need of the commission.

But Jenny knew nothing of this. She would always see the best in anyone, if they were offering help then they must be nice. He loved her for her complete lack of cynicism, her innocence, but when it rubbed up against reality, especially now, it always caused friction. She always thought he was being uncaring, thinking she was dumb, when in fact the opposite was true. He wanted to protect her. Her and Lewis, and right now, he was failing. She was right about one thing, the Authorities were going to take Lewis, sooner rather than later, especially after his outburst.

That moment seemed like a fever dream now. He still couldn't figure out what the trigger was, even though he'd gone over it multiple times. He wished he'd kept going to the anger management classes and not cut them out as soon as they were no longer tied to his parole. He thought that with Jenny, and now with his boy, he had it all under control, he wouldn't need to be The Savage any more, just Ian. It looked like Ian wasn't going to be enough, and The Savage was gone long ago, which meant they really had no-one to help them.

"I'm sorry darling." He got down on his knees in front of her, her head still only coming half way up his chest. "The only people we have right now are each other. That's all we've got and that has to be enough.

No-one else understands, except maybe Martin, I trust him, but he can't help us any more than he has."

"But he's the reason we're here now! We should have just run away, we could have been abroad by now." She covered her eyes with her sleeve, letting the tears soak into it.

"Princess?"

"Oh, don't say that..." she took away her arm from her face and shook her head.

"Princess?"

She tilted her head to one side, a sliver of a smile appearing for the first time in days. She could see past his roughened and scarred features and into his eyes and knew in an instant he was feeling the same pain as she was.

"My handsome prince." She cupped his cheek in her hand.

"Together yeah? We'll get through this together, because we have each other. We don't need anyone else. It's going to be hard, I'm not going to lie to you..."

"You never lie to me."

"...but we'll get there. One day, they'll see we can look after him, and we'll get him back full time, and we'll be a proper family again. I promise Princess."

She flung her arms round him, burying her head under his chin.

"I know, I know."

With his claws bent under his forearms he gently hugged her, staring at the wall behind the sofa, face rigid with fear.

CHAPTER 14
MARTIN'S APARTMENT

"Speech therapist is getting on my fucking tits." Maria was sitting on the breakfast bar stool opposite Martin. She was awkwardly positioned. The organic, curved metal frame around her left leg meant she couldn't hook it under the chair, so instead it dangled loose and heavy, pulling her down on one side, but she refused to sit on the sofa. She hated the coffee table being too low down and too far away, having to fold herself over to reach it. It was only trading one discomfort for another thought Martin, but even after the beating Charles gave her, it looked like she had lost none of her stubbornness. At least he knew that part of her was the same.

"Says I need to work harder on my 's' and 'z' differentiation and my 'th' isn't strong enough. I felt like saying 'You try saying, 'sizing thongs', with a jaw full of metal and screws. Imbecile."

She sipped her coffee while Martin tried to hide a smile.

"In any case, I'm not sure I like the guy. Seems a bit over familiar if you know what I mean? And 'sizing thongs'? Why that? Completely inappropriate. He wouldn't make a child say that would he, but that's fine for a woman?" She shook her head and swirled her cup slightly, the foam head rolling around the inside rim. "I'd be better off myself, I mean you can understand me fine?"

"Yep."

"And a lot of the function will come back on its own once the swelling is all gone and the muscles have had time to heal properly, etc., etc. No, I don't think I need him any more. What are you smiling about?"

"Oh nothing, I just... I mean you're already on your second physiotherapist so I'm wondering how many speech therapists you'll go through."

"Well that first one was an idiot, wasn't she? She had me in agony going up and down stairs, and doing fitness exercises like I'm some kind of body builder. Ridiculous! The way I keep fit is by walking. I always used to walk around the woods back home with my mother as a child and I still do that now. I told her this and she ignored me! No, she had her own completely inflexible programme that I was somehow supposed to fit into." She did a huge shrug, before tucking the thin scarf closer in around her neck and slipping her finger into the cup handle again. The operation scar under her chin was red and bulged slightly, like a blood vessel just under the surface. She never mentioned it though, just kept a scarf wrapped round it and avoided looking up. When she had to, she would hold the scarf in place with one hand.

"How is getting someone doing physical activities they never do in their normal lives 'rehabilitation'? Just get them back doing what they usually do. Gradually. Then they're more likely to do it, aren't they?"

"Yep. Makes sense."

"Exactly."

They sat in silence for a while, sipping their coffees. Martin was sat with his back to the sofa. The TV was on the news channel again. Martin had gone to turn it off when she arrived, but she told him to just turn the volume down a bit, she couldn't stand dead silence. Maria was looking around the room behind him with her remaining eye, a plain black concave patch sat over her right orbit. That was something else she never mentioned. Martin just left it. He knew that if she ever wanted to talk about either her eye, or the scar, she would.

"Tsk. Can hardly bear to go back outside again, thanks to those damn paparazzi. At least they left me alone when I started teaching and doing research. I guess that wasn't 'sexy' enough for them. But now that the hearing is almost here, they are everywhere. They've even been hanging around the campus and research labs, trying to get interviews or to spot me, and I'm not even there! Which is another thing that's pissing me off..."

"That's not all?" thought Martin.

"… enforced sickness leave. Two months. And then a full physical and mental health assessment before I can go back. 'For my own well-being', they say. Fucking bullshit. That's what it is. They are just scared of legal action if I slip and fall, or think I'll go crazy with a knife. I wouldn't mind, but it's the fucking Psycho-psychology department! Of all places they should know that's not how the brain works."

"I guess they think it might help keep the photographers away if you're not there."

"Bullshit! Those people would do what they want whether I was there or not. It's just an excuse. Plus I don't trust that Professor Carter. He's been trying to grab some of my budget for his tenuously related studies for years. I wouldn't put it past him to be laying it on thick to the Board for Health and Safety and, 'my own well-being'. Bullshit." She took a deep breath in, and exhaled hard, shaking slightly. Martin took another gulp of coffee and put the cup down.

"So… you ready for the hearing tomorrow?"

"No. Not really. I'm glad we only need to be there for one day."

"We don't have to be there at all you know…"

"Of course we do! I want to be there to see that son of a bitch sentenced for life."

Martin couldn't argue with that.

"At least he's pleaded guilty and spared all of us the indignity of having to give evidence in court and risk our dirty laundry being exposed, or some over-enthusiastic anti-Hero reporter deciding to go pulling up floorboards, looking for more bodies."

"There is that I suppose."

"You have got your story straight about him attacking you in your old flat? Just in case?"

"Pretty much."

"Pretty much isn't good enough Martin, it needs to be spot on! Any inconsistencies between his and your accounts…"

"Yeah, yeah, I know, people might work out it wasn't him who attacked me. It's OK, thanks to Jack I got hold of a copy of Charles' statement before I had to go in and change mine. I made sure they tallied up. It's all covered. But we won't be asked to give evidence anyway. He's admitted it, we've already given statements to the police, he's charged. All that happens now is we find out how long he gets sent away for."

This was the part he was looking forward to the least. Not only had he lied in a police statement but now he might have to lie in Court He probably wouldn't, but despite his reassurances to Maria he wasn't entirely certain of the procedure.

Of course it had been Jack, not Charles, who had attacked him in his flat. But to have admitted that would have led to revealing that The Controller had been alive all these years, manipulating Jack. If that fact got out everything that happened in 1993 would be made public, and none of them wanted that. It was a good job he couldn't be read by psychics, otherwise they would instantly know he was lying. Also the court weren't allowed to use psychics to confirm testimony as they had been deemed to be even less reliable than electronic lie detectors. That didn't mean that there couldn't be a psychic in the gallery, a member of the public or worse, a journalist, and that could spell big trouble. The lie was embedded now. They just had to get through this hearing and, as long as no-one challenged their version of events, it would all be over soon.

A quiet, yet confident voice behind him caught Martin's attention.

"...father and daughter powered team took down the entire gang, forcing the ringleader Malcolm Gleasdale to call the police to have themselves arrested. Office supplies worth an estimated twenty-eight thousand pounds were recovered by police from the warehouse and three vehicles, a firearm and over three thousand pounds in cash were seized. Police later arrested two other men in London, believed to be couriers for the gang. The two heroes remain at large and have been put on the PCA Most Wanted List.

And in other powered news, the 1980s physically manifested Hero, The Savage, has been charged with Manifesting Innate Powers In Public and Criminal Damage after destroying part of Element City Council Child Services department and threatening staff with his abilities."

Martin froze in his seat.

"Oh no. Ian."

"What?"

He turned to watch the TV. Maria followed his gaze.

"The Savage has been charged under his real name, Ian Randall, after openly presenting his claws in a threatening manner to Council staff who were interviewing him and his partner. He also punched a hole through a wall, knocking a door off its hinges causing it to almost hit an employee. Luckily no-one was injured in the incident and Randall has been released on police bail, pending a court hearing date. Element City Council released a short statement saying: 'A powered incident took place at our offices earlier today which was quickly resolved with no injuries. The matter has been referred to the local police force and, as such, we will be offering no further comment while their enquiries are ongoing. We would like to stress that, whilst events of this nature are very rare, we will be reviewing our Powered Security Procedures.' Randall gave no comment as he was released from custody."

"Raymond Billington has revealed that his application for a Hero Team Licence..."

"Oh Christ."

"What?"

Martin turned back to the breakfast bar and stared into the mocha depths of his coffee cup.

"He... ah, he was here last week."

"What!"

"Asking for my help." He looked up. "Ian Randall. The Savage. In my apartment."

"You have to be kidding me."

"He was with Jenny, his partner, and their son. He wanted me to 'disappear' them because… well, because they thought I could for one thing, and because they were afraid Child Services would take their boy off them."

"Don't get involved." Maria's face was emotionless.

"I didn't, they came to me."

"Why?"

"Well I guess I happened to be in the news lately, so that probably jogged his memory. And he said he trusted me. So I told them to trust me that the worst thing they could do was run, that they had to stay calm and do everything the Council said. I hoped they would listen… now this."

"Don't get involved. Listen to me."

"I hear you."

Maria placed her hands on top of his. He looked straight at her. She looked worried.

"Seriously, Martin. We can't do that any more."

"Do what?"

"You know what I mean. You think I don't feel it too? When something fucked up happens and you immediately think you can help? It's not real. Yes, we did it in the past, but even then it wasn't real."

"Wasn't real? What are you talking about?"

"The Heroic Instinct. The Call to Help. However you name it, it's bullshit. You are not born with it like you are with abilities, they don't come tied together. It's just a culturally conditioned reflex. You grow up hearing that that's what you're, 'supposed', to do, so that's what you end up doing. We both grew up with that expectation, but it's not real. You and I are just ordinary people. We don't have any special responsibility or duty to help."

"Yeah, but now you have a generation of kids who have grown up without that. How often do you hear on the news about people being beaten or up stabbed and people turn a blind eye and just walk past, ignoring their cries for help?"

"Don't. Get. Involved. It's seductive, the feeling that you can help everybody, but the truth is you can't. And most of the time you're better off not doing anything. You were lucky not to go to jail for not registering. That was stupid. You do something else stupid and you won't get off this time."

Martin's shoulders sank. She was right, he had felt it just then. It was an invisible tug at his chest whenever there was a bad news item on the TV. It was trying to convince him he could help. That he had to help, otherwise what was the point of having these abilities? But then he would reason with himself: he wasn't a medic or a policeman or a fire fighter. Or even a Hero. He definitely couldn't let himself be that. So he would forget whatever it was and carry on as normal. But then, what the hell was he doing with Hayley?

"I don't want to see you go to jail, I've... only just found you again." Maria had curled her fingers under his palms and was gently squeezing his fingers together. He hadn't felt her do that, one of the problems of having super-tough skin. He turned his hands under hers to palms upwards and held her by the wrists as they looked into each other's eyes and smiled.

He was actually happy. He hadn't felt that content in a long time. For years he had tried to kid himself that being on his own was the best thing for him, that he needed solitude to deal with the dark intrusions from the past, needed to keep away from people and keep himself busy with work and TV so that the memories wouldn't sneak up on him.

It took Charles murdering Vincent and nearly killing Maria to make him realise he was wrong, that what he needed was someone to help him make sense of it all, someone to care about in the present day to make the past go away. However wrong their relationship was back then, when she was married to Jack, it was still real. Everything that happened with The Controller, what he did to them, in the end it hadn't destroyed what there was between them, but he knew, they both knew it would take a lot of time to recover what they had once had. They had nearly twenty years to make up after all.

"In any case, they wouldn't be taking his son unless he had done something wrong."

"No, no, Lewis is powered. Already. At ten months!"

"No shit? That's very young…"

"He's the next Elemental apparently, can create things out of thin air."

Maria went, 'pff', with her lips and let go of him.

"The Elemental was a fraud, a puppet being played by those in power. All this nonsense about him winning the war was bullshit. He could create handfuls of gunshot and horseshoes. Unique power, I'll give him that, but that's all."

"There's those statues of his in Element Park…"

"Hah! Alone in a studio with a sculptor and no-one else saw him create them. Yes he made a bicycle once, that's now a star exhibit in the Museum, but that's the height of it. He was an illusionist, learned his craft from the travelling shows and plied it with the help of others to turn himself into a Hero that every powered person since has tried to compare themselves to. If this child can create anything more complicated than a rock *then* I'll allow myself to be shocked."

"I don't honestly know, they never said."

"Because it's something they've done, not the kid… Shit!" Maria suddenly leant back in her chair, clutching her side.

"You OK?"

"Aah, fucking, fucking, fucking…" She grimaced for a moment until she could breathe again and opened her eyes to see Martin out of his seat, about to come round to hold her. "The scar. Paining again. It's OK. They said I might get this until it healed fully. It's fine," she puffed out a lungful of air. "It's gone now."

Martin slowly sat back down again.

"I'm fine, really." She sipped her coffee as if nothing had happened.

Martin carried on from before.

"Anyway, like I said, I just told him to do what they were told to and not get into trouble. Some advice, that's all. Then he goes and does this…" he thumbed over his shoulder to the TV. "I just feel like…" He stopped himself, remembering what Maria had said a moment ago. It was an instinct. Years of conditioning.

Nothing real. Ignore it. "...I wasted my breath. He's done what he's done, and I can't change that now."

"Exactly. You're not responsible for other people's fuck-ups. It's not like he's family anyway, he almost gutted me during one of their bank robberies, remember? And gave you a beating a good few times. From the looks of things he hasn't changed one bit. Leave him to screw up his own life."

CHAPTER 15
RANDALL FAMILY HOME

Two cars and a van pulled up outside Ian and Jenny's house. Eleanor and Jane stepped out of the first car while three officers got out of the police car behind them. The side of the van slid open and two armed officers in black body armour and helmets climbed out awkwardly onto the pavement. Eleanor took the lead and opened the gate immediately as she tried to suppress her pounding heart. Everyone knew what they had to do. It had been planned meticulously, albeit quickly, as soon as the word came through. Eleanor knocked on the door. Jane stood behind her, the police officers behind them and the two armed officers stood at the back to the sides, weapons down, with a view past them to the doorway. They heard loud footsteps coming down the stairs and the glass in the door filled up with Ian's shape. She heard Jenny say to him, 'There's police there!', but she didn't catch his reply.

Usually she could predict how things would go, but right now she didn't have a clue. It all depended on whether Mr Randall could keep control over himself or not. She heard him undo the latch and the door opened slowly. Ian looked at her and Jane, then scanned his eyes over the officers before spotting the two clad in black. He visibly stiffened. He looked back down at Eleanor.

"What is this?" He sounded fearful but composed, thought Eleanor. He knew what was about to happen.

"Mr Ian James Randall? I'm sure you remember me; I'm Eleanor Cheadham."

"Ian? What do they want?"

The door opened fully and Jenny was standing next to him holding Lewis. Her face was crumpled up in terror.

"Oh God, they've got guns!"

"That's for me love, not you," he said, putting an arm round her. "Yes, I remember you. What is this?"

Eleanor thought he looked sad. He didn't seem as tall as usual, shrunken down into his frame. She took a deep breath and held out a brown envelope.

"As a Senior Child Protection Officer, and on behalf of Element City Council I have applied for an Emergency Protection Order for your son Lewis Randall because I believe he is in immediate danger as laid out in the Innate Power Amendment under Section 44 of the Children Act 1989. I have here a copy of the Order signed by a Judge and I am here to take your son into the protective care of Element City Council until we believe the Order is no longer required."

"No…" said Jenny, as tears began to well up in her eyes.

"The officers here are for our protection only, should we need it, but we hope the situation doesn't come to that. May we come in?"

Ian looked at the officers again. He could smell the fear in all of them, especially the armoured one on the left whose gun arm was twitching already. He gently shook his head as he kept an eye on them.

"No. You're not welcome in our house."

Immediately one of the officers behind Jane stepped forward so that he was between the two women.

"Mr Randall, these Child Protection Officers are here to do their job. This will go much quicker and calmly if you let them do it."

"Did I say I wasn't going to let them do their job?"

"If they need to come inside they…"

"Did I say I wasn't calm?"

The officer eye-balled him for a long time.

"No you didn't sir, we…"

"Then it might help if you listen to the words coming out of my fucking mouth instead of making up what you think I'm saying, yes?" He looked back down at Eleanor. She could see he was struggling to compose himself, neck muscles contracting, swallowing, blinking hard.

"You're here to take Lewis yes?"

"No, no, they can't do that can they Ian?" Jenny was crying, trying to pull away from the door, but Ian held her steady as she squeezed Lewis to her chest.

"Of course they can darling. Because of me."

"I thought you said you weren't going to take him away? You wanted to keep the family together, that's what you said?"

"Jenny, I know this is painful, but right now we have to take Lewis for his own safety. Please don't make this any harder than it has to be. And... we really would prefer to do this inside."

The neighbours were out by now. Standing in doorways, in their gardens and a few of the more adventurous ones had crossed the street and stood on the pavement, closely watching the house. The police officers, annoyed that they hadn't gained access to the house, and that Eleanor and Jane hadn't insisted on it, instead called on the onlookers to step away. One asked what was going on and was ignored. She turned to her friend next to her and said, "That was rude!"

Eleanor leant forwards. Even though she requested their presence, she was eager to avoid the police officers becoming forceful.

"If you give me him right now, we can be away in moments. Delaying things will only make it that much harder. Also it will keep the audience away." She tilted her head back and Ian spotted the neighbours gathering around. One officer was moving towards them, gesturing them to move back.

Ian turned to look down at Jenny who was sobbing uncontrollably. A small tear slipped out of one eye and slowly made its way down the twisting lines across his face.

"Give him to Eleanor love. This is my fault and this is the first step to making it right. Remember what

Martin said? Just do everything they say, don't give them any reason to make them think we can't look after him. If we do, we'll never see him again. This way, we will. And I'll make it up to you. I promise."

Jenny pulled Lewis up to her face and pressed her lips against his forehead, tears rolling down onto him. Ian rubbed a knuckle on the back of his head and swallowed hard.

"Please Jenny." Eleanor was holding her arms out to her. "We'll take the best care of him. That's my promise."

Jenny nodded and took a step forward so she was under the door frame. She slowly held out Lewis to her. She never looked away from his face. Eleanor took him, turning him round so he faced her.

"Hello," she said to him, as he stared at her bewildered. She then mouthed a, 'thank you', to Jenny. She held Lewis to her, covering his head with one arm to shelter his face. She spoke to the senior officer behind her. "It's fine, we have the child now. Thank you. We just need a few of his things, toys, blanket, clothes and such."

He gave a nod, and ushered her past him down the path.

"Mr Randall, we will need to..." the senior officer stepped towards the door.

"NO-ONE IN THE HOUSE!"

There had been a buzz, a chatter from the growing crowd, but it suddenly all went silent. The officer froze as the two in black pressed their rifles tightly into their armpits and bent their knees. Ian stared at the officer.

"I heard her. I'll get them." He said slowly, and disappeared upstairs.

Eleanor hurried over to her car with the boy in her arms. Jane followed and opened the rear door. She slipped Lewis quickly into a child seat that had been fitted before they left, making sure he was secure. The boy wasn't crying, but looked really confused. Eleanor took his hand and told him it would be OK.

Upstairs in the house Ian picked up his latest doggy from the landing floor, grabbed a blanket from his cot and opened a drawer with a claw, carefully lifting out some tops and trousers, and dropping them onto the open palm of his other hand. Everything was automatic. He was keeping calm, keeping rational, but he felt hollow inside. The world seemed to go slower as he came downstairs. Each step another hour into the past, another day when they still had Lewis. He kept thinking to himself, over and over, 'It will be fine', 'It will work out for the best in the end', 'Stay calm and you'll see him again', unable to truly convince himself. By the time he reached the bottom of the stairs, the doorway was clear. Jenny was outside on the lawn, crying, being supported by a female officer as Eleanor and Jane got into the front seats of their car. The armed police were standing by the side of their van. More people had gathered, the whole road was out, eyes on everything.

"...that's their boy..."

"...I hear they were fiddling with him..."

He ignored them. They didn't know, so nothing they said meant anything. He stepped outside, his body suddenly expanding in size as he squeezed through the doorway.

"I've got his things." Ian held out his hand, fingers outstretched, clothes, blanket and toy in his palm. Jenny quickly made towards him and picked them up. She was about to run over to the car when the female officer stepped in and put her hands on the bundle of clothing.

"No, we'll take this."

Jenny gave the items up reluctantly and the officer jogged over to the car. She knocked on the window and spoke to Jane before dropping the items on the back seat next to Lewis.

"...only a matter of time before he caused some trouble..."

"...had to happen some day..."

The senior officer was saying something to them both, but Ian wasn't listening, he was staring at Lewis fastened into a child seat in a stranger's car. He was holding his doggy in front of his face by both ears, looking intently at it. Had he picked up the right one? Ian cursed himself. If it was one of the older ones he would start crying any minute... no, he was chewing it now. He relaxed as Lewis turned to look out the window at them, frowning.

He had to believe he would see him again. All he had to do was stay calm and let these complete strangers do tests on their son while they kept them apart. He cursed himself again as his own thoughts betrayed him. He was losing his boy. He had to do something, hadn't he?

"...obviously unfit parents..."

"...shouldn't be allowed to have children if they're like that..."

"What was that?" Ian broke away from the cluster of people on his front lawn, stepped over the small wall onto the pavement and in a few strides was face to face with a plump middle-aged woman who lived a couple of doors down from them. She visibly cowered as he stood next to her, holding onto her friend. "What did you say?"

She said nothing. Jenny and one of the police officers moved towards them.

"If you have something to say about me or my family you say it to my FUCKING FACE, you hear?"

The officer hesitated in putting a hand on him.

"Sir, please, this isn't helping. Come back to your house. Let's go inside and calm down for a moment."

"Ian, don't."

"You hear me? Yeah?"

The terrified woman nodded, but her friend spoke up.

"You can't talk to her like that! I'm not afraid of you!"

"But she can talk to *me* like that, yeah? That's all right is it? Fuck you."

The officer gently moved the two ladies back and stepped between them.

"Not now Sir, please, let's move back."

Ian straightened up and looked around at the faces staring at him. Accusation. Fear. Disgust. Suspicion. Hatred. Nothing had changed in twenty years. Nothing.

"Fuck all of you!"

Eleanor's car started its engine, did a slow U-turn in the road then quickly pulled off, rising up the slight hill, shrinking into the distance. Ian turned and watched it go. His heart pulled at his neck and he gasped for breath.

"They've taken my boy. They've taken my baby." Giving in to the weight of his body he collapsed to his knees, cracking the paving slabs, and broke into sobs that shook his whole body.

Jenny gently put her hands on his head, whispering, "It's OK, he'll be OK."

He put both arms around her as she cradled him and they stayed there crying until it became too uncomfortable for the neighbours to watch and they went back inside.

CHAPTER 16
ROOMS UNDER THE OAK AND ARCHER PUB

"This is what I mean!" Bobby teetered on the front edge of a softly battered old wooden chair in the Pub basement. His whole body strained forward, as if fighting against an invisible, giant elastic band. His eyes were fixed on the small flat screen TV they had hooked up to the Pubs' old aerial. "This is exactly the shit I mean!" He flung a hand towards the screen as the news report finished and the anchor moved onto the next item. "Fucking dammit!" He got up, kicking the chair away from under him and stomped over to the corner under the thin slit windows. Carl and Rebecca looked at each other. They both knew he wasn't done, so didn't say anything. Jed sat behind them, playing a game on his phone. Steve had been injured and got spooked after the supermarket kill and they hadn't seen him for days. The new guy Michael, who was looking like his replacement, had been sent to get milk and coffee for the kitchen while they scanned the TV channels for updates. "Fuckers, fuckers…"

Bobby walked back to the spot he had sat, rubbing one hand through his curls, another on his hip. He stopped and stared at the TV again. A politician was talking earnestly about removing corruption from the European parliament.

"MUTE!"

It went silent at Bobby's command. He turned, panting, to face the three sat down. "Did you see that? Did you see that yeah?"

Rebecca nodded in sympathy, while Carl frowned.

"We didn't even make the fucking news! We've taken out two powers in the last two weeks, in broad fucking daylight, and all we get is a ten second headline for each one. Then we turn up outside the Court of that murdering powered bastard and not even a mention of us being there! All the news is about his hearing, about how he's going to spend the rest of his life in jail (good riddance), and now that fucking…" he waved his hands around "…Savage guy being arrested. I mean who fucking cares about these freaks! Jee-sus Christ! What about what WE have to say!" His face had turned red, contorted.

"We've doubled the number of daily visitors to our blog from the leaflets we handed out at the Court."

"Oh great, so we've got a hundred instead of fifty? Well that's going to make a great deal of fucking difference TO NOTHING."

"Hey, don't have a go at me!" Rebecca raised her finger to him. "We've had twenty-three new subscriptions which..."

Bobby made a rasping noise at the back of his throat.

"...which might not sound like a lot, but if even half of those get involved in the comments, and half of them can make it to meetings..."

Bobby walked back to the window shaking his head.

"...it all adds up, over time. People network, tell other people and in time it will snowball. Don't forget you only started this group a few months ago. There are other groups out there just like us who have much bigger followings..."

"NO!" He spun round to face her. "No other group is like us! We actually ACT on what we believe instead of fucking around, whingeing in chat rooms. Twenty-three might sound great to you, but we need hundreds, thousands of people if we're ever going to get these powered bastards off the streets."

"Well that's not going to happen overnight is it? We need to build up our profile first, and going to the Court was a start."

"Getting any kind of a mention in the media would be a fucking start! Did you see the paparazzi and TV cameramen out there? They didn't even acknowledge us, ran right by us to get shots of that Roadblock guy and the Professor coming out. And all the footage of the Court was edited so we weren't in frame..."

"That's because we're not allowed to stand..."

"I don't CARE where we're not allowed to fucking stand! It's the pavement! If there'd been another day of it, I would have stood on the steps right in front of them, let the police drag me away. Maybe then we'd get on the news."

"Or arrested."

"On what charge? Actually caring how much damage these freaks are doing to our society? Wanting people to pay more attention to their illegal activities than just one incredibly rare trial with that Charles Heathcote lapping it all up?"

"Bobby, we know all this, OK? There's no need to tell us again."

He closed his eyes and sat down heavily on the nearest chair, rubbing his hands hard across the top of his skull.

"I just don't know what we need to do. It's like they want to be blind. I can't make them see."

Carl kept silent. He never knew what to say when Bobby was like this. He never really knew what to say at all. He couldn't speak as well as him, put his thoughts together in the same way, or stand up with the same confidence and convince people he was right. So he followed him and watched him and made sure he did whatever Bobby asked, however he felt about it inside.

All through school Bobby had looked out for him. He never knew why, but one day when he was being routinely picked on by "Fat" Francis and his cronies, punched in the stomach for existing in the same country as them he supposed, suddenly Bobby came bounding along, hair even curlier back then, and stood right in the way. He never worked out how he did it. He told them the same things he had been telling them for years, "You're a bully", "Stop it", "Try that again and I'll do you", but somehow it worked for him. Sure, he'd seen him swing a punch since, but he didn't need to. Francis just spat some swears at him, telling him he'd better watch his back and walked off, and that was it. As far as he knew, Francis and his lot never touched him. He'd wondered about it since and realised that it wasn't the words, it was the way you said them. Not just that, but the way you moved and how you acted when you said them. He would try and copy him in front of a mirror in his bedroom, but he looked like a primary school kid in a play trying to act tough. He would get painfully self-conscious seeing himself like that and jump into bed face-first and start crying, frustrated at his stupid small body and inability to say the right thing.

In the end he gave up, he knew he couldn't do it. He just had to stay close to Bobby and he'd be all right, and he did, and he was. All he was asked in return were little favours, to go speak to these guys, to take this there, look out for police, get another name, distract the shopkeeper.

"You'll work something out," said Rebecca, seemingly out of ideas too.

Jed finally spoke without looking up from his game.

"I don't know man, just tell me where the next one is and let's do 'em."

"That's on Carl," said Bobby.

Carl hastily shoved a hand in his pocket, scrunching up the small piece of paper he was going to grab. He pulled it out, unfolding it carefully.

"Got two actually…"

"Sweet." Jed leaned over his shoulder and grabbed the list from his hands.

"Same as always guys, follow them, get their routine, work out the safest but most public place you can do it, then do it, yep?"

Jed nodded solemnly and folded the short list up with one hand, phone in the other, and slipped it into the outside pocket of his jacket.

"Your contact still good?"

"Hmm?" Carl wanted the list back, he didn't like it when it left his hands, typically to Jed.

"In the Council? The one with access to the list?"

"Oh yeah, he hates them more than you do. No problems there."

"OK." Bobby trailed off in thoughts of plans and wandered off into the kitchen, leaving them there and ending the meeting.

Jed tapped Carl heavily on the shoulder, making him spin round. He jammed his thumb towards the door and got up.

That was it then, Carl guessed, more detective work to do. He liked calling it detective work, it took the sting out of it. As he got up he gave Rebecca a weak smile. She was going to have to deal with Bobby now, the guy hated being on his own, especially when he was trying to work something out like this. He did think it was a bit weird she was still part of their group, seeing as the two of them had split up months ago, but that was Bobby he supposed, he could talk anyone into anything. Rebecca frowned back. She kept her seat and was still there when he looked back from the door, until Jed shouted at him from halfway up the stairs to the street.

CHAPTER 17
THE CHURCH OF THE NEW GODS

Two dogs barking at each other disturbed Clifford. He turned from his monitor and looked out of the window behind him. There was pitch darkness up to head height then, visible above the hedges out back, were the distant lights of windows from the new development. He turned his head left and right but saw nothing but night time either side. The sound must have been carrying from far away. All that was left of the sunlight was a blue and purple band of horizon illuminating a strip of thin clouds from behind, and soon that would be gone too. The phone had finally stopped ringing, giving him a few moments peace to do other work. Newspaper reporters and TV stations had been wanting quotes about the Charles Heathcote trial and The Savage all day, every day, for the last week. He had spoken publicly before, but the stand-up interview outside the Court had really brought him a lot of attention. Of course it was because the trial was so huge, lots of media attention and lots of talking heads needed for news spots.

Not only was there press interest, new faces had appeared at the Church during the past week. Some were just curious minds, people who came once and were never seen again. Others had been to his services and the 'Be Informed Powered Issues' meetings. Most of those had powers, according to Grant. All low level abilities, nothing striking, but then again, he thought to himself, The Elemental himself came from mixed-ability parents, only his mother having the power to cast light from her body. So he didn't feel too disheartened. In fact, the more the better.

He sat down again, rolling his neck to relieve the tension and continued on his latest blog post.

Emily had been watching him for a few minutes now from the darkness of the hallway outside. He worked late on his computer every night, either on a blog post, or emailing some journalist, or updating his studies. She knew she would always find him here.

The room behind the stage had a high ceiling with three tarnished bronze chandeliers hanging from long cables. The ceiling rose of one of them had detached from the plaster and rested where the cable entered the light fitting. The back wall had nearly full height windows made up of small squares along its length, making it look like some sort of factory. There were only a handful of pieces of furniture in the room. Clifford's desk had a well loved mahogany top, with two drawers and a green leather inset pad that had faded to pale yellow in the centre. On the desk were his computer monitor, keyboard and mouse (the computer case itself hidden underneath in the foot well), a letter rack, one of those classic dark green glass and brass desk lamps, several piles of papers and a round wooden cup brimming with odd pens and a novelty letter opener with a black precious stone koala bear on the top end.

Oddly, his chair was nothing special, a cheap black office model from Argos. Emily wondered why he didn't have a big leather one to go with the desk, which had followed him around for years. There were two bookshelves against the wall opposite the desk, filled with books on Heroes and their teams. There was a mix of historical non-fiction, biographies and books ranging from serious academic analyses to throwaway "tell-all" stocking fillers. One half of one bookshelf was cardboard magazine holders filled with copies of "Power up!", "Heroism Today" and scientific journals dedicated to Powered Studies. Another shelf was dedicated to Clifford's own research on The Elemental, printouts of notes, newspaper clippings in binders and a rare original copy of The Elemental's edited journal, printed after his death. The only other pieces of furniture were an old sofa, coffee table and sideboard at the far end of the room. A fairly new coffee maker sat on the sideboard and the table had several days' worth of newspapers on it, one half-read and open at a large picture of Charles Heathcote entering court for his hearing.

Clifford was a four-fingered keyboard hammerer. The keyboard almost imperceptibly moved with each downward thump and after every paragraph or two, he had to pull it back towards him.

Emily grinned to herself. He hadn't noticed her at all, and not because she was using her power either. She walked through the doorway and towards the desk.

"Clifford?"

For a second he didn't respond, then his fingers stopped, hovering mid-pounce, and he turned to look at her.

"Oh, Emily, dear, sorry… I didn't see you come in. You weren't ghosting on me were you?" he smiled.

"Of course not, you know I wouldn't do that to you."

Clifford stood up.

"I know, I know, I'm only joking with you." They embraced, he putting his hands flat into the small of her back, she wrapping her arms as far round him as she could reach. They separated and he lightly clasped her upper arms in his hands.

"How are things?"

She tilted her head to one side.

"I think Mark is getting a bit antsy with so many people around, thinks he's going to whisper to them all without himself knowing. Claire is still getting texts and calls from her family. I keep telling her she needs to dump the phone, but she hasn't separated properly yet. Everyone else is whingeing about the cheap beds and having to share a bathroom."

"I am trying to make things more comfortable up there for everyone, but you know that if I start moving too much furniture in someone will notice and wonder what it's for."

"I know, no-one is supposed to be living here, you don't have a residential permit and all that."

"And I don't have enough money left to get you all proper accommodation. You have no idea how badly I feel about that. I would love nothing more than to see you all comfortable in your own places, but... needs must for now."

"Hey, I don't mind, I've stayed in dorms before and shared at University, so it doesn't bother me at all. Just thinking...I'll maybe try and get Mark out more, helping with some of the local projects. Might take his mind off things."

Clifford tilted his head to one side and cupped her head in his hands.

"You are truly a good girl Emily. Always thinking of others."

She went slightly red, glancing down to the floor, but then took a deep breath in and brought her hands up under his and cupped his face in return.

"And you are a good man. A very good man, who spends far too much time down here on his own. More than is good for him. You need some company." She moved closer to him as his hands dropped to her waist.

"I can be your company?" Her glassy blue eyes gazed up into his as she went up on her toes, leant in towards him and kissed him lightly on his mouth. He didn't react at first, then pressed his lips to hers for a longer, second kiss. Then he started shaking his head and, taking her wrists, gently pushed her hands away from him.

"I'm sorry Emily. You know I care about you... so much, but we're not the right pairing."

Her crumpled smile wavered for a second, before it got bigger.

"That's not what you said last time Clifford."

Clifford gently pushed her hands down and moved towards her to kiss her. Emily tried to turn her head up to meet his lips, before awkwardly realising he was aiming for her forehead and dipping it down instead. He kissed her just under her hairline. She was looking down to the side, blinking when they separated.

"However much we care about each other, you know the cause is more important."

She nodded, her head still turned away from him.

"This is about more than you and me, this is about The Creator himself Emily. This is about... everything we've been striving for over the years. That everything I've been praying for would happen."

"But that's genetics, this is love."

"Genetics determines love." She turned her head to look at him as he went on.

"And genetics determines our future from the moment of conception. That's what we have to work towards here. We have been chosen because only we know The Creator is waiting for us out there, and it is up to us to help bring Him back into the world. Even if that means us having to create Him from scratch."

Emily had heard it all before, and knew it must be true. She trusted Clifford, but the mission made it hard for her sometimes.

"I know. I, I... just thought, there's no harm in... indulging in some mutual love as long as it doesn't interfere with... things? You know?"

"And how are 'things' with you and Kevin."

Her face changed instantly, her brow digging deep towards the top of her nose.

"He's a dick."

"Hey!"

She stood to attention, eyes wide.

"He may not be the most... thoughtful of people, but he is the best match for you, and he believes in the cause strongly."

"Yes, only because it means he's guaranteed to get laid at least once a week."

Clifford sighed.

"Look. I'm sorry he isn't a better match for you in personality..."

"Be nice if he had one..."

"...but, The Creator knows best for all of us. There is... nothing more I would like than to have you by my side all the time."

Emily did her buckled smile.

"But we have chosen the path of sacrifice to aid His passage, His return into the world. We must both be strong for each other, and the cause, to help bring Him back."

She moved away from his arms, over to his desk. She rolled her lower lip around between her teeth as she tried to blink back tears.

"Look, I know you're sure we can create The Creator, but I still think we will find Him out there.

Outside," she gestured towards the black night, reflecting a perfect copy of the room back at them. "He could already be there, anywhere in the world. I feel like we should be scouring continents looking for Him, not sitting here, handing out leaflets and mending fences."

"Well, if that is the case Emily and He is already born, then Element City is the place we're going to find Him. This City has been a magnet for powered people since it was renamed in His honour. Something like twenty eight percent of the population here are powered. That's the highest proportion of powered individuals anywhere in the world, and growing daily. If He is here we'll find Him. Or Her, of course," he smiled.

Emily put one hand on her belly, a small ring of flesh visible between the top of her skirt and her tight pink and black top. She swayed slightly, one hand on the corner of his dark desk.

"I think I would like a girl. Especially if it's Him. That would be ace."

Clifford smiled.

"I actually watched the ballet class earlier. Don't worry, they didn't know I was there, I was ghosting on the side of the stage. My mum forced me to go to ballet for a few years before I finally told her where to go. Felt an idiot dressed like that with black eye liner. But you know, seeing all those cute little girls in their pink leotards and tights... I kind of think if I had a girl, I'd make her do ballet too. Not to make her hate it as much as I did, she might love it, who knows? But just... I just think it would be nice to see that."

"And that's why I love you Emily. Because I know, wherever your child comes from, you will be not just an amazing mother for Her, but the best role-model She can have, giving Her the chance to try anything she wanted, expanding Her confidence and knowledge. You would prepare The Creator for this new world She was born into by granting Her every opportunity to learn Her place in it. I can feel this in my heart." He slowly walked over to her and took both her hands in his. "Go be with Kevin tonight. Right now he is immature and restless, unsure of his place in the world. As a father… trust me, that changes a man more than I could ever do with words alone. You can make a good family, and if your child should be The Creator, then I would be eternally happy in my sacrifice."

Emily rocked on one heel, chewing her lip again, then hugged Clifford. She pulled away, gave him a gentle nod and slowly made her way out to the corridor.

Clifford waited until he couldn't hear her feet on the wooden stairs any more before letting out a huge sigh and rubbing his forehead. He went back to his PC and with a few clicks brought up a spreadsheet. One sheet was a list of horizontally laid-out family trees of well-known Heroes, with their power classification written underneath, or left blank if they had none. At the top was The Elemental and his family tree stretching back to the sixteen-hundreds. A lot of those names had "?" underneath. Despite scouring records and journals and letters for years it was impossible to determine whether his ancestors had powers, as they were barely recognised as such, let alone talked about in that era.

There were some hints here and there, multiple trips to the doctor for one child, another relative who only had a handful of mentions anywhere, the assumption being she was kept hidden by the family, perhaps a PMA? He scanned over the list as he had done hundreds of times before. It made sense to him now, he could see the patterns he had worked out over years of study, but he still had to check. He had to keep checking in case he had missed something, got something wrong, but the patterns looked the same.

He clicked onto the next sheet. There was less text on this one. These were fictional family trees not with names, but types of powers belonging to parents and typical outcomes for Powered children. Some had a percentage next to them, some had question marks, some had notes like, "skips a generation?" or, "ONLY if mother is grade 3 or above". He clicked again. The final sheet had three trees. The top one had "Emily (perception affector)" and "Kevin (waveform generation)" paired with the outcome "(matter destruction??)". The second had "Claire (energy projection)" and "Mark (psychic - projective or tactile)" leading to "(energy projection/manipulation?)". The third one had no names, but listed the powers of The Elemental's parents, (none?) for his father and (energy projection) for his mother, leading to "(matter creation and manipulation - objects of will)".

Clifford tapped the screen with his finger under that cell.

"Where are you?" he said to himself. "Where the hell are you?"

Just then, a notification popped up on his screen from his BBC news feed. It was a follow-up story about The Savage. His child had now been taken into care under an Emergency Protection Order after the incident at the Child Services Department. Clifford shook his head then sat back, thinking. The child had to be powered. They wouldn't take it off him just because he had claws and a short temper, that wouldn't wash in Court, no matter how anti-powered the public sentiment was right now. If he could piggy-back off the Charles Heathcote trial onto this, that would keep his profile up after making a splash with the interview outside the Court, show he was really on the side of Heroes, and increase the flock in the process. He would have to find out the details. He couldn't go swinging in there if The Savage had done something else more serious to cause the child to be taken. That would ruin everything, he'd be dragged down by the negative publicity. He allowed himself a wry smile. It always paid to have contacts. Having a Detector, his network had been surprisingly easy to find. There were plenty of people hiding their abilities from their employers whom he was able to cultivate for information. He wondered if Peter in the Benefits Department had heard any gossip.

CHAPTER 18
BOYDEN BRIDGE SECURE
ASSESSMENT CENTRE

The Centre was kept mostly dark at night. The only full lights were on in the reception area, security office and bathrooms. The main corridors had orange night lights on the walls for safety, but all the residents' rooms were lights off at 8pm. The building itself was a red-brick new build, not ten years old, hidden in plain sight in that awkward part of a City where the big business and office district meets the residential areas. The offices were smaller, with fewer floors. Sat between them were apartments, flats, large buildings belonging to old clubs and societies and the odd town house, garden acceptably overgrown, that had escaped the regeneration programmes. The night security guard sat behind the reception desk, cords of his ear-buds dangling down the front of his shirt, mouthing and whispering along to his, "I Bet You Can Learn French Now!" app so as not to disturb those sleeping.

All of the residents were children. They usually stayed for a few weeks while their abilities were assessed and either returned to their families or were assigned specially trained foster parents if their own were considered unable to look after them. The oldest child was a month off his sixteenth birthday, the youngest was ten months. The older children were either given rooms to themselves or, if they were tight for space, shared a larger twin room. The younger ones shared bigger dorm-like rooms with three or four smaller beds or bunks. One small room was set aside for very young children but, as not many ever came, it was used for overspill during busy periods. The single bed had now been stripped and moved to the break room, sat up on its side behind the TV couch. In its place a cot had been assembled, (with much cursing and trapping of fingers), and in the middle lay Lewis, quietly snoring on his back, one hand lovingly throttling his bunny.

While the building had a night guard, security doors to prevent the children leaving, CCTV outside, and a high-security area for children with more dangerous powers, it was not the kind of place considered susceptible to break-ins. It meant that the rear fire-escape door was easily forced open with a crowbar and the alarm cord cut could be without anyone noticing. The smallish figure was clad all in black, apart from a navy blue top, and went up the staircase inside the door to reach the security door on the first floor corridor. They pressed a white swipe card with a blank grey face for a picture, against an oval plastic box on the wall near the handle. There was a quiet beep and a small LED turned green. Quietly, the figure closed the door behind them and started working their way down the corridor, room by room. The pale light from the corridor was only barely enough to illuminate the inside, but from the door they could see how large the room was, how many and how big the beds were, and that's all that was needed to confirm it was the right one. About halfway down, the main staircase interrupted the left-hand side of the corridor. The figure paused and peered down into the light coming from the reception area. It was mostly quiet apart from a humming drinks machine and somebody muttering in French. After listening for a while, the figure continued to check the rooms.

The smallest room was on the left, just the other side of the stairs. Lewis made gentle sucking motions with his lips as the figure scooped him up with his blanket and toy. Moving faster now, back down the corridor, back past the staircase. The figure cursed silently, struggling to get the swipe card from a trouser pocket while carrying the child. The sensor beep was far louder this side of the door and they paused again to hear if anyone had been disturbed. Nothing. Down the fire escape stairs, out the fire escape door and out into the night went the sleeping baby Lewis.

CHAPTER 19
THE CHURCH OF THE NEW GODS

You sit on the back row, near the exit. You're still not sure if you should be here, but something feels right about it. The pale-faced girl with the black hair and the cute smile who gave you the leaflet - she had powers. You just knew it. So did the tall and rather scary black guy who looked completely emotionless. He's not a gang member or drug dealer, you could tell, but he has something else about him. You scan the backs of the heads of the people sitting towards the front. Most are in the front three rows, but some, like you, sit a bit further back. The unconvinced? Or maybe they have tactile powers and avoid contact. You reckon they all have powers.

This Church of the New Gods is somewhere you feel relaxed to be. Calmer than you have felt in a long time. It seems right, but you sit at the back because you have been to enough churches in your time where the moment the sermon is finished the priest, or vicar, or one of their helpers launch themselves on you, asking for details, trying to get you to come to events or perhaps your children can come? Do you sing? We have a choir you know, they say. Yes, yes, you know they do and no, no you're not interested, you just came because it was Christmas and/or you were forced to come along by your wife or family, or you were restless one day, black thoughts swirling too close to the surface and you needed a quiet, contemplative place to let them settle, and your constant digging into my private life isn't helping get rid of these thoughts of a knife in your neck right now. You've been to enough places like that to know how they operate. But this one seems different. More of a safe haven, an escape from the world.

You look at the leaflet while you wait. It's an A4 sheet folded in three with, "Church of the New Gods. We're here for Heroes", on the front. You open it out and read information about the history of the Church. They believe that another Creator like The Elemental will return one day. He was unique, the only Hero to ever have that power. After helping the country win the Crimean War he returned home and was given his choice of city to be named after himself and to be transformed into a new capital city where people with powers were welcomed, somewhere where their talents could be harnessed to further British industrial and military might. The Church's mission is to continue his work and support all Heroes in the community with spiritual, financial and legal matters. You read in horror the stories of harassment of powered people, how differently they are treated in law. You don't recall hearing about most of these stories on the news. You read about their work in the non-powered community, opening the hall up for use by others, trying to regenerate the area by creating safe green spaces for children to play in, volunteering to fix damaged fences and walls, giving out clothes to the vulnerable in winter. They do a lot more than you realised. So selfless.

You think the world would be a better place if it was filled with more people like them, and less of the type you work with. Less of the selfish alpha-male sociopaths who care nothing for how they make other people feel. The things they say... it would be bullying anywhere else. Hell, it is bullying, but the moment you were to raise an official complaint, that would be the excuse they needed to get rid of you somehow, so it isn't bullying it can't be bullying, it's banter. Banter you laugh off before excusing yourself to the bathroom a few minutes later to sit on the lowered seat, trembling with tears. Yes, just high-spirited office banter. Just banter, that's all it is. Bastards. But you can deal with it. You've had years of it and you know how to deal with it. It doesn't matter how many times they call you an idiot or useless, which they do, regularly. You just ignore it. But do they call you an idiot because you aren't an alpha like Alex, or because you never rise to the abuse and give him the visible outcome that he wants to see, or because you never come back with a witty retort to show that the abuse doesn't matter to you, it's just banter? You have never worked out why and the risks of experimenting with responses, to try to work it out, are too great to contemplate, so you make yourself quiet, smaller, less interesting, so you have less chance of being a target in the first place. It's a coping mechanism that works sufficiently well enough to keep on using it.

Then there are the dark times where you work out ways to get him alone somewhere to kill him. Over the years you have been through hundreds of permutations of scenarios both inside and outside the office, trying to whittle it down to the sequence most likely to result in his death and you getting away with it. You've managed to get it down to two. The gentle applause startles you and you fold the leaflet up and place it on the empty seat on your right. You couldn't take that home, the wife would see it and questions would be asked, and you prefer to avoid questions as they lead to arguments.

That's him on the stage now, Clifford Gaines. You saw him on TV the other day, making a very eloquent statement about the rights of powered people. It was the first time you had heard of his Church, but then that's not surprising given the size of the City and your previous lack of interest in Heroes. Seeing him on TV made you think this man has got something. He's right. He knows he's right, and you believe he's right, and something… just felt right about seeing him, that made you want to search the internet for more information, for the address, for the times of the sermons, to look on Google maps for parking spaces nearby. He seems taller than he was on TV. Brighter too.

You say you were never interested in Heroes, but that's only because they've never involved themselves in your life in any way to change it. The closest you ever came to a Hero was in your late twenties, months before the Registration Act came into force. You were on the High Street at lunchtime, on your way to grab some sandwiches and a juice drink when you heard cries coming from above you. Then people around you started to scatter, ducking into shops and behind cars. You were a bit slow to cotton on, you must admit it, but you never expected something like that to happen to you during a normal lunch hour. Next thing, these two Heroes fell from the sky, landing on a Range Rover illegally parked on double-yellow lines, crushing it across the middle and sending tiny squares of glass spitting out in all directions. You covered your face but were peppered with glass and fell back against the outside wall of a shop, although you kept on your feet. When you uncovered your face you saw a middle-aged woman in a yellow costume straddling a younger man in blue and white one across the twisted roof of the car. She was pummelling his face repeatedly, screaming, "This is all your fault you selfish prick, you've ruined it for all of us!" She just kept hitting him, his head being forced further and further into the slowly yielding roof.

You wondered if you should, if not help him, at least say something to the effect that he didn't seem to be a threat any more and she could stop. He appeared to be conscious though, trying to grab at her weakly, so you stopped yourself. Not that you would have anyway if you were honest with yourself, you were terrified, pressed against that wall, tiny bits of glass stuck in your clothes and hair. Terrified to be there and terrified to move, you just froze and watched. After what seemed like a lifetime, but must have only been a minute, she stopped and stood up. The man lay there gasping, vaguely trying to wrest his head from the cavity in the car roof, blood splattered across his cheeks and down his costume. You had never seen such a face of anger before as you looked at the woman. Every crease in her face screamed resentment, utter hatred for this man. Even your wife never got that angry, ending every argument with dismissal and sniping before it got too violent.

Then tears started to pour down her face as the anger turned to sadness. You weren't the only one looking now, a small crowd had gathered, albeit at a very safe distance, and were watching in a mixture of awe and horror. You were the closest to them, only a few metres away, and you were the only one who heard what she said next.

"I could kill you, you know, but I won't, because you deserve to live in the world you've created, if only so you might know how badly you've screwed things up for everyone else."

The man tried to say something through his gasps. You thought it was, "I'm sorry," but you weren't sure. The woman shook her head and then looked right at you. She was beautiful, powerful, long, jet black hair, dark blue eyes and deep red lips. Her mask covered most of her face except for pointed oval eye holes and a diamond gap for her mouth and nose. Her costume was like a figure-skater's, a full-body leotard, bright yellow and shimmering with sequins or something down the seams and in patterns against dark blue curving shapes that matched her eyes. It was like she had dropped out of Heaven into your life, apart from the rip down one arm and the scrunched, dirtied areas of her costume, and the man's blood on her fists. You realised you were bent sideways, still leaning back against the wall, so you stood up straight and looked back at her. The other people didn't matter any more. It was just you and her in this moment as you waited for whatever was going to happen next.

Was this it? The moment you died? You had seen her close up, could ID her to the police, even if you didn't know her Hero name. You didn't even know if she was one of the good ones. Heck, even if she was she would probably still kill you for being there. Once punch would likely do it. Right in your face, snap your neck back or pop your skull open, however it worked, you weren't sure. Her eyes relaxed as she let out a small sigh.

"I'll be like you soon," she said quietly and, without even glancing at the other man, she bent her knees and jumped into the air, slowly rising at first, then faster, and in moments she was away over the buildings and out of sight.

You must have stood there for a good few minutes, mesmerised, until the scrunching sounds of the man peeling himself out of his car shell and the approaching sirens snapped you out of it. You had to get lunch. You walked off as the man angrily waved away the few who had come to help him and as they were shouted down by the rest who recognised him and what he'd done.

For days after you were in a state of hyper-awareness. You were constantly on guard for the police to come knocking on your door, which your wife would no doubt rush to answer then angrily call you down, or for them to turn up at work, standing in your bosses' office with caps under their arms as you looked up and they would all turn to look at you in unison. They never did, and eventually that feeling died, although the memory of that moment stayed as strong as ever.

Again you are drifting as the scraping of bench legs and the shuffling of feet signifies the end of the service. You look up and Clifford has come down off the stage and is talking to someone he recognises. A man with a long ponytail, who looks like a roadie for a rock band, steps up next to Clifford and whispers something in his ear. He must be one of the, "disciples", like the cheery girl and the scary black guy. You did a bit of research into this place before you came. Always prepared you are. There had been some controversy surrounding the man, none of it ever substantiated. There were rumours he was running a team, which would be illegal, that he had kidnapped people and forced them to join the Church, which they themselves denied, that he had forced girls to get pregnant, that he was psychic and slowly gathering together a flock of hypnotised people towards some unspecified, "but definitely a threat to your and your dear family", goal.

You were cynical enough to know to ignore all that. You put it down to Hero-hate. You take things at face value, and don't mind others' tattle. That's what your mother told you, and that's what you believe. Although saying that, the scary black guy has been looking at you for a while.

You are sure he's a really nice man, but decide it best to leave while everyone is occupied. In any case, you have to get those A4 pads and binders and prepare your, "reason for delay", excuse for the wife. It was a little ritual you went through when you needed time to yourself. She would see through it instantly, but she didn't care any more, and neither did you.

CHAPTER 20
ELEMENT CITY COUNCIL CHILD SERVICES DEPARTMENT

They had been pre-warned that this might happen after the boy went missing, but they hadn't expected him to get there so quickly. The alarm is raised by main security when he barges through the sliding doors before they have fully opened, smashing them, buckling the frames which then grind and crack the side glass panels as the mechanism hauls them in. One of the women behind the reception desk calls the emergency services when a guard who approaches him, baton out, is flung to the wall with little more than a gentle push to his chest. She panics when she sees his fingers, outstretched into pale yellow claws, but notices he keeps them flat out or curled under when he scatters two more guards and punches a door off its hinges.

He is bellowing, "Eleanor!", and is staring at the blue Department signs on the walls.

The increased security detail outside the Child Protection Department start evacuating people from the waiting area, while shutters close over the glass booth windows separating them from the offices. Parents with children scramble and scream through double doors being held open by security guards as the man appears halfway along the corridor. They are quickly ushered down a side route as he approaches the doors, his shoulders knocking pictures and door frames off the walls. Three security personnel stand in his way brandishing batons. One of them manages to say,

"Mr Randall, we have been authorised to use force if you...", before a sweep of one arm drops them like skittles. The double doors are flung open as he calls for Eleanor again.

The waiting area is empty and the shutters are down. A handbag lies dropped on the thin carpet. An alarm starts.

He stares at the shutters and uncurls his claws. He hasn't used them in anger for years. He hasn't sharpened them for even longer. He hopes they will still do the job. He takes an open-clawed swipe at a row of three windows in front of him. The plastic snaps and shatters into fragments. The metal tears like ribbons of fabric, one of the shutters rips from its fastening and crashes onto a small flat-screen monitor that snaps apart and bounces off the desk. He looks through the opening and sees staff squeezing through a fire exit at the back of the offices. Twisting his head he sees Eleanor standing behind a desk, waiting for him. With the back of his hand he breaks the other shutters free and awkwardly steps over the counter. He approaches Eleanor. She has a hand resting on the back of an office chair, but isn't running away.

"Where is he?" he says. "What did you do to him?"

"I am so sorry Mr Randall. It appears somebody has taken him from the..."

"How? How could this happen? He was supposed to be safe! Safe with you. Safer with you than with me, remember?" He pointed a long, sharp finger at her. There is a scuffling noise of footsteps behind him and in the corridor outside.

"You are right Mr Randall. You are absolutely right. He was our responsibility, he was supposed to be safe, and we lost him. It is our fault and we... I, am so sorry."

Muted radio noises can be heard outside the door to the corridor.

"You said you could look after him better than we could. I think you're wrong Eleanor. I want my son back now!"

"We are working with the police to..."

He roars and plants his fist through the desk in front of her. It crumbles as folders, pens and notes are flung into the air.

"I don't want apologies or 'we're working on it', I want my son!"

A tiny voice says, "Go, go, go!"

A metal prong buries itself under his left shoulder blade and there is a clicking noise as his back convulses. He twists round, swiping and cutting the thin wire. He grabs a chair and flings it at the black-clad officers standing the other side of the hole he cut through the booths. It catches one on his head and he falls back. Eleanor looks around in surprise as all the doors to the office open.

"No, wait! He hasn't done anything to me. Let us just talk."

Another prong in his left side. Another in his right leg. Officers come through the door to the corridor and the fire exit.

"No. No don't... There's no need to... I can talk him...". Eleanor is grabbed round the waist by a large officer and firmly directed out of the room as the man swipes at the wires, roaring in pain. She looks back and sees him pick up a desk above his head. He seems larger than before, like a bear raised on its hind legs, and only now does she see the true size of him. In the corridor outside she is moved past a line of armed officers pressed against the wall as they move into the offices one by one. She protests, saying there is no need to do this, they were talking, she was going to calm him down, but she is escorted outside in silence at a jog, like a freed hostage. All she can hear behind her are his screams. More prongs dig into his flesh than he can swipe at. He feels his muscles starting to fail as he drops the desk to the side of him. He needs to get out, but all the exits are covered. He tries to use the desk as a shield as he backs away towards the corner of the booths where the officers haven't reached yet.

"Where's my son?", he yells, as a hail of darts hit his left side from the fire exit. He moves the desk to cover them and more hit him from the right. He tries to pick some out of his body but there are too many and his fingers are suddenly fat and clumsy and when he does he let's his guard down allowing more to hit him. A prong jams itself into his shin and the current slices through his leg like a blade. His knee gives way and he goes down onto it, dropping the desk.

"Now! Keep him suppressed!"

"Ready the net!"

He tries to get up by pushing his fists down into the floor, but it seems a long way down now, slowly dropping away from him. His arms tremble and fail to get him to his feet. For a moment he thinks he sees his son's face below him, falling, and he wishes he could be there with him, to keep him safe. Then he drops to the ground. Peppered with dozens of darts, some stuck in his hair, and bleeding from Taser prongs, his breathing slows as his bladder empties itself. A weighted net is thrown over him. He hears muffled shouts, a vague sensation of movement. Is he being kicked? He can't tell and doesn't care any more. They can have their fun and beat the shit out of him while he's down, because when he comes round nothing is going to stop him finding his son. With that thought, he passes out.

CHAPTER 21
THE CHURCH OF THE NEW GODS

Jenny stared at the shiny gold metal plaque on the wall. It read:

CHURCH OF THE NEW GODS
DR. CLIFFORD GAINES
ALL DENOMINATIONS WELCOME
POWERED OR NON-POWERED

It looked expensive, she thought. At least she had found the place in the end. It was a nightmare to get to from the house, two long bus journeys and a ten minute walk with a heavy shoulder bag. She was exhausted, but she needed to do this. Lewis was gone, possibly forever, and now Ian was gone, for how long she didn't know. Her mum had consoled her as much as she could, but she wasn't well and needed carers just to get out of bed. With no other family and no way to contact his old team mates, (who all sounded too dangerous or dead anyway), and no friends left after she started going out with him, there really was nowhere else to go. She gently knocked on the door. There was hardly any sound it was so solid. She waited for a few minutes but nobody came, so she knocked again, a bit louder. A few more minutes went by with no sign of anybody.

Her lip started to tremble. She'd come all this way for nothing. She was thinking that was it now, nothing left to do, when she heard a clunk and the door slowly opened.

"Hel-loo?" said a voice and a white-faced girl popped her head into the gap.

"Oh... hi!"

The girl opened the door all the way.

"No need to knock, just come in, our door's always open." She smiled. She reminded Jenny of a doll she'd seen in the store once, striped grey and purple leggings and tight purple top, black hair and dark make-up.

"Thanks." She stepped through the door and into the hall. It was bigger than it looked from the plain outer walls. There was a large open area by the door and front windows that must have been four times the size of their living room.

"You were lucky I was down here cleaning up, I wouldn't have heard you otherwise."

"Oh right, I just wouldn't have come in like that though, my mum always taught me to knock and wait."

"Sounds like you have a lovely mother." The girl smiled but her eyes seemed sad. She shook it off and perked up, "I'm Emily!" she held out a tiny hand.

"Jenny."

They shared a weak handshake.

"Welcome to the Church of the New Gods. We accept powered and non-powered alike and..." she could see Jenny growing increasingly awkward, "...you've never been in a church before have you?"

Jenny gave a nervous laugh.

"No, never. Not even a proper one." It took a few seconds. "Oh no, sorry! I didn't mean you're not a proper church, sorry!"

Emily put a hand on her arm.

"Hey, it's OK. Truth is we're not like those other churches anyway. We're inclusive to everyone and don't force you to come every week with the threat of going to Hell if you don't!"

Both girls laughed as Jenny relaxed. "So how can I help you Jenny?"

"Is Clifford Gaines here? I saw him on telly and wanted to speak to him about something he said."

"Not at the moment, he's got business to attend to on the other side of town, but you can come to any of us for help or advice, that's what we're here for."

"OK I..." She had really hoped to speak to the man himself. Talking about it to anyone else seemed odd. She'd been warned off church people not just by Ian, but by her mum when she was younger, who would curse Jehova's Witnesses on the doorstep. "They only ever want to brainwash you into believing in God by pretending to care about your troubles.", she would say. "They don't have the answer to anything. You talk to your family about troubles, no-one else."

Clifford Gaines seemed different, like he actually cared. He set up a church for Heroes because he actually cared. So she supposed that anyone working for him would think the same way too.

"You look really stressed out, are you OK?" She guided Jenny to one of the long seats and they sat, turned to face each other, at the end of one by the aisle. It took a little while for Jenny to compose herself while her leg muscles pained from the sudden rest.

"It's my son. And my partner too. They..."

"Hey, wassup?" A young man in a green polo top and dark jeans had appeared from round the side of the stage and was approaching them up the aisle. He had a square face with prominent cheekbones, a big smile and short brown hair, spiked on top. He seemed a bit more "churchy" to Jenny, a slightly out of place well-dressed look, a little over familiar. Both women immediately tensed. Emily quickly spoke.

"Kevin, Jenny here has come for a private chat..."

Kevin stopped on the spot, put both palms up in front of him and made a big "O" with his mouth.

"Oops, my bad, I'll give you girls a moment."

"Actually, Jenny, do you fancy a cuppa?"

"Oh, I'd love one, it's taken me so long to get here."

"Milk? Sugar?"

"Mmm," she nodded.

Emily looked at Kevin who gave her a wink.

"Two teas coming up ladies."

Emily waited until he had left the hall.

"So, what's up? You mentioned your son?"

"Lewis. He's ten months. I've got a..." She fished in her bag for her phone, took a couple of seconds to bring up a photo and showed it to Emily.

"Aaw, cute. Big eyes he's got! And he's giving that dog a good munching."

"It's a rabbit really, but, you know, they don't really look like anything these toys."

"Yeah, don't see many blue dogs do you?"

Jenny laughed and took back the phone. As she stared at the picture she suddenly exploded with tears.

"Oh god, I'm sorry, I can't…" Emily slid closer and put an arm round her. "Hey, It's OK."

"No. No, it's really not. They've taken him."

"Who has?" said Emily.

"Child Services. They took him because he has powers and they said we weren't good enough to look after him. And then Ian, my partner, he got angry and broke a door in their offices, he's a PMA you see, really huge and strong and they came to our house last week with the police and took him away from us, and then a few days ago someone stole Lewis from the Assessment Centre and they don't know where he is, and Ian went mental and attacked the offices and he's in jail now, and I don't have either of them, and I don't know what I'm going to do." As Jenny had been speaking, it slowly dawned on Emily who she was and what she was talking about. It was like a black hole in her stomach at first, tugging at everything so much she felt ill. Then she realised she had to get Clifford over here as fast as she could. When Kevin came back with the tea, she'd get him to call his mobile, all interviews were off for the rest of the day.

Jenny was sobbing over the phone, tears running over its screen. Emily pulled her close in and took her hand.

"Clifford looks after everyone who comes here, especially those being persecuted for having powers. I know he'll only be too glad to help. Don't worry Jenny, you've come to the right place."

CHAPTER 22
HM WOODHALL HIGH SECURITY
PRISON

"This place looks bloody grim", thought Martin, as he hitched up the handbrake and turned off the engine. Woodhall Prison was seven miles to the North of the City, hidden in a small dip in the landscape, a long narrow road through checkpoints after a gated entry off the main road. It was built as the replacement for the overcrowded Scarrington Prison, the old Victorian building which was closed after the abuse and experimentation scandals came out in the early two-thousands. This place was much more modern but no less depressing. Surrounded by miles of electrified fencing, arranged in three concentric rings, it was a squat, two storey building made up of five separate wings, each catering for different classes of inmates requiring their own specific security and care.

The wing at the back of the complex was separated from the others by a much longer connecting corridor and had its own outer wall. Barring HM Tillford in Hertfordshire, the maximum security powered prison, this wing alone was the second most expensive building in the system, constructed, as it was, entirely from special materials that could resist all types of energy and shock damage. This was where Charles was being held while he underwent inmate risk assessment for his powers. The two wings in the middle were more specialised, one for tactile powers which had strictly enforced separation procedures and a specially designed internal layout, the other was mixed for psychic and emotional affectors, with an array of psychic-blocker machines running night and day, courtesy of the company belonging to his old Team Leader, Jack. The remaining two wings that faced the front of the complex were for the bulk of the prisoners, enhanced strength, agility, invulnerability, lowest-grade energy powers and the like. They also had special facilities for PMAs who needed medical care or enhanced supervision. It was this wing Martin was visiting today.

He had never been near a prison let alone inside one. As he was driving up he bleakly amused himself by wondering if they were going to let him out when he was done visiting. He hoped Agent Morris hadn't secretly gone back on his word of not charging him for being an unregistered Hero.

He felt sorry for Ian, he could tell when they came to his apartment that he and Jenny were really happy together and that he seriously wanted to make a go of a family. If he hadn't been, why come to your biggest enemy, as it were, and ask for help? That must have taken a considerable degree of self-reflection and humility, and in itself told Martin how much the guy had changed over the years. Despite being aware of this, he had hung back from coming here, unsure how much Ian blamed him for recent events. It was his advice they had followed after all. Not just that, he was keen to keep it from Maria, and had to wait to arrange it on a day she was "otherwise engaged" getting angry at her therapists.

There was a slight slope to the car park as he walked up to the main doors. With the barren landscape around it Martin felt like he was approaching a castle, except instead of being a symbol of power positioned at the highest point of the land, it was hidden away where no-one could see. The main door was buzzer entry. A woman's voice crackled in the speaker, asking him his name and who he was here to see. He gave the details of his appointment and after a pause he was told to turn right as he came in. As the door opened by itself, he spotted the signs on the wall in front of him:

<- Non-powered visitors only
Wings A-D

All powered visitors and ->
visitors for Wing E

Well that was him told.

He was taken into a large room with a table and chairs but not much else. There was an interview with a large prison officer called Paul, with a similar build to his, except a few inches taller and no hair. He spoke in a thick Black Country accent to confirm all the details they had of him on the Innate Powers Register and run through what he was allowed to do and not do, and what would happen if he were to use his abilities during his visit.

"Not a good idea," he summarised at the end, with a serious face.

Martin nodded in agreement, very aware of the two guards in the room that had been staring at him throughout, one standing at each door either end of the room. He was then presented with a small tray in which he dropped his phone, wallet and anything metal on him, including his belt. The tray was locked in a numbered safe in the next room, and the number written next to his name in a log book. Then he passed through a body scanner before the four of them, (one guard in front of Paul, another behind Martin), went through another door into a wide corridor that turned immediately to the right.

Martin was expecting to be led through a maze of corridors and gates, but there was only one set of double-gates opened by Paul's palm pressed against a black glass scanner. One guard remained standing by the last gate while the other went into a side room with a large window. Martin could see a desk and several monitors inside, much like the security room back at the shopping centre where he used to work. Straight ahead of him was a solid metal door.

Paul nodded to his colleague through the window and a there was a loud buzz. He pulled at the handle with some effort, and as the door opened, stood back to let Martin go in.

"Five minutes only."

Martin nodded and went in.

The room was much longer than it was wide, divided in the middle by a two-inch thick metal wall with a central rectangular super-glass window. The window had a yellowish tinge to it, the fierce halogen lights above giving it a dull urine-coloured glow. It made it difficult to see through from certain angles, but Martin could just make out the other half of the room was unoccupied.

There was enough space for two tubular metal frame chairs this side, both bolted to the floor, and one larger chair on the other side, also secured. There was no shelf, nothing to hide your hands under while three cameras, two at each top corner of the dividing wall and one directly behind, watched proceedings. He was sure there would be a matching trio across from him. As the door was locked behind him, he took the right-hand seat and waited. Through the window he could see the top of the chair and another solid metal door in the far wall.

Five minutes was hardly any time at all, but more than he knew what to do with. They had no friendship or shared history to talk about, as long as you didn't count the fights they got into, but that seemed part of the past Ian hadn't wanted to rake over when he came to his apartment. Nothing good to reminisce about he supposed, not when you'd been given drugs and steroids and psychic intimidation to deliberately pump up and enrage you before being let go like a giant clawed whirlwind while the rest of the team did their thing. Wind up and let him go, break him out of jail when you need him again or stun him when you're done and drag him unconscious back to the secret base. It had become a strange relationship, something akin to Stockholm Syndrome except he was never a captive. He joined willingly and then they gradually abused him more and more and he couldn't see it, always going back to them, ready for the next mission. More like a drug addict dependent on his dealer, thought Martin, sticking with them so that he could get his next fix guaranteed. How long it had taken to break his dependency on them he didn't know, but he seemed to have done it. He brought Jenny and their son to him instead of contacting any of his old team. That was something.

There was a buzzing noise and a loud click and the door through the glass swung open. The first thing Martin saw was the shoulder of a blue-jumpered guard, stepping sideways into the room. Then just behind him he spotted Ian's hair as he dipped his head below the top of the door frame. Then they turned and he could see the other guard holding him by his right arm. They approached the glass quickly, filling up the view, making Martin lean back. Ian was manoeuvred into position in front of the chair then sat down heavily with a clacking of chains. One of the guards pulled out something like a large wing nut attached to his belt by an extending cord. While the other held Ian by his shoulders, he bent down in front of him, pulling on chains and spent a few seconds twisting something into the ground. Then he stood up and they both left, the door clicking loudly as it shut behind them.

Ian's head drooped down, his face obscured by his dreadlocks tumbling over his forehead. He looked like he was dozing.

"Ian?"

Slowly Ian lifted his head and his face came into view as he breathed heavily. Martin wondered about whoever was watching them, whether they knew anything about their history and thought it odd that an old Hero and Villain were sitting here face to face for a chat, or whether they cast them both in the same light, the only distinction being that one of them was in the right place.

Ian seemed to be struggling to keep his head erect, and it took a while for his eyes to roll up to meet Martin's gaze.

"No... feeding... the animals, OK?" His speech was slurred, head tilting slightly as a dreadlock slid down and swung across his jaw.

"Ian, what the hell have they done to you?"

"They're keeping me... nice and calm."

"They're sedating you?"

"Know... what they say... better safe than... bother to learn anything about me. Levels the playing field. Nice and simple."

Martin leaned forwards.

"They can't do that can they? Does your solicitor know about this? You do have one?"

"Mmm-mmm, court appointed. All... above board. This too." He took a deep breath, and braced himself to enable him to lift his arms up into view. His hands were clasped together with thick-ringed cuffs, a foot long metal brace separating his two wrists, a chain attached to the middle that fell down to the floor where it had been secured. All his fingers were folded down, claws buried in a block of a grey-coloured synthetic mouldable material, which was then secured by thick tape around the back of his hands. Martin could see blood spots and irritated rectangular pink patches of skin where successive days of tape had been ripped off. Ian dropped his hands into his lap and breathed out, slumping.

"What the hell? You're not dangerous, you haven't been for years?"

"Ah but... when's the next one? Then next one? Nobody knows."

"That was only because of Lewis. Any parent would get angry about that! Just because you can do a bit more damage than most parents doesn't mean you deserve this done to you."

"Ooooh no, no, no." He shook his head gingerly, "Got to be safe you see. I'm a bad man. What's... what's it they say? You can run from your past... but you can't hide."

Martin wished that whenever somebody said something like that he would stop feeling as if they must know what had happened with The Controller and The Pulse all those years ago. Not everyone was psychic. Nonetheless his face still tightened as fractured images of the past were flung into the back of his eyes again. He squeezed them shut a few times and the images disappeared for now.

"Yeah, I know all about that."

"Yep, you do. And now… we're here." Ian sat back slowly, his chair squealing as his weight pressed down on the back rest. They sat silent for a while. "Well at least he doesn't seem to be angry with me," thought Martin, unsure how deeply Ian could think about recent events with all the sedatives pumping through him.

He could see Ian looking around his side of the room.

"Just shy of three years… I was out. It's like being back home."

"Well don't get comfortable. I know people who can get you a good solicitor, someone who can get you home, get you in a better place for getting Lewis back, OK?"

"These… the same people who couldn't have helped us… run away, yeah?"

"Ian, I know right now it must seem like that would have been for the best, but like I said it…" He stopped as Ian started to laugh drowsily, a slight rattle on his chest.

"I'm only kidding." He paused. It seemed hard for him to think. "Shit happens. You deal with it.", he said eventually.

"I'm getting you a better solicitor, no discussion. I'm not having them chain you up like that."

Ian just stared at him.

"Is there anything you need me to do out here for you?"

Ian shook his head but then his eyes widened and he sat upright.

"Jenny. See... Jenny. Not heard from her, no contact. Nothing about Lewis. I just... I just want to know she's OK... and what Child... police... people are doing about my boy. I don't know..."

"I'll find out for you..."

There was a harsh buzzing sound and a woman's voice said, "One minute remaining, one minute."

"She was banging on... about that New Gods Church, said guy on TV could help us. If she's not home... bet that's where she'll be. I know her."

"OK. I'll make sure she's fine and keeps away from those odd people. Child Services aren't going to look favourably on her if she gets involved in that."

"Exactly."

"And I'll try and find out what's happening with the investigation into Lewis. The police will be all over it anyway, but I know someone I can ask to find out more. I'll pass it on to you the next time we get five minutes in here."

Ian narrowed his eyes, studying Martin carefully.

"You're a good man... Martin."

Martin looked away.

"No, don't say that. *You're* a good man for having changed so much since back then. That must have been hard. I'm just doing what I can to help."

"Visiting time is up, please wait until the inmate has left the room."

The door behind Ian clicked loudly and swung open. Two large guards moved in quickly, one unscrewed the chain from the floor, then both picked him up under his arms and within seconds had walked him out of the room. Martin watched their shadows move along the wall into darkness as they went out of view and the door closed behind them.

CHAPTER 23
ROOMS UNDER THE OAK AND ARCHER PUB

Carl's phone call to Bobby was garbled, full of panting and words that didn't make sentences. He wasn't able to calm him down, but did finally get that he wanted to meet him and Becca at the meeting hall, and that it was urgent. He was already there when they arrived, hiding in the kitchen, and was peering round the door to the main room when they came down the stairs. They both looked around expecting signs of a struggle, but there was only a silver laptop computer sat on a chair at the end of the room, missing its power cord and sleeping to save power. Other than that, the place was unchanged.

"Carl? What's so urgent that..." Carl emerged from the doorway holding a ball of blankets to his chest like a rugby ball.

"I've done something... I... I think it's the right thing."

Bobby and Rebecca had been walking towards him but they stopped and Bobby took a small step back.

"If that's a... head, or something... that can't be here..."

"NO! Christ, no, it's a baby."

They all froze. Rebecca's face curled up in horror.

"You...?"

"NO! Jesus Christ, it's alive! What do you think I am?"

"I know what you are, and what you do for Bobby OK?" said Rebecca, "So what are you doing with a baby?"

"It's the..." He went silent as he relaxed his grip on the blankets enough to let Lewis's face appear. He was a little red from the tight bundle around him, and was glad to get some air, but was comfy enough to let this strange man hold him for now. Bobby's brows dropped as something clicked in his brain.

"Which child is that Carl?"

"The one from the news. From the Assessment Centre."

"Holy shit Carl! That was you?" Rebecca grabbed the back of a chair as it dawned on her.

Carl looked at his feet and mumbled,

"Yeah, kind of..."

"You stole a baby mate."

Carl stared at the floor, glancing at the boy now and again.

"Yep. And a laptop."

"From a Government Assessment Centre."

"Yep."

"A… powered baby."

"Well, he's more a toddler really…"

"Carl, what have you done? We're criminals now!", Rebecca shook her head at him, open mouthed. Carls' stomach twisted. Lewis screwed up his face. Bobby leaned in to her and said in a calm, low voice,

"We already were."

Rebecca bristled, pulling her shoulder away from him.

Carl knew she was right. If they were discovered with the child they would be going to prison for a long time. Bobby walked over to him and pulled the edge of the blanket so he could see the boy's face. Lewis looked at him, eyebrows dancing.

"But why this kid? And why did you take it instead of just killing the little freak there and then? All of them, when you had the chance!"

"Bobby!"

"This one's something different though," said Carl. "It was… separated from the others, and I've seen it make stuff."

"What do you mean 'make stuff'?"

"From thin air! Like The Elemental, but it's like, still only a baby. It does this blue rabbit toy thing, I've already got three of them!"

Bobby took a couple of steps back, mouth and eyes wide open as his face glowed.

"That's it." He started pumping his arms and walking around. "That's fucking it! You're a bloody genius Carl, you know that?"

Carl looked at him blankly. Rebecca looked at them both with the same amount of confusion.

But Bobby's mind was racing away with him. The frustration that had been bothering him for months had gone and a plan was slowly forming in its place. A plan to get The Real Heroes name into the papers in a big way. He suddenly approached them and pointed at the baby.

"This kid is our ticket to the big time. He's all over the media, everywhere you look. We get it out there that we have him…"

"And we'll have armed police storming this place! They know who we are from the blog you idiot! The people from the meetings will tell them where it was held, and somebody must have seen Supernanny here running around with a crying laundry pile under his arm."

"He didn't cry! And nobody saw me, I swear…"

"Then we don't use our group name, obviously. We use another. We haven't done a video about our other work have we?"

"Work? Jesus…"

Bobby stood his ground.

"They can't get away with it Rebecca. You should fucking know that better than either of us after what they did to your sister."

She hovered on the verge of saying something, torn between two halves of her brain, but in the end just shook her head and stood back.

"Good. OK. We keep it here, feed it, clean it, keep it happy, whatever. Rebecca, you're in charge of him…"

"Oh right, because I'm the female?"

"No, because neither of us has done that shit before and we've got other stuff to plan."

"Sure, 'man stuff'." She rolled her eyes. "I'll leave you to it. Give the little fella here..." she gestured at Carl to give her the baby.

He was even less sure how to hand a child over to someone else than he was to carry it, but thankfully Rebecca just scooped the boy up, leaving him cradling the air until he became awkward and dropped his arms.

"Hey there, Lewis isn't it? Fuck me, I'm an accessory to kidnap now. Cheers guys." She gave them a list of seven or eight supplies they would need, three of which the two men promptly forgot between them as they moved away to the wall under the high windows. Shaking her head again, she went through to the kitchen and could be heard running water.

When he knew she was out of earshot, Bobby spoke to Carl.

"You're errand boy now, right? I've got another list to add to hers..."

"What's going to happen to the baby?"

"Don't you worry about that. You did the right thing bringing him here. Ignore her, she just hasn't been laid in a while, puts her in a mood."

"You said I should have killed him?"

"But you didn't." said Bobby as he leant forward, swivelled his eyes up to meet Carl's and pressed a finger into his chest. "And neither will I. I promise, all right? He's not going to die. But he is going to be useful. But I need you to make yourself useful first, all right?"

Carl looked over to the open doorway and could hear drawers opening and closing and Rebecca cursing out loud. Bobby placed a hand on his cheek and turned his head back to face him.

"Look at me! I'm going to give you a list of what I need, and you're going to get it. This is the most important thing we have ever done. You started it off and I'm trusting you to help me out here, yeah?"

Maybe he wasn't just going to be the distraction or the errand boy this time? Sure, he was going to fetch stuff, but this was different. He'd started it off, a big plan, he could tell by Bobby's face. Only the three of them knew about this and he was in the inner circle now. He wasn't about to be left out. He smiled and nodded.

"What do you need?"

CHAPTER 24
THE CHURCH OF THE NEW GODS

You sit closer to the front this time. You felt... compelled? Is that the right word? Compelled to go back? No, not really, that presumes you had reason to go back. You have none. After the last visit you couldn't stop thinking about the things Clifford had said, or at least the words you heard before your mind distracted itself with the past. You listen more intently this time. He talks about the changes in government policy The Elemental started, to officially recognise Heroes and head off discrimination against them. Then he compares His forward thinking against recent events involving an old Hero called The Savage who had his son taken from him by Child Services because he had powers, because of his history. He says that all of us blessed with powers are discriminated against now, but none more so than those whose powers change than physically, because they are unable to hide. None of us should have to hide anyway, but they bear the brunt of it. Then he says the child has been stolen from a supposed place of safety, to gasps from some of the congregation, (but not from you, you heard it on the news the other day), which just went to show how little the Authorities cared for even a baby with powers.

That's exactly what you thought too. How on earth could anyone let such a thing happen? To a baby? The most vulnerable of people in care need the most protection. Where was the protection for this child? Has everything The Elemental fought for been lost?

Clifford goes on, hatred is easy to feel in circumstances like this, it's the default setting, but as Heroes, we have to remain resolute to our need for justice.

"This isn't time to get angry," he says, "this is the time to make sure this does not, and cannot, happen again." He tells you all to contact your local MP, demand an inquiry into how this happened but tells you not to interfere with the police investigation. Any hindrance could jeopardise the safety of the little boy. You have to come together as a community to demand a proper place in it. Wow. You love how this man speaks so clearly, gives form to those stray thoughts in your head. He makes everything make sense.

The service ends and you join the others in a standing ovation. He shakes his head, raising his palms, meek in the face of such obvious adulation. How does he do it? He wants nothing more than for Heroes to be equal, that's all he speaks of. He wants nothing for himself, he is so committed. Your heart sinks as you wish you had a cause to feel so empowered about. But you're not even a Hero. You don't even fit into this community and you feel more a part of it than any group you've been with in your life. You suppose that doesn't mean you can't call your MP. You don't have to be a Hero to care about this stuff! How have you only just realised this? Heroes are part of your City, your country, it would be remiss of you if you didn't care, and it would show your MP that it was an issue that not just Heroes cared about. The more non-powered people felt this way, the more he would be inclined to do something about it. At least you think your MP is a he. You're not sure. You didn't even vote in the last local elections so it's not like you can claim your MP is even your representative...

"Harvey, glad you could join us again."

You are so startled you almost fall back into the seat, but Clifford grabs your hand with both of his and gives a firm shake, steadying you upright. He must have slipped down the side of the benches towards you while you were daydreaming again.

He looks young even close up, but you know he is forty-three to your forty-nine. Not that much between you. He must have been given good genes though, he has a full head of hair for a start. If you didn't know who he was, he wouldn't look out of place in large pair of sun shorts on a beach, surfboard under one arm, draining a can of lager and ready to launch into the waves to impress the ladies. Like a proper Aussie! Instead, he's here in dreary England, dressed in fitted charcoal suits and pale pink shirts, acting somewhere between a businessman, politician and your best friend. A fear suddenly grips your throat, he said your name!

One of his disciples must be psychic, otherwise how would he know? Or maybe he is? You look behind him and standing next to a pillar watching the two of you is the old roadie with the ponytail, smiling. You guess it's him, you couldn't imagine Clifford prying into your mind.

"I can reassure you that no-one has pried into your mind, merely skimmed your most projected thoughts, your psychic tags. Like glancing at the labels on food in a supermarket, if you will. Most people don't know but they share this stuff openly all the time, their name, age, job, etcetera. It's no more invasive than analysing body-language, but in much the same way it does make a lot of people very uncomfortable upon being "read". I'm sorry if I have made you feel uncomfortable Harvey, but I knew you would understand if I explained it to you, because I know you."

"You... you know me?"

"Why yes. I know you understand things. How things are and how they should be. You know that in these times filled with anti-Hero sentiment, that while we welcome one and all into our Church, we are never quite sure who is genuine and who is watching us, listening in to report back somewhere."

You gasp. Surely they don't mistake you for a Government agent, do they?

"I'm not reporting back anywhere!"

Clifford, still clasping your hands, leans in.

"I know. But you understand how careful we have to be."

"Absolutely I do, yes Mr Clifford. Gaines! Mr Gaines."

Clifford gives a huge smile and leans away from you, leans back.

"Please, just Clifford." He laughs.

"Clifford, yes, of course." You laugh nervously. You just made yourself look a proper fool and don't know yet if he is laughing with you or at you. No, it couldn't be at you, he's not that sort of person.

"Harvey, can I bother you for a moment to talk? I am in need of some of your advice in a more..." he looks around the hall, some people still standing around and chatting, "...private setting?"

You are stunned. He needs your help? But he knows nothing about you. How deeply did they scan you? Your mind starts to buzz with questions as you experience something you haven't felt for years. No, haven't felt at all. Is it... needed? Is this what it feels like? You are so buffeted with conflicting thoughts at the moment you can't focus on anything. He leads you away from the hall to a large office behind the stage. On the way you pass the guy with the ponytail, who smiles and nods, and the short girl with dark hair who says, "Hi Harvey." as she hurries past. This all feels very weird. Not worryingly so, just delightfully strange. You are filled with anticipation as Clifford closes the door behind you and directs you to a sofa at the far end of the room.

"Harvey..." he says as you both sit down, "...no, there really is no better way to put this..."

He pauses, deep in thought. "What? What is it" you scream at him in your head. "Have you ever noticed..."

he continues, finally, "...that at work, at home, when watching the news, you see all these events unfolding, these micro- or macro-dramas of humanity and it all seems somewhat strange to you?"

A lot of the world feels strange to you. People do odd things all the time that don't make sense, or they don't react normally to things.

"Kind of."

"I mean, you live in a state of confusion over how things always seem to turn out, because they never turn out right, do they?"

"Hardly ever."

Clifford moves slightly closer, seems more intent.

"But over the years you have brushed it off as 'one of those things' haven't you. You stopped questioning things. You let others get their way because it's... easier. Less hassle."

It's like he's reading your mind right now. "You watch the news but are more and more detached from it the more nonsensical it becomes to you, am I right?"

"Yes!"

"That's because you have a power Harvey."

You feel all the blood rush to your legs and almost faint backwards. You steady yourself on the arm of the sofa next to you.

"A subtle power. The kind of subtle power most go through their entire lives not even realising they have: intuition, Harvey. That is your gift. You see how things should be so clearly that when events fail to turn out that way it causes confusion, a feeling of hopelessness. How many times in your life have you felt that way and shaken it off as too many hours worked, not enough sleep or, even worse, you thought you were simply stupid."

There are claws in your mind, tearing away at layers of doubt formed from years of self-torment and abuse, sending chinks of light piercing into your brain.

"All the time."

"But that's your power. You do understand. Completely and totally. You simply know what is right, what needs to be done and how to do it, instinctively. You have built up so many mental defences over the years, but the clarity and surety of thought you could possess if you were to reveal it is… astounding. More so than I possess."

Of course. That's it! You knew this all along. You are right. You are simply right, about everything.

You feel angry. You now understand why those bastards at work are always on your back, because they know you are right, they know you understand the work, the job, better than they can ever hope to, so they have to repeatedly put you down so you are never heard, so they can climb the corporate ladder instead of you. Your wife, constantly belittling you to control you, assuming her versions of events as the correct ones, annoyed that you aren't as compliant and supplicant as she would like you to be. All because you always know deep down what is right.

"Harvey?"

"All… all these years…"

Clifford grips your upper arms with his hands. You're a ship broken free from anchor in a storm, being tossed and turned about by so many conflicting thoughts and emotions. He seems to know you need steadying right now.

"Don't focus on the past. What's done is done and can't be changed. You need to look at the present, what you know now, and where you want to be in the future. I can help you Harvey, if you will let me. I can help guide you safely to port, through all the rough weather until you are safe and steady enough to plot your own course. Will you let me do that for you Harvey?"

This man understands you like no other person you have met.

"Yes. Yes! Of course I will Clifford."

"Oh Harvey! You have no idea how pleased I am." He stands up suddenly and you do the same, to find yourself embraced in a bear hug by the man. You go with your emotions for once and reciprocate. He smells of forests.

He releases you, laying his hands gently on your shoulders, tipping his head slightly to one side, beaming a perfect teeth grin as the light from the window behind him makes his blond curls glow.

"I am going to help you, no... *we* are all going to help you fulfil your life's potential Harvey. But first, and I... hate myself for asking this of you in the moment your Heroic soul is bared to the world, but I need your help. The kind of clear-headed, absolute advice only someone with your ability can give me. Is that... too selfish to ask? Please tell me if it is."

The man needs your help. You can give him that help, the help that only you can give. That's not a selfish ask at all. You know what selfishness is, you experience it every day. This is someone in need of help, someone who has just freed you from your mental shackles. You owe him this. You owe him everything.

"Clifford, you can ask me anything."

CHAPTER 25
THE CHURCH OF THE NEW GODS

The hall had apparently been done up recently, but it still looked like a barely used community centre to Martin. There was a heavy-looking new door, new windows, a lick of paint and a shiny plaque on the wall, but the brickwork was dirty, the roof bowed in slightly on the right side as he faced it, and the land inside the walls around it was a mix of plain concrete slabs and rough stony soil punctured by weeds. A six-foot grey wall ran around the sides and back of the plot, along the rough tarmac footpath that disappeared down the side between the hall and a row of terraced houses. At the front, the wall was only knee high with a gap for the path. From his quick scout earlier he also knew a pedestrian and cyclist path went along the back of the hall and houses. There was no rear access – always know your exits.

He had tried Ian and Jenny's council house in Mellfields earlier, but the place was empty. After a calmly antagonistic conversation with one of the neighbours, who came over when she saw him at their door, he discovered Jenny hadn't been seen either there or at the local shops for a few days now, and nobody was particularly bothered about it. The only other place he knew to try, was the Church that Ian had mentioned. But he wasn't about to walk in to an ambush of any kind. He had been sat in his car watching from a hundred metres or so down the road for nearly an hour, nipping round the back for a look when the meeting had started.

About a dozen people had left forty minutes ago, a mix of different ages and backgrounds. The congregation he guessed. Since then two girls, one short with black hair and patterned leggings, the other taller with long blonde hair and a flowery top, had gone out and returned a few minutes ago carrying shopping bags. Other than that there hadn't been much activity around the place. He'd seen some figures moving inside the large front windows but the glass was rippled so he couldn't make out who they were. He hadn't seen any sign of Jenny.

These sorts of places had cropped up pretty frequently since the 1960s. They would either be dedicated to a team, one specific Hero, (usually dead), or to the idea that all Heroes should be worshipped as Gods. There was a big spat in Nottingham that he remembered seeing on the news in the 'seventies between two, "rival", Churches. One held the, "actual Gods", view that they should be revered no matter what, while the other was more Christian-based and believed that the good ones were angels sent by God, the bad ones demons sent by Satan. There were rallies and protests outside each Church by both sets of members and it was all stoked up by a local bishop of the Catholic Church at the time, who said they were all damned to Hell anyway. In the end the police moved in and arrested both groups. Not one Hero got involved during the whole dispute, which was a pretty accurate representation of how much the actual Heroes cared about it all. To be honest, they were generally too busy beating the crap out of each other at the time. When the Restriction of Innate Powers Act came into force most of the Churches and cults closed shop, or moved to America or more permissive countries on the continent. They weren't illegal in themselves, but the mood was against them. So it was rare to have a place like this exist nowadays. This Church was fairly new too, but Martin had no idea how long they had been planning it, it had probably been years in the pipeline.

The door opened and a middle-aged man with a comb-over and glasses came out. He carefully closed the door behind him and walked across the street to a Volvo which drove off a moment later. Probably their accountant thought Martin, who decided it was now or never, got out of his car and headed towards the building. The outside of the place didn't look as bad when you couldn't see the whole of the building.

He didn't have to wait long after knocking before the door opened. It was the blonde-haired girl, more-or-less his height. For a split-second Martin saw Inna standing there, waiting to tell him everything was OK, until she spoke with a strong Cockney accent.

"Bloody 'ell!" Her long face seemed to stretch even further down to the ground and she reached up and grabbed onto a chunky brown necklace that was tangled up among her loose-fitting layers of flowery and lace-patterned tops.

"Erm, Hi. My name is Martin Molloy, is there a Jenny Crossdale here? I'm a friend of her partner…"

"I know who you are. Christ, yeah, come in, you're more than welcome. Take a seat while I get Clifford."

"It's OK, I don't need to speak to him…"

"But he'll want to speak to you."

She opened the door wide. Martin could already tell this wasn't going to be quick or simple. He took a deep breath and went in. The first thing that hit him was the smell of solvent and new wood. It smelt like his father when he came home at the end of the day, except he would also have that musky stink of car grease and oil. The second thing he noticed was it felt a lot bigger than it looked. It seemed cramped and boxy from the outside, but it was bright and airy when you got inside. It was newly painted in lighter colours, rows of low benches, a pretty big stage at the far end and although the ceiling had been built in to hide the rafters, there was a good sense of space. The third thing he noticed was all the eyes turning to stare at him. The blonde girl had closed the door and was half-jogging down the side of the benches, constantly turning around to check he was still there.

A tall thin black guy of indeterminate age wearing baggy jeans and a t-shirt was standing in the far aisle by the wall, absolutely motionless, sunken eyes gouging holes in Martin's head. A Detector or psychic perhaps? Martin knew that haunted look well. A young guy in dark jeans who had been at the far end, fixing something under the stage, came bounding up the central aisle towards him.

"Roadblock! Oh my God. My name is Kevin. Thank you for coming here! You are so welcome. Please, take a seat while Claire goes and gets Clifford for you. Is there anything I can do for you sir?" His enthusiasm was like a physical attack, hitting Martin backwards with each burst of it.

"Nothing. Except... call me Martin. I'm not Roadblock any more."

"Oh but you always will be in my eyes. You were with The Pulse. You guys were amazing! You've met them all. You've worked with them, done actual Heroics." He beamed. His face suddenly dropped. "Is this about Ignite? Charles Heathcote? There is no way that was an unbiased hearing, what with all that crap in the media about him over the last few months. It's no wonder he pleaded guilty just to save himself the ignominy of trying to defend himself against..."

"He pleaded guilty because he's a murdering bastard."

Kevin stopped, open mouthed, finally silent. Martin heard the tall black guy give a grunt that could have been a suppressed laugh, except his face hadn't changed expression.

"And I'm not here about him, I'm looking to speak to Jenny. Jenny Crossdale? I believe she's here with you guys?"

"She… ah…"

There was a rampaging, creaking thunder of several pairs of footsteps rushing down a set of wooden stairs and moments later three more people appeared from the side of the stage area, the dark haired girl he had seen earlier, a slightly podgy ginger-haired boy and an older man with a tight, drawn face, greying hair tied back in a ponytail. It was him that spoke first.

"Holy shit. Yeah. I was right. I knew I could feel a powerful Hero here, but… shit."

Kevin tried to regain his composure.

"Ah, this is… Martin, guys. He's here to see Jenny and more than welcome in our place of worship."

The girl and the older guy came up the aisle towards him, the ginger lad, who looked much younger than any of them, hung back.

What had been a large, airy hall was now feeling very small to Martin. Kevin was standing far too close, and as these other people approached they seemed to be dragging the stage with them, shrinking the walls in. He could swear that if he took a step back, the front wall and window would be right behind his heels. His pulse started to race as his face tingled.

"Emily. Emily Roberts." The girl held a hand out to him, which he shook gently while she stared into his eyes, a huge smile curling her mouth up.

"Grant. It's an honour to meet you Martin."

He shook the older guy's hand too. He had a stronger grip.

"If you don't mind me saying…" Grant had a puzzled look on his face for a reason Martin couldn't work out, "… you're not what I expected."

"Grant, please!" burst out Kevin like a cannon next to him, "He's our guest here!"

"I didn't mean it as an insult, I just assumed…"

"No it's fine, that's actually one of the nicer things people have said about me recently, so I'll take it." There was a nervous laugh and Martin felt the space around him widen slightly.

"You've just missed a service, but Clifford will still speak with you… can I call you Roadblock?" said Emily.

"No, it's Martin please. And that's great, but I'm not here to speak to him. I'm just looking for Jenny to find out how she is."

"She's great Martin." The girl moved closer, her eyes widening as she gazed up at him, lips curling into a smile. "She's among friends, as are you."

"Claire's just gone to get Clifford actually," said Kevin.

Emily took his hand.

"I'll take you to his office."

Kevin's face visibly hardened as she slowly led him down the side of the hall.

He was glad to be away from that gathering as he felt himself cooling down, legs feeling more solid again. How any celebrity could cope with the constant haranguing by fans trying to get a photo or signature or just to be close to them, he didn't know. Not that he considered himself a celebrity. Not like Charles had. He never had any inclination to throw himself into the limelight, to seek the appreciation of others for what he did and he really hoped he could avoid those people on the way out. Not that they didn't seem nice, it was just too much pressure to feel people acting that way around him. It made him quickly uncomfortable.

Emily led him down the side of the stage into a wood panelled corridor. He saw a narrow passage with three steps leading up to it on his left, while on his right he passed a wider wooden staircase disappearing up into the space above the hall. On the walls there were framed photos of groups of people in a line. Some were in colour, some black and white, all had Clifford standing in the middle. Either side of him stood people, mostly youngsters, but some older ones too. He spotted Grant and Emily in a few of them, but some of the older ones were taken in bright sunshine with nobody he recognised apart from Clifford. He guessed these were from back in Australia. Past the stairs at the end of the corridor was a single heavy black door that he guessed must lead to the waste ground at the rear. He thought he was heading through that until a wooden door that almost blended into the wall opened on his left. Claire, the blonde girl held it open as Emily let go of his hand and gave him a gentle push in his back. This room smelt different, like a strong pot-pourri from the 'eighties. Clifford was standing in the middle of the room waiting for him, hands clasped in front of his chest. He gently nodded to the girls and they left, closing the door behind them.

CHAPTER 26
ROOMS UNDER THE OAK AND ARCHER PUB

Carl walked briskly down the street carrying two wide, shiny DIY store bags. He was pissed off.

He was pissed off because he thought he would finally have earned enough trust from Bobby to be given a meaningful job. Something important. Of course, Bobby made it sound like it was vital, managed to convince him to run stupid errands again. He was pissed off because his back ached from the heavy black backpack, stuffed with two pairs of workman's boots, four old orange boiler suits, eye protectors, hats and masks they had used for a rap video they made in their last year at school. He was pissed off because the two bags filled with rolls of lining paper wouldn't stay straight. They had been swinging round the whole way here from the store, cracking off his shins and calf muscles so often that each bump now felt like being hit with a metal ruler.

"This had better be worth it," he thought to himself.

Truth is, he had no idea what Bobby was up to. He had given him, Jed and the new guy Michael different tasks without telling each of them the full picture. Yes, it made sense so that nobody knew everything about what was going down in case one of them got caught, but it didn't make it any less infuriating to be left out. He turned off the main road into a quieter one. He was glad to be away from the eyes of people. Bobby had told him to try and not look conspicuous. He hadn't known what he really meant, so he just kept his head down and walked as fast as he could. He'd thought about leaving the group loads of times. Always because he would never get the full picture from Bobby. He would always be left hanging with half the info he needed, get more and more annoyed until he stopped turning up, stopped answering his phone. Next thing, Bobby would turn up at the house or find him hanging out on the street and act as if he'd just seen him yesterday, all best buddy and friendly, take him for a drink, tell him about his latest plans and that he knew just the thing Carl could do to help. And that was it, he was back in. That pissed him off too, but it was outweighed by the feeling of being needed again, so he went along with it.

He was the one who had been with Bobby for the longest. Even though Bobby found him, surely this meant something? What about what he had to say, his ideas? He was just ordered around like a minion. And another thing... he'd brought the baby there. That was him. But now nobody could get it from Rebecca and it was like it just appeared there magically. No-one ever mentioned his part in it. He just hoped he had done the right thing about that. After all, he could hardly have taken it to the police...

"SHIT!" One bag split silently with no warning, spilling rolls of paper over the pavement. One rolled straight into the gutter, another got wedged into a railing while the other three made a break for it down the hill. He dropped the other bag and gave chase. He managed to kick one to the side. Another slowed down enough that he bent and grabbed it. The third one bounded for freedom until it rolled over the feet of a man who stood in its way, running up his shin like a cat up a wide tree, before dropping back down in defeat.

"Almost got away from you that one did!" The man was almost bald apart from a bad comb-over, his round glasses making him look like a cartoon mole. He held up the roll to Carl as he jogged to a stop in front of him.

"Yeah, thanks mate."

"Ha, no problem."

Carl turned round and started gathering up the other rolls under his arms until he realised he could only fit two under each. He jammed them in.

"Can I give you hand with those?"

"No, you're all right." He could have done with some help if he was honest. The rolls were heavy and awkward to hold. He had to squeeze his arms in to keep them from dropping, but that pressed them against his ribs and they rolled painfully over them as he picked up the other bag and grabbed the fifth roll in his free hand. The guy was still there when he turned back.

"You heading to the meeting today?"

Carl didn't move.

"The Real Heroes Meeting? I've been following your blog for a while but never got round to coming."

"There's no meeting today mate." Carl walked past him, head down. The Pub was on the corner at the end of the road. He just had to make it that far with crushed ribs.

"But I'm certain it was at two o'clock?" The guy was following him. He couldn't have him follow him, so he stopped and faced him.

"Two o'clock *tomorrow*, but it's been cancelled anyway. Sorry mate, you'll have to go home."

"Oh dear, that's a shame... I came a long way..."

"Sorry." Carl stood his ground as the bottom rolls slipped down into the backs of his elbows.

"Are you sure I can't give you..."

"Positive mate."

"I guess you're busy redecorating, that's why the meeting is cancelled!" he smiled.

"Yeah, redecorating. Make the place look a bit nicer. See you later." He turned and tried to walk away again.

"When will the next meeting be then?"

The bottom roll under his bag arm started tipping forwards, not quite centrally balanced. He bent his arm slightly, taking even more strain, to keep it from sliding out.

"Keep watching the blog mate, it'll be on there." He couldn't hear the man following him as he half-ran down the rest of the street to the top of the stairs leading down the side of the pub to the basement.

He looked back up the road. The man was still standing there and gave him a cheery wave. Carl gave a nervous nod and hurried down out of sight. He only just managed to get through the door before the roll slipped out and slammed to the floor. He gave up and dropped them all on the spot. He cursed as he took the backpack off, almost tipping himself over and dropped it on top of them. Bobby had come out from the kitchen at the noise to find Carl shaking his arms out, rolls of paper around him.

"Did you get them all?"

"Yeah. They weigh a bloody ton you know? It's only supposed to be paper... what do we need these for anyway?"

"Papering walls, what do you think?", he said, screwing up his face. He walked over to where he had set up the laptop Carl had brought with the baby, connected to a smart phone on a small tripod on a chair. He had found several out of date Yellow Pages, and put them on the chair to boost the height of the phone. Jed was sitting in the corner on his own mobile. He hadn't looked up since Carl came in. Carl sighed, guessing Bobby would want rolls somewhere other than the floor and picked them up, one in each hand. He left the room. He looked to his left but the old cellar area, now a makeshift kitchen, was quiet, no sign of Rebecca. Lewis was lying on his back sleeping in a cheap plastic cot she had brought from home earlier, a halogen heater set to low next to him. To his right, there was a smaller room, some kind of washroom or cloakroom with a nasty toilet off to the side of it. It was empty too.

Or rather, it had been emptied. The piles of old cloths and boxes of random stuff must have been moved into the main room, but he hadn't noticed. Looked like it had been given a bit of a clean too. That wouldn't have been Bobby or Jed.

He looked straight ahead at the bottom of the stairs leading up to behind the bar. There was some light coming down from above, but it looked like faint daylight, not like someone was up there.

"Becca?"

"Just put them in the empty room. Did you get the costumes?"

"Yeah, they're in the backpack," said Carl as he left the corridor into the spare room and started propping the rolls up in the corner. When he came out, Bobby was posing in front of the camera. He then went to the phone and played back the video, looking disappointed.

"Do you know how to increase the brightness on this thing? Comes out really dark.", he said to Jed.

"No idea mate, I just found it for you," replied Jed without looking away from his phone. He had also come into possession of a power cord for the laptop and the tripod the phone was screwed into. When it came to that sort of stuff, Jed could find anything you wanted pretty quickly. Bobby started fiddling with the touch screen.

"You guys seen Becca?" asked Carl as he grabbed two more rolls.

"Don't worry about her, just get those rolls in there and start papering."

"What, me? With what?"

"You did get the paste didn't you?"

"I've only got two bloody hands you know! Didn't realise you needed that now as well."

"Of course we do, what's the fucking point of buying all this lining paper without getting the paste for it?"

Jed snorted.

"Well how am I supposed to know what you want to do with stuff, you never tell me everything!"

Bobby's face was screwed up again, his grip tightening around the frame of the phone.

"Fine, well I'm telling you now we need paste too. Not that ready-made expensive crap, get the powder and you can mix it yourself."

"And a pasting table," said Jed out of nowhere.

"What? Shit, yes of course. Get one of those fold-down tables too. They're cheap. You still got change from what I gave you?"

Carl had about £15 left from buying the paper.

"Yeah."

"Well fucking hurry up then, I want this done by end of today."

Bobby was in one of his moods, distracted by whatever it was he wasn't telling anyone about and it seemed to Carl like he was the only one that cared what it was.

"There was some guy hanging around outside. Didn't you notice him?"

That made Jed look up.

"Some old guy with glasses, asking about us…"

He gave a small shrug and went to go back to the emptied room. Bobby was over to him in a flash.

"Whoa whoa whoa whoa whoa… what old guy?"

"I dunno, thought you knew about him. In a grey suit…"

"Cops?" said Jed, standing up.

Carl looked at them both for a moment. That moment was long enough to make him feel better.

"Nah, just some guy who follows the blog, wanting to know when the next meeting was."

"And what did you tell him?"

"I told him it was cancelled! Exactly like you told me to say to anyone who asked! Jesus Christ, you think I'm dim or something?" Carl walked away into the corridor, glanced at Lewis who was grasping at air with one hand, and went into the empty room. As he leaned the rolls against the wall next to the others he allowed himself a little smile.

CHAPTER 27
THE CHURCH OF THE NEW GODS

"Welcome, Martin, to the Church of the New Gods. You are most welcome."

Clifford hung on the spot for a moment, before taking several huge strides forward, reaching both hands out towards his. He clasped Martin's hand and shook it, keeping hold of it while he made eye contact.

"Please, let's take a seat while my coffee machine does its wonders." He definitely had a presence about him thought Martin. With just a few words and simple movements he felt relaxed and almost compelled to do as he asked as they crossed the room.

"I'm sorry but I'm not really here for a conversation with you, I need to see..."

"Jenny Crossdale, Ian Randall's partner. You are here to see how she is coping with everything."

"Well, yes."

They sat down on the sofa, Martin with the sideboard to the right of him, bathing him in a scent wave of coffee that nearly hid the flowery smell he hadn't yet spotted the source of.

"She is as you would expect, very upset, desperately missing her son Lewis, unable to go home because of the abuse from her neighbours, and all made worse because her rock, her only source of support, is in prison. So we, the Church, all of us are acting as a surrogate form of support for her, trying to help her through this. For you to visit us here is great support for her as well as our Church."

"It's not an endorsement, me being here you know. I'm here on behalf of a friend. I'd like to talk to her please."

"That's what we're arranging now. The girls will be telling her you're here and seeing if she wants to see you."

"If she wants to?"

Clifford pursed his lips together and gave Martin a look of concern.

"I know you did what you thought was right, telling them to put Lewis at the mercy of Child Services, and in any just and equal society that would be the correct course of action, but... she does put some blame on you for what has happened to him. To them both, in fact."

Martin sighed.

"I did wonder about that."

"For what it's worth, I wouldn't have done what you did, but I don't blame you for doing it. I would have spirited them away somewhere safe from a system in which discrimination is built in. I know the frustrations, living in a world where you are hated for being yourself, having to hide part of yourself constantly because a Government has convinced itself and the masses that we are dangers. But you have to let go of the past."

"Really."

"Why yes. Your old moral code is... refreshing to see in this day and age, but it is just that, old. When you are oppressed you don't give in to their way of doing things. You have to fight against them, sometimes loudly and publicly against their decisions, but sometimes quietly and with subterfuge, against how they would wish to treat you. I wish it wasn't this way. I wish it was as it was when you were at the height of your powers Martin. Things were much simpler then. Trust was taken as a given, that Heroes would always do the right thing and the system would do right by you. But that's gone. Dead."

"I know that Dr Gaines..."

"Please, call me Clifford," he smiled.

"I know that, but when fighting makes things worse, when it makes things more difficult for you in the long term, sometimes you just have to follow procedure."

"The path of least resistance, yes? But we are resisting. We have to resist! You could no more tell and expect a non-powered person to not use their arms. They are an extension of their being, an intrinsic part of how they interact with the world. Our powers are an extra limb that we use without hesitation, but... the difference is in how we use them. Any person with a pair of fully functioning arms could use them to strangle another person, yet they don't. Compare that to Heroes, who use their abilities to help others. They realise this extra limb is special, it makes them special and gives them an extra level of responsibility."

Martin laughed.

"We don't *all* use our abilities to help, not if I remember correctly the number of Heroes I had to beat the crap out of to stop them killing people. With all respect Dr Gaines, that's a fantasy you're living in. There was never any pure golden age of Heroics and morality. There are and there always have been good and bad people, with or without abilities."

"But that's because human nature is seductive Martin, and those with little resolve always give in. No Hero is born with the will to kill and Heroes are no more likely to kill than anyone else. Now we are not one of those churches that believe Heroes are Gods beyond judgement. We believe Heroes are humans born in the image of the Gods that created this world, one of whom, The Elemental, graced this world in recent time. We are born equal to non-powered people until we discover our abilities. We celebrate the Hero who is naturally good by default and we help those who worry they are being seduced by their humanity. We show them the correct path to the true Heroism that is in all of us."

"Still sounds like a fairy-tale I'm afraid. These Churches have never meant anything to me. Nothing I've ever heard about them makes me think they know about the real world out there. They make up their own nice little story about how things should be and pretend that will somehow change the world."

Clifford smiled meekly and looked down at his clasped hands for a moment. The coffee machine started to splutter as the bitter scent made him dizzy. Martin could gulp a mug down in one right now.

"Let me tell you, if you will humour me, a story about a man, much like yourself."

Martin bit his lip. He knew something like this was coming. If Clifford was the gatekeeper to him seeing Jenny then so be it, he would let him talk. He just hoped he could stay awake until he was finished.

"Sometime in 1845, a small farmer's boy discovered he could fill a bowl with water just by thinking of it. Fearful of what it meant, he hid this ability. Told no-one. Almost ten years later he found himself in the middle of a battle, about to be slaughtered, when he imagined a bayonet striking through the heart of the enemy upon him, and it became true. Except this time, someone saw what happened, because he did the same thing again, and again and again. He saved over forty men's lives that day and forced the enemy infantry to retreat from his position, changing the course of battle. From a small boy hiding away in fear, to a young man finally accepting his powers and turning the tide of a war. That is what we can accomplish when we are allowed to be ourselves. What if *you* could change things Martin? What if *you* could stop hiding part of yourself every day? My goodness, what incredible things you could accomplish."

"No-one is hiding. Well I'm definitely not hiding any more, not that I had much choice about that. We all live our lives pretty normally, get jobs where we can, have families, run businesses. You know, normal."

Clifford brought a hand up to his mouth.

"You can't see it can you? Oh dear, no."

He stood up and walked towards his desk.

"You can't see it, because it's in plain sight. There are hundreds of Heroes in this City, hiding every day. Walking past you in the street, hiding. Sitting next to you in the coffee shop, hiding. All of them, all of us are hiding. They try to remove our extra limbs by denying us the use of them, hoping they will shrivel away through lack of use. But the danger there, is that hiding breeds resentment. How many Heroes are being turned to evil when, if given the chance to use their powers for good, they would not turn? And the Government can't see what kind of country they are creating." He stepped towards Martin, arms wide open. "Imagine Martin, if you could use your abilities openly again. What would you do. Still be a security guard? Possibly. But what about that fight breaking out in the street, those people trapped in a burning flat, that car accident with the doors mangled shut. You would save them wouldn't you? You would intervene with your abilities to do the right thing, because it is what you intrinsically know to do. But they have disabled you. Cut off your limb. And the worst part of it is, you have let them do it."

Clifford was right. Of course he would help those people if he could use his powers openly. Damn it, he would do it even now! Because he had to. Martin could almost hear Maria chastising him again, but what was he supposed to do if those feelings were genuine?

Ignore them? Let people die? What neither of them knew of course was he was back doing Heroics again, in secret. Which reminded him of something he had been meaning to ask.

"So, what power of *yours* are you hiding from the world?"

Clifford smiled, almost embarrassed and looked down at the floor.

"Well, I'm sorry but I hope you'll forgive me for not telling you." He looked up at Martin again. "When I grew up back in Australia, telling anyone you were blessed meant being removed from your family. I had it drilled in to me that you never told anyone about your true nature. I guess some of that programming has stayed with me now I'm older, but... do feel free to ask my disciples about themselves. They'll be more than happy to tell you their stories. And they're all stories of discrimination, hiding their secret from their family and friends. Half of them aren't registered. And I feel comfortable telling you that, putting that burden of knowledge on you, because I know that's where you come from too. You hid away from the world for eighteen years. You, more than anyone, know what it's like out there for gifted people like ourselves. You will find many kindred spirits here my friend. Come, take a look around. Let's see if Jenny is ready to talk to you." Clifford was halfway down the office, gesturing him to follow.

Martin wasn't sure about him at all. He was much like all the other Hero religion people he'd bumped into during his time, a slick politician with all the right words but no meaning. He hoped Jenny was going to be all right here. In any case, all he had to do was speak with her for a few minutes, find out about Lewis and be gone. That should be simple enough.

CHAPTER 28
ELEMENT CITY COUNCIL CHILD SERVICES DEPARTMENT

"There should have been a security detail posted at the centre at the very least. He shouldn't even have been there Jane, the moment the initial assessment came back he should be been transferred that day to Coppham!"

"You know as well as I do that transport services have been cut back as part of cost-cutting measures. There are set days for transfers and he was going to be moved on the Thursday."

"Thursday!" Eleanor threw her hands in the air, shaking her head. She walked over to the window in Jane's office and looked out at the car park, the nearest spaces filled with white vans and a highly visible police car. Jane was sat behind her desk, surface objects geometrically arranged, peering at Eleanor calmly from behind a pair of reading glasses.

"Eleanor, there was no known information that he was at any risk."

"Apart from the fact his father smashed a door out of the wall? Not that I didn't understand his reasons, and it turned out that he wasn't a risk to him at all, but that should have been enough for an emergency transfer?"

Jane raised an eyebrow over the top of her thin black frames.

"The father wasn't a risk? At all?", she nodded towards her office door. Workmen were buzzing around outside in the corridor, laying strips of plastic and other materials in piles, carrying sheets of MDF into the offices opposite where the damage from Ian's attack was still visible, the police having only just released the offices to them two days ago. Now and again the neck-tightening squeal of a circular saw sliced through the air, heavy with the odours of earthy fibres and sharp glue.

Eleanor shuddered as she remembered the partitions and metal shutters peeling apart before her eyes. She remembered the size, the smell of him as he stood next to her, the breath on her face.

But she wasn't frightened. She wasn't frightened because she knew that *he* was. His son was missing and he had no-one else to blame but them.

She was angry however. Angry at the response team shooting him, netting him, dragging her away as she was trying to calm the situation. She knew she could stop him, but they didn't listen to her, despite her angry protestations at the time and later, during the, "debriefs", first by the police, the PCA and then to hastily gathered staff counsellors. They treated him like an animal, when he was just a terrified father. She couldn't forgive them for that. Jane peeled off her glasses, letting them dangle by one arm between her fingers.

"Look, I understand how you feel. It's not your fault. It isn't anybody's fault. You did everything right, your process is logged and agreed upon by all of us, and I will say as much in any official enquiry, which there will have to be unfortunately. This was something nobody could predict or prevent."

"This was an organised group who knew what they were doing Jane. They knew who they were looking for and where he was. They had the resources to get hold of a swipe card to gain entry and knew to remove his tracking chip..."

"And the Powered Crime Agency is following up on every lead to find him. You can't be the police as well Eleanor. Let them do their job and stop blaming yourself."

"I'm not blaming myself, I'm blaming the Department! There needs to be a fast-track procedure for high-risk children, with access to immediate security and transport to an appropriate facility."

"And I agree!"

Eleanor stood surprised by her boss's reply.

"It's something I've mentioned to Philip several times before. Please, put your suggestions in writing and send them to me. Your experience will only add weight to them. I'll add my own recommendations, again, and pass them upwards. If anything can get us that budget back it's this tragedy."

Something positive could come out of this after all, thought Eleanor. She had to focus on improving processes, everything had to be about helping the most vulnerable children. She took a deep breath in, noticing she was slouching, and pulled herself up.

"Fine. I will."

Jane slipped her glasses back on.

"Good. Now, you can go back home. I appreciate the thought, and yes, there is a lot of work to catch up on, but the counsellor you spoke to said you should have at least a week off and I agree with him. You've been through a traumatic incident and our protocol says..."

"I'm not going home, I need to speak to Mr Randall and Miss Crossdale about their son. Someone should be following this up with them."

"Absolutely not." Jane's voice had lost its calmness.

"They are still the child's parents, they still have to be included in..."

"No. Not at all." Jane took her glasses off in one move, folded them and placed them parallel to a small pile of folders. "One, Miss Crossdale is in the care of police liaison, so there is nothing we can do for her until her son is back in our care. Two, Mr Randall is in the care of the Prison Service and will be for a great many years. Only if he is considered for parole, should that occur before Lewis is eighteen, will we get involved with him again regarding access and structure for any contact with his son. Three, on a personal note, there is no way anyone here is going to help that... man, in any capacity, and that goes for everyone from myself upwards. He is, "persona non grata", as far as this Department is concerned."

Eleanor stepped towards the desk.

"So that's it? We disown him because, instead of hammering on the partition like dozens of other fathers who we have successfully reunited with their children, he was able to tear it apart? It was a natural reaction Jane."

"It was natural for him to attack you? Are you saying you're fine with that?"

"He didn't attack me! How many times do I have to explain this?"

"You don't Eleanor, the evidence for it is next door! Look, I know you care, genuinely care, about the families assigned to you, but sometimes you need to dial back the empathy a bit and look at the actual facts."

"The only fact I see right now is that my Department has given up and I'm the only one trying to save this family!"

Jane stared at her, unblinking. Both her eyebrows were high, the whites above her irises visible.

"Go home Eleanor. That's not a suggestion. I don't want to see you until this time next week. In the meantime we can all hope the child is recovered safe and when you return we can look to the next stage of the process. Am I clear?"

Eleanor knew she had spoken out of line. Never, in all her time here, had she raised her voice to a manager in that way. She knew she should consider herself fortunate that Jane, despite her abrasiveness, was clear-headed enough to not take it personally. In any case the decision was made. She dipped her head and rubbed her temples to a backing track of hammering and workmen's phones chiming with text messages.

"Yes, perhaps you're right."

Jane picked up her glasses, opening up the arms.

"I know I am. Take some time off, go to counselling, come back refreshed. Yes?" She slipped her glasses back on and woke up her monitor by shaking the mouse.

Eleanor nodded, slouched again, and left the office. She immediately tasted chalk in her mouth and could see, through a door propped open by a can of paint, one of the men cutting a huge sheet of plasterboard on a saw bench. The shredded partition lay in a pile in a corner of the room near the fire exit ready to go to into the skip outside. All the furniture they couldn't squeeze into the smaller interview rooms had been piled up out of the way in the other undamaged corner. She went back to her temporary desk in interview room four and slowly gathered her things together.

CHAPTER 29
THE CHURCH OF THE NEW GODS

"Hello Harvey." The blonde girl called Claire smiles at you as you come through the front door. She is sitting on the end of a bench tapping at a mobile phone.

"Oh, hello." You smile back awkwardly, closing the door behind you. You haven't spoken to her much. You haven't spoken to any of his disciples really, mostly just Clifford. You had to suppress a smile when he told you they were called disciples though. Very religious and somehow amusing, you didn't know why and didn't want to insult the man by laughing at him.

"Is Clifford here?"

"Yep, in his office as always."

You nod and head to the back of the building. You knock on the office door and go in when you hear a quiet,

"Come in".

"Harvey! My friend! Please, you don't need to knock. My office is always open to you. Here, take a seat. Coffee?"

"Oh yes, don't mind if I do. Just black is fine."

"Of course, a man who likes things simple, none of these fancy coffees with froth and vanilla shots and all that nonsense."

You make a face as you take your coat off and go to hang it on a coat rack next to the bookshelves.

"Goodness no. A waste of good coffee." You suddenly become aware of your over-familiarity and hesitate until Clifford nods and, relaxing, you hang your coat up before taking a seat on the sofa. Clifford stands near, back towards you as he presses buttons on the coffee maker.

"So!" he says, spinning round and clasping his hands together, "How goes the investigation?"

"Very well Clifford. I watched the Pub for the whole day."

You pull out the diary from your inside suit pocket and open it. You were glad it was a "day-to-page" one, the number of notes you ended up taking.

"At nine twelve, a.m. I saw a girl go in the side entrance to the rooms underneath it. She was carrying a square flat box in a black bag. I could just make out the bright label through the bag, it was a cot."

Clifford's eyes light up.

"Go on."

The coffee maker starts to growl.

"Well, then a young lad left shortly after. He came back at eleven thirty three. I spoke to him…"

"You did what? You were not supposed to reveal yourself, remember?"

"But I am the only one of us that they have no chance of recognising. Anyway, you said my ability is to know what has to be done. I knew I had to speak to one of them."

Clifford's face tightens as the coffee maker vibrates on the sideboard.

"I had a plan. I told him I followed their blog website and was wondering when the next meeting was. Apparently they are all cancelled until further notice."

Clifford relaxes.

"He wasn't suspicious about you?"

"No, no, he was far too busy trying to gather up rolls of lining paper he had just bought. I gave him a hand."

"Really…"

The machine starts hissing, wafting out waves of coffee aroma.

"Yes, and he left again soon after and came back with a bag filled with boxes of wallpaper paste. I'm pretty sure he's one of them from the photo you showed me too, you know, the police shots of those attackers who've been going around killing Heroes?"

Clifford sits down next to you, brow furrowed.

"Are you one hundred percent sure?"

You know you have to be honest.

"Not one hundred percent no, but I think there is a very high chance because I did see the black lad from the photos go in and out the same way at…"

You scan your list of events. "…ten forty eight, returned at eight minutes past two, left again at…"

Clifford lays a hand on your forearm and you stop. You feel a tingle creep up and down your arm from his palm through your suit jacket.

You look up from the diary and see him looking deep into your eyes. The machine is bubbling gently, rumbling the floor.

"Anything else?"

"Er…" You're sweating. Something about this man makes you nervous when he's close, but not in a bad way.

"There was another lad, looked only about twelve, probably not though, the older you get the younger kids look eh?"

Clifford smiles encouragingly at you.

"He… he had brown hair, brushed forward like those teen pop stars have it done. Thin lad. He came out with the black one at…" You go to check the events list, but remember Clifford's arm on you. Too much detail Harvey, just the basic facts. If he wants any more he'll tell you. "… sometime in the afternoon, and they didn't come back till late. They were all still in there when I left half an hour ago."

"So, that's four at least, one of which is definitely the black lad from the security footage…?"

"Definitely."

"Another one is a possible. Another young boy we don't know about and a girl. And they've brought in a cot, rolls of paper and paste and they've cancelled all their meetings."

"Yes. Yes, that's about it." You close your diary gingerly. You hope that was enough. You could stay overnight to watch them. You should suggest that. It would be difficult to explain to the wife as you've never had to do that before for work, or for any other reason. It would be odd and you wouldn't know how to explain it. You've only managed to get out of work by telling them it's a family emergency. That gives you five days maximum before you have to explain yourself.

You hope that's enough time. Any longer than that and they will call home to find out where you are and end up speaking to the wife. And that can't be allowed to happen.

"Excellent work Harvey. Excellent!"

You smile as Clifford stands up. He slides open the sideboard and takes out two small cylindrical cups and matching saucers. He places one cup in the hollow at the front of the machine and presses a button.

"So, what does all that say to you Harvey? Taking into account what I told you about their group and the suspicions I've had of them for some time now."

"It's them. They've got the child."

"Why do you say that?"

He takes out a cardboard carton of long life milk from the sideboard.

"The cot, the cancelled meetings. They must have him there. Not sure about the paper and paste. Preparing a room for him I suppose, expect to be there for some time? Of course! You don't do up a room somewhere you're only using as an occasional meeting hall in a building you shouldn't even be in. That would be pointless!"

"Exactly Harvey. Exactly. I suspected they were behind the killings and as soon as I heard about the missing boy, I was certain they were involved. But of course, I had no evidence for any of this."

Clifford turns round with two cups in saucers and hands one to you before sitting down next to you again.

"You've only gone and worked out what the Powered Crime Agency has failed to. You are amazing."

Your heart swells so much it feels like its going to burst out the front of your chest. You feel yourself go red. You take a quick gulp from the cup to hide yourself. It tastes rich and hot in your throat.

"Mmm, lovely coffee," you say to try and change the conversation.

"Only the best Harvey, only the best."

You return his smile and take another sip. Your arm trembles, so you put the cup down carefully so it doesn't clatter on the saucer.

"So what now Clifford? We can't get the PCA involved because, like you said before, a child with that power is too useful and too much of a danger to the Authorities. Who knows what they would do with it."

"Well now my friend, I must formulate a plan. I reckon we have a few days grace before the Authorities catch up with our level of information, formulate their own course of action and act on it. I must come up with an intervention to rescue the child before it is too late."

"Goodness me." You stare across the room to the door, thinking of the disciples upstairs. He must mean going in to take the child out by force. He would be breaking several innate power laws in one fell swoop, not to mention all the regular ones. But... you can't think of any alternative that guarantees the safety of the little boy.

"I will be of any assistance you require Clifford."

Clifford is drinking as you say that. He mutters, "mmm", from a behind mouthful of coffee, nodding. You fool, you could have waited until he could respond. You are as bad as those waiters that come up to your table to ask how the meal is just as you take a bite. Inconsiderate. You don't want to be inconsiderate. Clifford swallows.

"I know I can always count on you Harvey, but this one is on me and me alone. It's a potentially dangerous exercise I can't have you involved in. Besides, I need your help on another matter, something I no longer have the time to look into personally."

"Anything Clifford," you say.

You worry about the time off work, about your wife, about explanations and excuses, but you push them all to the back of your head. Priorities Harvey. Your priorities have changed. Heck, your life has changed. You just need to reorganise things to accommodate it.

"May the Creator bless you Harvey." Clifford rests the cup and saucer on his lap. "Now, I recently had a visit from a man who calls himself Martin Molloy..."

CHAPTER 30
MARTIN'S APARTMENT

"What the crazy fuck did you think you were doing Martin?" Maria was still inside the doorway of Martin's apartment, jacket on. He had only just let her in and closed the door when she started. He wasn't too sure what she was on about to begin with. Was this about him going after Jack? It was a bit of a delayed reaction if it was, that was months ago, and he was sure she didn't want to talk about that anyway. She was staring at him. He supposed she was waiting for an answer which meant he really should know what she was talking about.

"When?"

"When? When you did the exact opposite of what I told you to!"

Martin was tempted to say, "When?", again, but held his tongue. No humour was going to defuse this. Had she found out about his Heroics with Hayley? But how could she, they had been very careful, not spotted by anyone since the stationery gang, just doing their normal nightly rounds when she wasn't on shift, trying to track down Mr Fitzpatrick. Thankfully Maria quickly tired of his blank look, dug into the black shoulder bag hanging by her hip and pulled out a newspaper, which she thrust towards him.

He unfolded it, checking himself again when he thought about reading the sports pages, and turned it over to the front. As he did, it suddenly clicked in his head and he felt like someone was pouring freezing water down his spine.

It was a copy of the Daily Mail. The main headline, in fact the whole front page, was about Charles'ss hearing, same as yesterday. What caught his attention most of all was a box-out with a zoomed-in picture of him, stepping out of a large pair of black doors, brass wall plaque just in shot. They got him coming out of the Church of the New Gods.

"Shit."

Maria remained silent as he turned the page. Pages two and three were about the aftermath of the sentencing, revelations from a former lover of Charles about hurried sex in a TV centre store room, but pages four and five ran the headline, "As Ignite goes down for murder, are The Pulse going up in flames?". There was a picture of Maria getting into a taxi outside her apartment titled, "The face of the Witch shows the strain", and there were more pictures of him at the Church, along with a stock photo of the prison.

"Oh Christ."

The captions and boldface text read, "cracking up under the strain", "bizarre behaviour", "visits the vicious Savage in the clink, the only other Hero to nearly kill him", "does he think he's some kind of God?".

He didn't read the rest of the text, he knew what it would say anyway, that's why he never read any of those rags. He folded up the paper slowly, planning out his words.

"OK. I went to see him in prison because I felt guilty for not helping him. I didn't want to break the law to help him earlier, but I thought I could at least do something now."

"I don't care about your reasons. I told you not to get involved! And what did you do?"

"Look, what the hell is wrong with trying to do something right?"

"You got INVOLVED. That is what you did wrong. Full stop." She was panting heavily and her face was red. "Leave the past in the fucking past. That's all I asked of you."

"But this isn't about the past, it's about right now! He isn't the animal who attacked us back then. He has a family and he's trying to…"

Maria gave out a yell, threw her hands up in the air and stomped awkwardly past him to rest her hands on the arm of the sofa. Her leg was still encased in metal and she flexed it up and down as she bent over slightly.

"I don't care what he is now Martin. I'm sure he's a really nice, well-adjusted person who only destroys Council property and attacks armed response teams when he's having a really, really bad day. I don't care about anything he has or hasn't done. I care about you. I care about you not getting messed up with Heroics again, and the first step backwards to that is 'getting involved'."

"A bit late for that", thought Martin. He kept his eyes low, picking out the curves on the metal leg frame rather than make eye contact with her.

"Focus on your own problems before anything else. Yes? Do we agree?"

Martin let out a guilty sigh.

"Yes."

There was a sucking-in of air and Hayley appeared six feet behind Maria, in her safe spot between the TV and the wall, holding a tablet device. She was mouth open, about to speak, when she caught sight of Maria out of the corner of her eye and jumped away. Martin heard her reappear in the bedroom.

Maria looked puzzled and turned to an empty space, then looked at Martin.

"That noise?" he managed to say with an innocent face, "Gas boiler coming on. Noticed that not long after I moved in. Bit loud isn't it?"

She still looked puzzled, but satisfied. She was too distracted by her own thoughts to give any more time to it.

"And the Church? That's... not you. Really?" Maria was halfway between concerned, at not picking up on some obvious sign about his mental state, and accepting that he may have found a genuine belief in something like this. She had read enough about religious belief and Hero psychology to be worried.

"Oh no, Christ, nothing like that... no pun intended. I was looking for Jenny."

Maria tilted her head.

"Ian's partner. Lewis's mum. I found out she is staying with them now. Ian asked me to find out how they both were. She hadn't been in contact since... the incident."

Maria snorted.

"No fucking surprise. What did she say?"

"I never saw her in the end, she wouldn't speak to me. I only heard about Lewis through Clifford and I still need to go tell Ian, to give him an update..."

"NO! You are not going back there." She pushed herself up straight from the sofa and faced him.

"But can I at least tell him about his son? Find him a decent solicitor?"

"No buts! You can't be seen any more, you can't get any more involved. How much more clearer can I make this? We're still in the media storm surrounding Charles's conviction, hoping it will die down soon, and you're off visiting The Savage in jail and popping into Hero churches. Do you have any idea how that looks?"

"I don't care how it looks. I've told you before, I'm not interested in what the papers say about anything I do. I know the truth and that's all I care about."

"Well you should care about it."

"OK, fine then. How about... I'll just say... I thought Charles was trying to kill me, I thought I was going to die. I've realised how short life is so I've made a decision to... I don't know... help people who weren't expecting any help. Like Ian and the Church. They do community work. There!"

"Bullshit. They won't buy it. They'll still just say you're losing it."

"And again, I care because?"

"Because I thought you were trying to get your life back in order after everything that's happened. I thought you were trying to find a job."

"Oh come on, no one is going to hire me..."

"And no one will, if they keep seeing you on the front of the papers every day." She shook her head. Her eyes, which had been wide in alarm, suddenly drooped and she put her hand to her forehead and rubbed her temples.

Martin felt guilty for getting her so wound up when she was supposed to be recovering. He was supposed to be giving her stability right now, what with everything going on. She stepped towards him, and rested a hand on his shoulder.

"I just want things to be normal again. For both of us." She looked Martin in the eye, piercing his cloud of uneasiness. "Things have to be normal for us both to move on. Do you understand?"

Martin didn't know what the future held for the two of them. They had only met again because of Vincent's death, and they still hadn't spoken about their affair eighteen years ago. It seemed to be a conversation that was always about to come up, but one that was never started. It was the only truly honest relationship he had ever had, not that there had been many before they met, and there had been none since then. He didn't want to jeopardise their current relationship, just as they had found each other again, even though he didn't know where it was leading. Especially because he didn't know. He put his hands either side of her waist, just to reassure her. To his surprise she was bonier than he had expected.

"You're right. We both need some kind of normality. I promise I won't go back to see Ian OK? Or to that Church."

"Good. That's a start.", she said, picking a piece of fluff from his jumper before brushing it flat. "Anyway, I have to get back now…"

"I thought you were still on sick leave?"

"Are you kidding? I *had* to go back. I've got trial data to go through before Professor Carter claims my study has passed some time threshold which allows him to claim my funding. The bastard!" Maria hobbled towards the door. "God-damn! These Exo-legs are supposed to be lightweight, designed so you can walk normally while your leg heals. Walk normally? Bullshit! And you know who makes them? One of Jack's companies. Figures."

Martin smiled, relaxing slightly as he opened the door for her while she muttered, "cheap rubbish", under her breath.

"Just promise me one more thing…" she said as she rested on the door frame. "No more secrets between us, yes?"

Martin involuntarily stood up straighter, as an image of Hayley, hiding in the bedroom, popped into his mind.

"Yeah. No more secrets. Promise."

CHAPTER 31
MARTIN'S APARTMENT

"Wow Dad, she really beat you down!" Hayley had waited until she heard the lift door close before coming into the living room.

"And of course you were listening in…"

"Beat you down like a bitch."

Martin screwed up his face.

"I'm not hers, or anyone else's 'bitch'. I'm going to get Ian a decent solicitor whatever she says, get him out of those damn shackles and off those meds. If I can't visit him then that's the least I can do. Anyway, I don't like that term, it's not nice."

"Sorry Dad. Hey, I just realised, I met The Black Witch! That means I've done four of you guys now," Hayley beamed. "I mean yeah, one was possessed, the other a murderer and I only saw this one for a second before she almost clocked me, but… that's not bad is it?"

"And can you please stop calling me Dad."

"Why not? It's what the news is calling us, and it's good cover isn't it? Takes the police's scent off us for a bit." Hayley thought for a second, "Wait, *I'm* the police, so does that mean I'm stopping myself finding myself? Maybe I should become a guru in not finding yourself…"

After Maria's visit, Martin wasn't in the mood for any babble.

"Look… what do you want?"

"Hmm? Oh yeah, you need to see this." She held out a tablet device for him. Shaking his head he took the glossy rectangle. The screen was dark apart from a black triangle in a grey circle.

"So what is this?"

"Oh God, you Neanderthal!", said Hayley, as she reached over the top of it and tapped the circle. As she did so a video started to play.

There were three people standing against a wall covered in plain paper. They were wearing mixed camouflage gear, with dark balaclavas and sunglasses covering their faces. Martin was confused, expecting them to have Kalashnikovs, thinking this was some sort of terrorist video, but they were empty-handed, apart from the one on the right who was holding a small child in his arms. The one in the middle gave a nod to someone behind the camera and stepped forward.

"We are The Hero Killers and we have the Creator child." He motioned to the person holding the baby, whom Martin was fairly sure was a girl, and she turned the boy towards the camera.

Martin went completely cold. It was Lewis. He would have known that face in an instant, but if there had been any doubt, Lewis was chewing on the same blue-eared rabbit he saw only a week ago.

"We have watched you self-titled, 'Heroes', you entitled 'Heroes', fly and smash your way through our lives for years with impunity. You evade the law as if it has no meaning, so we have been bringing the law to you."

"Is this happening right now?"

"No no, it went up on YouTube within the last few hours, I don't know when it was recorded, now shh…"

"Betty Henshaw AKA Mother Nature from the 'fifties' team Havoc, responsible for the deaths of at least eight civilians and one police officer, we took her down in her local grocery store. Chris Barnes AKA The Mighty Bastard killed a young boy and left another in a wheelchair, so we burned him alive in his flat. Jacob Harrison AKA The Interviewer, tortured dozens of people for his crime boss, his throat was cut open on the street where he lived. All of them were living their lives out like they had done nothing. Nazi war criminals had to spend their lives hiding because they knew people were after them, and they would be found and put on trial and charged, no matter how long ago their evil acts had been. But these…Heroes and the things they did…?", he made a sweeping motion with his hand, "brushed under the carpet. 'Oh it was a different era', 'Immunity for information' - bullshit! They killed and injured innocent people, normal people, and got away with it. And now, 'Heroes' are supposed to be kept on a leash. These dangerous freaks living among us are supposed to be monitored so they can't hurt us, and yet we hear about them every week, killing guards to rob a jewellery store, or flying down to help save someone from muggers by beating the shit out of them. I thought the law was supposed to stop all that? Yet it goes on, and PoCA don't do fuck all. Well it's about time someone made them." He stepped back into line and leaned over to Lewis, rubbing a finger under his chin.

"We're not going to hurt this little fella. Well, not as long as we start to see a change. We have demands, and we are going to see them met. Here's demand number one, from tomorrow no newspaper or news programme, national or local, printed or online will use the words, 'Hero' or 'Heroes' to talk about a powered person. We don't care what you call them, as long as it's neither of those words, because we're taking them back. We're going to make them mean something again. We're going to have more demands in the coming days, but first we need to be sure you're listening, because if you're not, you're going to have the blood of a dead child on your hands."

"We are The Hero Killers, and we're going to make things change."

The image froze and the grey circle reappeared over it.

Martin and Hayley stared at the image in silence for a long time, until Martin finally spoke.

"Oh shit."

"Yep. Major media have already picked it up and have been calling the Department non-stop for the last half hour, according to my mate Alice. I'll probably get a call to come in to help field phone calls at the station in a moment, while they set up an incident room. It's been verified as genuine too, that's definitely his son."

"They can't hurt him though. I mean they wouldn't?"

"These are the guys who smashed an old lady over the head with a baseball bat, slit the throat of an old man on a busy main street, (and got away from me, the bastards), and apparently killed someone else in an arson attack. So, yeah, I think they probably would."

"Oh God. Ian can't see this. I hope he doesn't get to see this." Martin handed the tablet back to Hayley, got to his feet and started walking around the living room.

"We have to find them. Get Lewis back. We need to track them down. Can we find out where they are? Can they do that with computers?"

"Unless they've been very clever and disguised it somehow, it should be possible to get the IP address of whoever uploaded it to YouTube and track them that way, but I don't know how long that will take to arrange…"

"Then we need to find them before the police or PoCA do!"

"Why?"

"You said it yourself, they're vicious thugs who hate powered people. They get one sniff that someone is onto them and Lewis is dead. We need to find them and get in and out in seconds, and I only know one person who can do that."

Hayley smiled and stood to attention.

"I'll try and get as much info as I can while I'm at the station, because I'm like ninety-nine percent sure I'll get called in once this hits the fan. I'll feed it back to you, and we can take it from there. You OK?"

Martin was standing still, hand on his chin, thinking hard.

"Yeah…"

"Hey, don't worry, we'll find him. He'll be OK," she said, putting her arm on his shoulder. "Anyway, gotta go and wait for the call. Hell, I might as well get ready. See ya." Hayley leapt away, leaving Martin standing in the same place.

He thought again about the advice that he gave to Ian and Jenny, and about his promise to Ian make sure both she and their son were both OK. He had to fulfil that promise. Martin knew that everything Ian had gone through to try and build a normal life for himself would be lost forever the moment he saw that video. He would become The Savage again, and nothing would stand in his way.

CHAPTER 32
OUTSIDE MARTIN'S APARTMENT

You chew and swallow the last piece of your prawn salad sandwich. You wipe your lips, fold the tissue twice and put it in the plastic bag with the coffee cups, empty sandwich container and orange juice bottle. That will go in the public waste bin just up the road before you head off. You had told the wife there was a presentation coming up in a few weeks and that everybody had to be hands on deck, working extra hours to prepare. She hadn't been bothered, feigning enough interest only to say that she would keep dinner in the oven for an extra hour and if you weren't home by then it would be in the bin. You had just nodded and said, "OK dear," as you both sat up in bed reading. When she turned off her light and went to sleep, you had quietly pulled out your Private Investigator's Handbook and read it for a few more hours.

You had watched stakeouts on American cop shows when you were growing up. The emphasis was on the tedium of them, but there was always a pay-off, i.e. they always spotted the suspect arriving or leaving somewhere, or doing something suspicious. You are beginning to suspect that ninety-nine percent of the time there is no pay-off at all. Just a lot of waiting. You had been outside Martin Molloy's apartment since six-thirty that morning. It was now nearly half-past eight at night and already dark. He hadn't been out once. Well he may have been, when you went for your toilet breaks in the coffee shop up the road, but you doubted it. This man was a hermit. You had hoped he would go out so you could rifle through his rubbish, maybe find some paperwork or hand-written notes, something to go on. He didn't of course, so at lunchtime, when you hoped everyone was busy, you went across the road and down the alleyway.

Round the back was a private car park with a dozen spaces, their access blocked by a row of metal bollards. It looked like the bollards retracted into the ground when a key-card was swiped against the yellow box set on a pole next to the wall. There were five cars parked up, all models from the last two years. You had checked the prices for these apartments online last night. You undoubtedly had to have money to live here, and it showed. The back wall of the building had a small exit door and two silver-grey shutters. The one next to the exit was closed, but the other was open and you could see the bottom halves of several large bins inside. Your mood dropped. There was no way of knowing which rubbish would be his, or even which of the bins were at the bottom of the disposal chute he used. It was a wild guess at best. There was a CCTV camera watching out over the whole area, a black ball on the end of a cream metal rod fixed to the back wall of the building. There was no chance of being discreet, the camera probably already had you in its wide field of view, so you figured you might as well commit yourself to the act. If you were caught you would just have to bluster your way out, playing the dull, boring Harvey that everyone ignored. So with a deep breath you walked through the bollards and straight up to the open shutters.

Your heart was leaping into the bottom of your neck. While you knew you had to do this, you couldn't believe you were. You weren't the same Harvey you were last week. You would never have dreamt of trespassing on private property, tracking down criminals and following powerful Heroes. That burning in your veins wasn't fear, it was purpose, and you knew then that wherever it would lead, you would go. Willingly. This was the Harvey that knew what needed to be done.

And right then you needed to get elbow deep in a rubbish bin. Your luck was in. There wasn't the putrid smell of rotting food you were expecting, but the dry musty smell of paper and card mixed in with the sweet smell of ripe milk and wine. These were the recycling bins. There were no chutes above here, which made sense as nobody wanted to be woken at three in the morning by the sound of bottles clattering down a metal tube from the top of the building. That of course, meant an increased likelihood of being disturbed by residents, not to mention any security that might have spotted you going in. So this meant you had to work fast. The paper and card bin was pretty full, so you didn't have to lean over too far. You shuffled through the top layers, a mix of flyers, magazines, Amazon boxes and frozen ready meal cartons. You had never eaten a ready meal in your life and it seemed strange to you that people with this much money would be dining on these terrible concoctions. You sighed. It must be the rush of modern life. People too busy earning money to take the time out to learn to cook a decent meal. As you lifted a large and badly folded cardboard box, you spied paperwork underneath. Looked like utility bills. You grabbed a handful and started checking the addresses.

It was then the door opened behind you. You had to try and keep your cool, keep searching with purpose, but you stopped breathing entirely when Martin Molloy himself came in. He wasn't as tall as you had imagined from the photos Clifford showed you, or from the pictures you found in a cursory web search, but he was wide, muscular, built like an Eastern European weightlifter. He didn't look outwardly like a Hero. You realised that was a silly thing to think of course. It's not like he would be wandering round in a costume, not like that woman you saw pounding that man's face all those years ago, but he did have a certain aura about him. You're not a Detector, but you would like to think that if you hadn't known who he was and hadn't seen him in the news over the last few months, that if you bumped into him shopping in the supermarket you would be able to tell he was like you.

He was carrying a small plastic box filled with beer bottles, a wine bottle and some papers, including an old catalogue.

"Hi.", he said.

"Oh hello, don't mind me, just trying to find some bank statements I threw out by mistake."

Martin Molloy chuckled.

"I've done that before."

"I can't believe you have to keep them for two years. Ridiculous really."

"Need a hand?"

"No, no, I think I'm getting there. But thank you."

"No problem."

You kept searching while he started dropping the bottles into the small brown bin next to you.

You had no idea where all your patter came from, the bank statements thing. Out of nowhere. Off the top of your head. And it was so easy! And you made it sound convincing too, because he didn't seem suspicious of you. Martin Molloy had stayed relaxed and continued sorting his recycling.

Clifford said they couldn't read him, but they knew he was involved somehow, and that's why you had to follow him, to find out his routine, who he knows, where he goes, (which was nowhere as it turned out), and what he does.

But that's the thing that had been bothering you. He's a Hero. There is no way a Hero would be helping an anti-Hero group kidnap a powered child to let them threaten to kill him and try to turn society against people like himself. Like yourself. Even if he was connected somehow, what was the point of following him? It was obvious where the child was being kept and that was the primary goal right now, the safety of that baby. Whatever Martin Molloy was up to wasn't directly related to this, and Clifford didn't give you any hints as to what it might be, besides a nebulous, "watch him". It didn't make sense to you, but it was what Clifford needed of you, so you obliged all the same. He had dropped his newspapers and the catalogue into your bin when you noticed he was eyeing the papers in your hands.

"Ah, not mine these ones. Should be shredded really, for security. Anyone could pick them up. Identity theft, isn't it? Cybercrime, where they steal your details and buy things on the internet?"

"Wouldn't know, never been online," he had said.

"Really? Heh, to be honest I don't blame you, not much worth bothering about on there anyway." You shared a laugh as you dropped the papers back and lift a handful of flattened cereal boxes.

"Well I hope you find them."

"Me too, otherwise I'm not getting that loan my wife has been bothering me about!"

He smiled at that and left you to it, disappearing back through the door into the building.

You immediately left the way you came and sat back down in your car with a heavy thud. You exhaled deeply, your arms and legs shaking, but you smiled to yourself. You did it. You can do this.

Seven hours later and you aren't smiling as much, but the confidence hasn't left you. The light is on and you see no movement. Same as the rest of the day. This was a waste of time. You decide to give it another hour. Not because you think he will do something in that time, but because that's the latest you reckon the wife will accept you returning home without too much of an argument. As you let yourself smile about how much you won't care about her anger directed at you, you see a large figure, good grief... the man must be well over six feet tall and just as wide. He hurries from down the street trying to keep to the shadows. There is nobody else around apart from some kids much further down your side, and they're walking away from the area.

You see a mass of thick hair bouncing around as he pulls a raincoat across his chest and disappears down the alleyway where he stops halfway down under some security lights and looks up. That couldn't be, could it? But he's in prison! Oh my. This could be interesting.

You sit up in your seat and train your eyes on him, glancing up to the fifth floor window and back down. Well Harvey, whatever happens next, at least you'll have something to report back to Clifford.

CHAPTER 33
MARTIN'S APARTMENT

Martin had spent the day waiting for any information from Hayley. He only received two texts from her in the end, the first one to say it would be difficult for her to text as she was in Central Command again, and another one saying the investigative team were still trying to track down who The Hero Killers were. So not much movement there.

While waiting, he had dusted the apartment, done a small amount of underwear and t-shirt washing, taken some old bottles, free local newspapers and flyers to the recycling bins on the ground floor and a dozen other small tasks. That took him three hours. Since then he had been online, tapping fearfully at his new computer, somehow managing to search for, and find, Clifford Gaines. He read with interest that Gaines went back to Australia after his exile when they changed their Hero laws in 2002, and founded the first Church of the New Gods in Adelaide. There were several stories about local councils refusing planning applications, about attacks on the Church and his followers, that one building they were using was fire-bombed. Complaints smearing his character, allegations of, "breeding programs", with young girls and rumours that he had fathered several children with some of his followers. These were all unsubstantiated in the end. Eventually he left and returned to Scotland. Following that, there were several UK news articles about him setting up a similar Church in Glasgow six years ago, then of course the new one in Element City, which took him up to the present day.

In the background, the BBC News 24 rolling coverage alternated between Charles's life sentence verdict, construction magnate Raymond Billington applying for a Hero Team Licence, the new father and daughter hero team, (he just shook his head and didn't listen), and the kidnapping of Lewis. They replayed that video at least once every fifteen minutes, with zoomed-in stills of the kidnappers' masks and Lewis's face cross-cutting the interview and discussion segments. Various talking heads, such as the head of INNATE, Hero historians, retired hostage experts and Clifford Gaines popped up over the course of the day. The discussion ranged from speculation over the kidnappers' identities and motives, to potted histories of The Savage. Questions were posed for debate, were Heroes discriminated against by Social Services and the law? How would the police trace the child and, when they did find him, how would they tackle the situation, negotiation or the SAS? It was in the middle of yet another recap of the sequence of events that Martin heard the thuds. He immediately placed them as outside the building, but couldn't work out exactly where.

Then, he heard a tearing noise emanating from the bedroom. There was a short sequence of sounds like ripping plastic and then the entire window and frame in the bedroom flew in, bounced off his bed and crashed onto the floor. Martin got up from the sofa and walked into the kitchen area as Ian climbed through the hole. They locked eyes and Ian pushed himself through the doorway into the main room. He was wearing a huge raincoat over his slate blue prison clothes, the hood buried under his trailing dreadlocks. He was breathing heavily. There were long, thin, red gashes on the flesh of his face and exposed arms and legs. His feet were dirty, hairs stuck together with blood and mud.

"Well, I guess you're not in prison any more. You haven't been on the news yet, so you couldn't have escaped long ago."

"About two hours."

Martin nodded. He had to be careful. When he visited Ian in prison he had been friendly enough and seemed to understand what Martin had, or rather, hadn't done. There, Ian had been behind a security wall, cuffed and drugged. He wasn't himself then, but now he was different. The question was, which version of Ian was he now?

"How did you…?"

"Thanks for the solicitor. He helped me get out of those restraints and get the dosage lowered." Ian brandished his claws, "You forget I can cut metal and climb walls with these things. I scaled the Earth Building once, remember?"

"Wow, yes, I'd forgotten that. I had to take the stairs to get you after your buddies knocked the power out."

Ian nodded.

"I'm not going to have to go after you again am I Ian? I mean, I don't think my knees could take it any more."

Ian smiled.

"Depends how much help you think I'm worth giving, doesn't it?"

Martin sighed.

"What the hell are you doing here? You shouldn't have broken out! You think you'll have any chance of parole in the next twenty years now?"

Ian said nothing. He kept his claws held out, their brick dust covered tips pointing up towards the ceiling.

"I'm sorry I couldn't help you, but you can't carry on like this. Everything you are doing is making it more and more likely you will never see your son ever again."

"Because you're the expert, right? You know exactly how to keep families together, yeah?"

Ian was shifting his weight between legs. Martin recognised this from the old days. This was his anger building up, hopping around to try and release the frustration before it got too much and sent him wild.

"Look, we're going round in circles here, OK? I get it, we'll never agree about what happened. Fine. So… why are you here?"

"Where's Jenny?"

"Why are you asking me?"

Ian roared and leapt forward, catching Martin in the chest with the back of his fists, sending him flying backwards. He slammed into the kitchen units, granite worktop in the small of his back, his head flipping backwards, cracking a cupboard door in half. As he shook his head to recover, Ian was on him, claws either side of his body, thumb under his armpits, pinning him in position.

"Because you *know* Martin! You know every fucking thing, that's why I'm asking you yeah? I told you to find her and ask about our son and let me know. Thanks for not doing that by the way. You know where she is, I know you, and you're going to tell me."

"Or what? You'll cut me open like the old times? Properly disembowel me this time?"

Ian was staring at him, his pupils had swallowed up his irises and seemed intent on pushing the whites of his eyes under his eyelids completely. Martin had to calm him down. Fighting wasn't an option, Ian could kill him in seconds if he wanted to.

"What do you want with her Ian? Hasn't she gone through enough?"

"She needs me."

"What, like this?"

Martin looked at the claws, perilously closed around his arms.

"She can't be alone right now. Not with Lewis missing. I've got to find him. I have to find him." Ian was panting hard.

"I know. I want to find him too."

"You? So you can hand him back to the very same people that lost him in the first place? Yeah, I think I'm done with your help thanks." Ian pushed himself away from Martin, flicking an impaled metal utensil holder from one of his claws. It bounced and scattered its contents angrily across the tiled floor. Martin straightened up with a wince as his lumbar muscles twanged back into place.

"Tell me and I'll be gone. Where is she? She's not at home, I've already been there. The police are watching the place. She's not at her mum's either."

"How do you know that?"

"How do you think?"

Martin shook his head. If nothing else he had to stop Ian putting himself in more danger.

"She went to that Church of the New Gods place."

"Oh Christ...", Ian twisted his head around, disgust on his face. "After I told her not to."

"She was scared and had nowhere else to go. They're... odd people, I'll admit, but they're looking after her OK from what I saw."

Ian looked sideways at him.

"Where is the place?"

"Balden Green, where the steelworks used to be, it's the old workers' hall. If you're going to go there, go in the back way, below the new development. If anyone knows you're there you'll put the lives of all those people in the Church at risk."

"Heh. I'm surprised you care about other people's lives."

"That's not fair."

Ian was breathing easier now, and used a hand to flatten out his locks.

"You know, it wasn't easy coming to you for help. Sure, all those years we spent battering seven shades of shit out of each other, I had respect for you. Yeah, it was buried somewhere in here...", he circled his finger by the side of his head, "...among the haze of drugs I was on, but I knew you weren't some stuck-up twat like Charles or Jack. You were a genuine guy. Even so, having to come to you of all people... well it helped that we were both desperate, but still... it was a bigger step forward than any of the therapy I've had." He grunted. "Anyway, I convinced myself it was the best thing to do. And then I convinced Jenny too. I said I figured you'd know the right thing to do because you spent your life helping people. But now I realise you care more about preserving some kind of, 'Hero code of honour', than you do about people. Your, 'right thing', is to follow the system, not actually do any good by anyone. It doesn't work like that any more. You've been hidden away too long Martin. We're both of us bits of history that don't fit any more. I'm getting out while I can."

"Ian, I'm not going to stop you from trying to find Lewis. I'd never do that, but when I find him, I'm giving him back to the Authorities, for his sake, and that's all there is to it."

Ian moved in close to him again. Martin tensed.

"Then I guess I'm not worth giving any help to after all." Ian stepped away through the hallway and into the bedroom. He slid his frame through the window opening brushing one wall, causing the brick and plaster to split in a wave of arcs, thin curved strips falling clattering, shattering onto the wood flooring. Then he dropped out of sight. A moment later, a crunching thud in the alley below and the quiet pounding footsteps that disappeared into the rain. Martin stood staring at the gap in the wall for some time, trying to get his thoughts in order. In the end all he could come up with was to find Lewis. He tried to pretend it didn't matter to him who found him first, as long as the boy was safe, but it did. Maybe it was just the way he was programmed, nothing he could change. Whatever the reason, it wasn't important right now. All that mattered was a young boy's life.

CHAPTER 34
ELEANOR'S HOUSE

It was only when Eleanor put the bag of clothes in the boot of her car that she stopped to consider her actions for the first time. What the heck was she doing? She had been on autopilot since her manager put her on forced leave, sorting things out for this. It was a massive risk, what she was preparing to do. She closed the boot and went back inside to the kitchen where she had left her mobile phone, torch and spare batteries on the work top next to the sink.

She couldn't believe Jane, her manager, was acting like Lewis was just another powered child. She had been very particular in detailing his abilities fully in her notes, and had tried to impress on Jane how unusual his case was, but she seemed to be treating it like any other. Even *after* the kidnapping. And now that Eleanor had been sent home for a week, it would be her manager who was liaising with the police, not doubt failing to make them aware of the unique circumstances.

She had barely had any sleep, thoughts racing through her mind constantly. She had to do something. She couldn't sit at home drinking coffee and watching that horrible video replayed over and over on the news. Lewis was an innocent in all this, none of it his fault. He didn't deserve to be a pawn in anyone's power games. Not only that, the longer that poor boy was out there, the bigger the risk to himself and other people. Those Hero Killers had no idea what they were dealing with. That boy needed proper care. That is, not his parents or a minimally secure care centre, not some anti-Hero group or even powered foster parents.

Earlier that day she had been to her mum's to sort a few things out. When she let herself in she found her mum sitting in the living room drinking a cold cup of tea. She had forgotten to boil the kettle and poured it unawares. She told her it must be broken and she'd have to buy another one, that they didn't last long these days. She had been and bought six in the last four months. They all worked fine.

She sat down with her and explained that the carers would be coming in four days a week, instead of two, from now on. Her mother nodded, made eye contact, but seemed lost in a world of her own. Eleanor wondered how much her mum took in and actually remembered of what she told her. She had been deteriorating more rapidly this last year or so. Eleanor had tried to convince herself it wasn't happening, but then she spotted the little things: the uneaten ready meals, the high blood pressure tablets still in their pill organiser, the kettles. She had been secretly petrified at what she might find in the evenings, after racing here from work before heading home, but in the end she needn't have worried. But another six months or so and she would have to go into a care home. She wouldn't be able to cope with her any more. And if things went wrong with her plan, she might not be around to look after her at all.

She checked the batteries were in the torch and that it still worked. This was so dangerous. This was too dangerous. They were too unpredictable. If the police were already involved she could get herself arrested and lose her job, then who would make sure all those powered children got the right care? She could get herself killed, then who would sort her mum's care? No, there was nothing else for it. Her department was too happy to let the police handle this, the police themselves were dilly-dallying around too much, the boy's father was in prison unable to do anything and the people in that video were too serious to be ignored. She had some information about their location, only hints, but she knew she could track them down. She hadn't passed this onto the police, not just because Jane had made it clear she wasn't to be involved, but also because she was fearful they would send in an armed team to get him out. The risks of a bad outcome from that were too high. She couldn't have that on her conscience.

She set the house alarm, closed and locked the front door and got into her car. "Damn it all", she thought to herself as she fastened her seat belt and started the engine. She drove off with only one purpose, to find Lewis before anyone else did.

CHAPTER 35
THE CHURCH OF THE NEW GODS

Clifford heard a tumble of feet down the stairs and seconds later Grant's drained face peered round the doorway.

"He's here," he whispered.

Clifford nodded.

"Good."

Grant waited, leaning round the frame, looking blearily puzzled, glancing towards the back door.

"Aren't you going to let him in?"

"Not yet."

"But people will see him!"

"No they won't. Not at this time of night. They are all safely tucked up in their houses, worrying about their own small little worlds without a care for us. We wait. We wait until he knocks, then we let him in. When he's ready."

Grant straightened himself up

"Oh. Right you are."

The only light on in the office was from the desk lamp, creating a glowing orange ball in the middle of the room that surrounded Clifford.

"Are you sure about letting him in here at all?"

"You know I am. That question tells me that *you* aren't."

"Well, not really, no. He's violent…"

"You used to be."

"The main thing is he's unpredictable, we don't know…"

Clifford looked up at him for the first time since he came downstairs.

"And you weren't? Remind me how I found you again?"

Grant said nothing.

"Pissed and confused and angry with the world, sleeping rough in Manchester. The police knew you by name, had a cell set aside for you at the station to sleep it off before they threw you out in the morning. 'Violent and unpredictable', I think was how they described you before I took you in."

Grant dipped his head, always embarrassed about his past when it came up in conversation.

"Clifford, you know I would agree, but this guy is on a different level. Anger is part of his ability, not just part of him."

"You may be right, but he deserves the same chance as you had. After all, his girlfriend is here, we're his worshippers, there is no need for him to attack us." Clifford leaned forward onto his elbows. "Plus, we need him. You know that."

Grant nodded.

"Yeah, I know."

There was a short, careful series of knocks on the back door. Clifford smiled.

"There, see? He's ready for us. Let him in. Bring him in here, then wake the others so we can all greet the Hero together."

"Yes Clifford."

Grant scuffled his way out of the office as Clifford stood up and moved to the centre of the room, closing his eyes. He took a deep breath in as the pressure in the room dropped with the back door opening, breathed out as it closed, the air full of the large figure in the corridor. As he brought his hands up to his chest and clasped them together, the quiet conversation got louder, heavy footsteps closer. He opened his eyes as Ian ducked under the top of the door frame.

"Welcome, Mr Randall, to the Church of the New Gods. You are most welcome."

CHAPTER 36
THE CHURCH OF THE NEW GODS

"But Clifford, I know I can be of more use saving the Creator! You need to know details about these Hero Killers, and I can get that for you." It had been an exasperating conversation so far.

You had told Clifford about yesterday's uneventful day of observation, enlivened only by the arrival of The Savage. He didn't seem surprised for some reason. You had thought this would be of vital importance to him, the one gem of information from an otherwise wasted day. That he would be leaping around his office dying to know more, but he barely reacted. Disinterested even. That meant your stakeout was even less useful than you had convinced yourself it had been.

He had told you off about speaking to Martin Molloy too, said you had a bad habit of getting involved, getting too close when you needed to observe from a distance. He said that you needed to listen to him. You wanted to say, "But I know what I have to do, that's my power," but you didn't, because you remember he wasn't happy when you said that the last time. Still, it was true.

You guessed it must be hard for him to let go in a sense. He is the head of the Church, to whom so many look up to for guidance. Now here he was, having to be guided by you. Your natural ability trumped all his years of leadership. That would be a bitter pill to swallow even for a better man than Clifford, so it was only natural for him to be pushing back against you, trying to reassert himself.

So you bit your tongue and allowed him his moment of being correct. He stands in the middle of his office as you sit on the sofa looking up at him. His eyes are tightly closed, his elbows pressed tightly into his sides as he moves his hands up and down, palms out towards you.

"There are plans in motion to rescue the child. Don't worry about Him Harvey. I need you to focus your energies on Martin Molloy. You have already discovered invaluable information about him with regards to The Savage turning up at his apartment..."

You're not convinced it was that valuable to him.

"...an incredible turn of events! So who knows what more there is to learn? Now, I can't spare anyone else to do this task..."

Oh, so you're the, "spare", now? That's nice. At least he's opened his eyes and is looking at you.

"...you are the only one I trust to do it. Discreetly though, from now on, please. Yes?"

"I told you, he didn't suspect anything, although..." you cut off Clifford as he was about to step forward, "...

I do accept that I have used up my one chance to be an unknown entity to him. So yes, I will keep my distance from him and anyone else, unless life or limb are in danger from his actions. I won't be an accomplice to a terrible act through my inaction. I would have to act."

Clifford is silent. He is staring at you, looking around your face. You feel yourself going red.

"You… you would do that Harvey?"

"In an instant, Clifford."

"You would take one man's life to save another, even though you would be putting your own on the line?"

Well you hadn't quite intended it like that but, now that you thought about it, yes, you would. It was always a question you had posed to yourself, and you guessed many people wondered about it too. If it came down to it, could you kill another human being to save your own life? To save someone else's life? Thankfully most people never had to find out for real, but you could not think of such a concise test of character. How exactly you would kill an invulnerable man who had enough muscle on him to feed you for a month you had no idea, but you supposed there must be ways.

"I would."

Clifford had been hunched up, tight, during his argument with you. He straightened himself up now and lifted his head.

"Of course. If you knew it was the right thing to do. That's your power."

"Precisely."

He seemed to be in a better mood now. That was something positive. You had shown him your resolve by being honest with him. He seemed to appreciate that.

"Well you have the good fortune to have no need to commit such an act now. All I require of you is to keep following Martin Molloy. He has connections to this case, to the Child, and I think he may suspect our involvement."

This was news to you. Your motivation was dulled by being asked to watch him for another day, but at least Clifford was being more open and sharing with his reasons.

"But how?"

"Because while he may look like an ageing fitness addict gone soft, he is not stupid. He is more intelligent, has more surprises about him than he lets on. If anyone is going to work it out first it's going to be him, not the Powered Crime Agency. So I need you to keep monitoring him. Can you do this for me Harvey?"

You bury your disappointment deep down for now.

"Of course Clifford, whatever you say."

"Good. Thank you my friend."

You only had a couple of days of leave left. You didn't really want to spend them all sat in your car eating production-line assembled sandwiches.

"Oh and by the way, there is no need to come back here to report. You can pass any information to me over the phone. Things are... sensitive here at the moment. I wouldn't want you getting wrapped up in something outside of your control. It wouldn't be fair of me to put that on you."

He nodded.

Oh, right. Was this it? Was he done with you? Pushing you away? Why? Were you no longer of use to him, or does he view you as a threat? You have no desire to take over the Church if that's what he is worried about. You're not a leader of people like he is, you couldn't do it.

So was that it? No, it couldn't be. Clifford would know this already, he knew what you were like.

But for how long would he need you now? They had found the Creator Child that he predicted would return to Element City. Then, when they rescued him, what would your purpose be? Would you have to go back to work? You choke at the thought. You couldn't. You couldn't do that knowing what you know now. You would have to pretend you were normal again. You would have to sink back into the routine of misery, the daily despair crushing the will from you. Deceiving yourself into the belief that returning home to a detached and angry wife is something to look forward to. Yes, her. What was she to you before? What is she to you now? You can't go back to that. You slowly pull yourself up from the sofa.

"I'll get right on it," you say, the lack of enthusiasm obvious in your voice. But Clifford doesn't notice, he's already at the office door, holding it open for you. As you leave the hall into the chilly morning air you tuck your scarf tighter round your neck and realise that you can't carry on like this. Something is going to have to change.

CHAPTER 37
ROOMS UNDER THE OAK AND ARCHER PUB

An old inflatable paddling pool had been pumped up in the main room under the Pub. Inside it, Carl sat with Lewis in his lap as he babbled something about water and doggies, holding his bunny down on the bottom of the pool, occasionally lifting it up before banging it back down again and laughing. Carl asked if he had ever been swimming. Lewis looked at him curiously, then went shy and pressed bunny into his face, one eye peeping round his cotton head.

Rebecca sat next to them trying not to smile too much as she held one hand out supporting his back. He was slightly wobbly, but she only pressed her hand against him gently so as not to make him think he was being held. She remembered when her baby sister was that age, ever independent, absolutely hated knowing she was being supported in place.

Jed and the new guy, Michael, sat in the seats under the thin windows, both on their phones, sometimes chatting to each other, showing one another pictures of Hero porn, smiling, looking over at Lewis like lions sizing up their next meal.

"Ow, my leg's gone to sleep!"

"Here." Rebecca lifted Lewis off Carl's legs and sat him on the floor sideways to her as Carl stood up and shook his limbs out.

Lewis revelled in his new freedom, grabbing a nearby bright green shaker toy vigorously before tapping it against bunny's head.

"I think he's enjoying this pool." said Carl.

"Well... we've had no use for it for a few years now. Thanks for looking after him while I was gone by the way."

Carl shrugged.

"S'alright." He smiled at Rebecca as she smoothed a tuft of Lewis's hair down.

Across the other side of the room, Bobby was sitting on an old chair, plastic tube legs splaying out under his weight, tapping at the laptop. Carl was glad only he knew the password for the protected files on it. Partly because he still wanted to be useful to them, and if they could get to those files he wouldn't be much use any more, just putting up more lining paper and fetching things, but mostly because he didn't trust anyone else with that information. Especially not Jed. They could hear Bobby's disguised voice playing quietly now and again before being abruptly cut off with a tap of a finger as he shook his head and swiped heavily at the touch pad.

"That's me in those videos," said Rebecca. "I can't believe it. I'm in this now. I'm fully in this... whatever it is."

They had filmed two more videos earlier in the day. One was already up online, calling for equality in investigation and prosecution for Heroes who commit crimes. A second one, queued to go up tomorrow, wasn't asking for anything in particular, but a short speech, more of a rant from Bobby, calling out the hypocrisy of the tabloids for using Hero-critical headlines one day, then Hero praising headlines the next, depending on which would get them the most sales.

Bobby was energised, intensely focused from having the media listen to his last video. No broadcasts or newspapers used the word "Hero" in today's editions, and they were mostly scrubbed from their websites too, apart from a few that slipped through but which disappeared during the course of the day. The truth was that the police had been quick to act and call on the papers to do as their video had demanded, to avoid anything happening to the child and to give them enough time to find him. Lewis was his not so secret weapon, and he knew it.

"You're disguised," said Carl, "and you don't say a thing. So they don't know it's you, do they?"

Rebecca gave him a disdainful look.

"They'll know it's me sure enough, when they find us all together in here, won't they?"

Carl thought of something to reassure her.

"I guess... we'll have to hope they don't?"

"I just wanted to stick close to him you know, give him another chance?" She was looking across at Bobby again, who was sharply adjusting the tilt of the screen back and forth until he finally got the angle he wanted.

"And now I'm going to jail for him. For a long time."

"He might..." Carl knew his words weren't going to make much sense, but he had to say them anyway. "He might let you out, you know? Before things get any worse?"

"Any worse than what?" She was staring at Bobby, eyes out of focus, thinking. Lewis had noticed and was following her gaze, but saw nothing of interest. "Could you watch him for a minute?" said Rebecca.

"Sure!" said Carl, a little too eagerly he realised, but she didn't notice.

He sat down next to Lewis as she picked herself up, stepped over the lip of the pool and walked across the room.

"Bobby?"

He turned and looked right past her to stare at the child next to Carl.

"How's the freak?"

"The baby is fine, I just..."

"Scares the shit out of me that thing. I mean yeah, it's fine now, making dolls for itself, but when it's an adult and it can make anything it likes... guns, a fortress, copies of itself? Scary shit right there. You know, people think The Elemental was some God like he could make whatever he wanted? Truth is, he couldn't. I've researched this the last couple of days. The most complex thing he ever made was a bicycle, and that took him hours and hospitalised him afterwards. It's all spin. It was all about some politicians of the day wanting to move power from London to up here. They found a guy the papers were hailing as a war hero, (to sell more copies), got him on side by giving him his own city and convincing the people he was the future of Britain, and encouraged all other Heroes to come here and set up a new centre of the country. A new 'powered Utopia' that would take us into the future. And now look at the country that plan has given us today. That kid…" he pointed at Lewis "… he's already making complex objects with different materials with barely a grunt of effort. He's way more powerful than The Elemental ever was. Imagine all the bad that could happen if someone with an agenda got hold of him. It could be the end of us normal people. Nobody should have that kind of power. Should have been put down at birth."

Rebecca turned to look at Lewis too, as Carl waved the bunny's floppy ears in front of him and he tried to grab at it. She couldn't see anything dangerous about him, he was just a baby.

"You can't predict what people are going to do. What they are going to become."

Bobby grunted and looked back at the screen.

"Speaking of the future, what are we going to do next Bobby?"

"Well the second video didn't get as many hits as the first, so I think we should do another one explaining the name, 'The Hero Killers'. We need to tell people yeah, it's literal, but also metaphorical, you know?"

Rebecca sighed.

"I know."

"We need to explain we're trying to kill the *idea* of Heroes too, so that people can see them for what they really are. And so that they know what we are."

"Wanted. That's what we are Bobby, wanted. And going to spend the rest of our lives in prison."

Bobby smiled at her.

"They won't find us OK? They're not going to track us through the blog, I've gone on there saying, 'The Real Heroes', don't endorse any kind of violence, we're not affiliated with and don't know these, 'Hero Killers', people, yadda yadda, covering our arses basically."

"I'm not talking about the blog, I'm talking about Lewis."

"I never said this was going to be easy you know."

"You never said anything at all, that's the problem! You just said you had an idea for a video with the kid, to get the word out. You never said what it was about until we made it, and it was too late by then!"

Bobby looked puzzled. He turned round in his seat to face her.

"Becca, haven't I been talking about this for years? About being able to change society, reset it back to the way it should be? You don't get to do that without society kicking back. It's lazy, self-absorbed and doesn't want to change and the police don't like change because it means they have to do some actual work. Of course we could go to jail, but that was always a risk from the start when Carl started getting us names of those in hiding. You've been with me all this time, I didn't think any of this would come as a surprise to you."

"Yeah, I know, it's just... I guess none of us thought you'd actually do it."

There was a moment of silence, during which the only thing Rebecca could hear was Bobby's breathing.

"What?"

"Look, I like you Bobby, we all do. We always liked hanging out with you but... things changed after... you know, your dad..."

Bobby stood up suddenly and pointed a finger right in her face, making Rebecca jerk back.

"I'm not talking about that piece of shit!"

"I know, it's OK, calm down. It's just that... after him, you got a bit intense and this anti-Hero stuff started up. I don't like them either right? Before you say anything yeah? So I went along with you, we all did, 'cos we all agreed in a way. But it's just got too much lately, bringing in Jed and the others to go after those oldies like that."

Bobby spoke through gritted teeth.

"War criminals have to hide, those bastards were just walking around the same City, amongst the families of the people they killed!"

"I've heard it all before Bobby! I know OK? Jesus..."

Bobby was breathing heavily now. Rebecca took a tiny step back.

"We turned a blind eye and all that, OK? Like, as long as we couldn't see it, it wasn't happening. But now there's this baby, and the police are after us and... my life's fucked. We're all fucked, because we're the criminals now."

Bobby's head wobbled as his eyes slowly lost focus on her and started to wander round the room. Rebecca put a hand up to her mouth, suddenly aware of what she had just said, then brought it down and fiddled with the silver flower necklace Bobby bought for her when they were still an item.

"Well fucking thank you." mumbled Bobby.

Rebecca stayed ready to take another step back.

He turned away from her, walking round the chair, breathing heavily, then he leant on the back of it to look at the laptop screen.

"Thanks."

He nodded to himself, lips paling as he pulled them tight against his teeth.

"Thanks guys!" he shouted.

Jed and Michael looked up from their screens, confused. Carl and Lewis both looked over too.

"Bobby…"

"Thank you for your support, you BUNCH OF WANKERS! You think this was an after school club? A few friends gathering around to talk shit before going to get pissed? Well I wasn't talking shit, I meant it. I meant it ALL! This…" he pointed at Lewis, "…is our chance, our ONE chance to change things, to show those powered bastards who we are. I'm not scared. I'm not scared of where it could take us. I'm excited! But if anyone here is too scared, if anyone here doesn't care what those freaks have done to any of us, to our families, then the door's there. Help yourselves and don't come back 'cos you're not worth my time."

He sat back down on the chair heavily making the legs bow out, the plastic end caps skittering over the floorboards. He pulled himself closer to the table and started tilting the laptop screen back and forth again, muttering, "Damn you bastards...", to himself.

Rebecca hovered near him. She hated seeing him so alone and angry like this, just like when he found out about his father. That was when they first got together. They had been close friends for a while, although nothing had happened between them. She couldn't bear to see him so unhappy and unfocused. She wanted the old Bobby back. In hindsight it probably hadn't been the best time or reason to start a relationship.

At the other end of the room, Jed looked at Michael and nodded. He slipped his phone into his front pouch pocket and got up. In a handful of steps he was over next to Carl in the paddling pool. As he crouched down, Lewis looked round and tilted his head back so he could see this new person's face. Carl asked,

"What do you want?" he was shaking and put a hand on Lewis's shoulder.

"Names."

"Not now." He looked over towards Rebecca. She was standing behind Bobby, one hand on the back of the chair. They seemed to be having a quiet conversation. Or at least she was saying something and he was ignoring her. Jed reached across Carl's face with his hand and back-handed his right cheek, forcing him to turn to look at him.

"Yes now."

"Fuck you! If Bobby wants to give you another name he'll ask me for it!"

"Oh. Right. You a quitter too, yeah? You think this is enough now, yeah?"

Carl was hyperventilating, finding it hard to swallow against his dry throat.

"We've got stuff to do. Here. We can't go…"

"I don't care what you think. Give me a name. No, two names. I'm sick of fucking sitting around here doing nothing."

Carl glanced over at the laptop.

"I can't get…"

Jed slapped him again.

"Will you stop…!"

Jed slowly curled his hand around Lewis's neck, pressing his thumb under his chin.

"No, don't!" hissed Carl.

"Contact your guy. Get us some names. Simple, yeah?" Jed rubbed his thumb up and down, squeezing into Lewis's skin. Lewis had grabbed onto his hand and was gently tugging at it, eyes wide.

"Leave him, please?"

"It's only a bag of meat. A tiny waste of space. It's not done anything wrong yet, apart from being alive. There's some of them out there who've done some really bad shit and need sorting out. Get me their names and I won't need to end this one. You get me?"

Carl felt cold from his scalp down.

"Give me a few hours. I'll get you some names."

Jed slowly let go of Lewis's neck and patted him on his head.

"Cute little fucker eh? Gonna murder loads of us normal people one day though. Can't let him live forever." Jed stood up and took his seat back next to Michael. They shared a smirk and both looked over at Carl before going back to their phones.

Carl checked Lewis but he seemed OK. He was huffing slightly, a little scared, so he picked him up and cuddled him, his tiny feet digging into his thighs.

"What did Jed want?", said Rebecca when she came back over. She obviously hadn't noticed the hand round the throat.

"Um... nothing. Just checking stuff."

She sat down cross-legged opposite him as Lewis snuffled in his ear.

"So. What's the plan then. We stay here?" he asked as she stared at the sole of her trainer, picking at a loose edge, peeling off a strip of rubber and rolling it between her fingers.

"What other choice do we have?"

CHAPTER 38
THE CHURCH OF THE NEW GODS

"No Clifford, I can't let you do that. I want my son back, but not like this!" Jenny walked away from him to the small square frosted glass window between the beds, folded her arms and shook her head with anger. Ian was too large to fit between the beds, so he stood at the end of them and stroked her back with a bent knuckle.

"Please honey, listen to him. We're past the point of arguing for custody or trying to prove ourselves as parents. We've just got to take him and run. Like we originally planned to do, yeah?"

She turned round to face them all. Ian standing a few feet away, Emily sat on one of the beds opposite and Clifford stood by the doorway. They were in one of the small rooms above the hall that were being used as a dorm, without the knowledge of the Council. It was square, with four single beds snugly arranged, two on either side. A bedside table stood between the beds and there was a wardrobe and three-drawer chest of drawers for each bed against the walls. The ceiling sloped up across the doorway from the only windows in the room, three square ones on the low ceiling side that looked into the red brick side wall of the house next door.

Clifford had convinced Jenny to stay at the Church for her own safety, so that they could support her and so that she could avoid any unwanted attention. She had been sharing this room with the two other girls, which was very strange to her, having always had a bedroom to herself when growing up. But the sleeping arrangements had been the least of her worries.

She hadn't slept for several nights now, snoozing instead during the day, whenever she sat down for too long in one of the comfy armchairs in the small common room up here. Then she would wake up groggy and spend an hour shaking off the feeling, until reality settled back in and she retreated to her bed to cry. She was awake when Ian arrived last night. She heard the knocking and the back door opening. She heard the voices from below and got up out of bed to go down. Grant had stopped her at the bottom of the stairs, said that Ian and Clifford were talking, but she pushed past him and went in the office anyway. When she saw it was him, she fell to her knees, sobbing with a mixture of relief, exhaustion and confusion. She was still incomplete, but at least part of her had returned. Now fear gripped her. He was going away and she would be left alone again. She couldn't bear to have that happen again.

Clifford spoke. "These evil people pose a real threat to the life of your son. I can't make it sound any less horrifying for you I'm afraid. The only way to ensure his safety is to go in and take Lewis back. We will be in and out quickly and bring him straight back here. The three of you then will be finally reunited."

"And after that?"

"Like I said, I have already reached out to people I know and trust those who can help you disappear. They can take you somewhere safe where you will be with our kind, a small community that looks after each other, invisible from the Authorities. I'm already arranging transport. I know this must be stressful for you Jenny, but it's all taken care of. Didn't I say we were here to look after you?"

"Yes... I. I just didn't think it would all happen so quickly."

"It has to be tonight," said Ian.

"But I've only just got you back. I've missed you so much."

"And I've missed you too baby. You have no idea."

Jenny walked down between the beds towards him and they held each other tightly. Clifford gave Emily a glance.

"Let's give them a moment alone."

When they had left the room, Ian relaxed his hug and looked down at her.

"You said yourself that when you heard I'd broken out you knew I was going to get Lewis back. Well you were right, I am. These guys say they've got a plan to do it quick and quietly, which I know for sure I couldn't do on my own, and then they'll get us all the hell away from here. Sounds good to me."

"I'm afraid that if I let you out of my sight I'll never see you again..."

"I know. Look... I'll be honest. I'm not completely comfortable with these guys. They're weird religious types. I didn't like it when you said you wanted to go to them, and I'm not very happy you're here, but they've looked after you when..."

Ian cleared his throat and looked away.

"...when I couldn't."

They stood in silence.

"I'm sorry. About punching the door out at the Council, about going after that Eleanor woman, for not being here, for not putting you before my rage. I thought I had it under control, but Lewis being taken just..." he made a switch-flipping motion with a claw next to his head.

Jenny looked at him thoughtfully.

"I just want to make it right, as it was, the three of us together again. Yeah, there might be some more of those weirdos around wherever they end up taking us, but as long as they keep to themselves, I'll just be happy to be with you."

She leaned her head against his chest as he curled his arm round her again.

"That's all I want too. I understand why you did what you did, but it can't happen again. It can never happen again."

"I promise, with everything I am."

She tucked her head in tighter and they stood together next to the beds.

***

"Emily, you know what you need to do, yes?"

They stood at the T-junction of the corridors. The girls' dorm was behind them, the boys' ahead, and the common room down the longest corridor past the toilets and bathroom, with the steps down to Clifford's office hidden behind it out of sight.

"Yes Clifford, I know my part. Wow..." She took hold of his arm, slipping her hand down past his elbow before grabbing his hand. "...we've actually found Him. We've found the Creator. Just like you promised!"

Clifford smiled.

"I know. I knew He was here waiting for us to help Him. It didn't quite happen as I had planned, but then what are my plans next to the ones He has for us. Nothing. He is here for us to guide Him, but we must follow Him at the same time. It is the most difficult thing to understand..."

"Oh but I understand it. I want Him in my life. And He's only a child too, He has so much to learn and so much He can teach us. I am just so excited!" she beamed.

"Hold that excitement for a moment longer Emily. We still need to secure Him first."

"And it means we're going away aren't we, to The Keep? I've never been."

"You'll love it there. It is its own community, hidden in plain sight where no one bothers you. You can live alongside your abilities as The Creator intended. It's perfect."

"It'll be perfect for us. You and me, taking care of Lewis. It'll be like our own family. It'll be a family done right."

Clifford raised his free hand and brushed her cheek.

"It will be a family done right."

They quickly separated a few inches as Grant bounded up the stairs, bustled through the common room and along the corridor towards them.

"Are we all set?" asked Clifford.

"Got the van from storage, no problems. Checked the engine over, topped up with petrol and some extra in a couple of jerry cans. Should see us all the way there." He looked at them both, wondering where Ian was.

"Is the plan still on?"

"Yes my friend, it definitely is. We'll have the Child tonight. Make sure everybody knows to be ready to go within half an hour of him coming here."

"I mean, the plan with… him in it?"

Clifford's face tensed slightly.

"Yes. It is crucial he is involved, it's the only way…"

They all turned as the handle to the girls' dorm squeaked and the door opened. Jenny came out first, then Ian ducked and squeezed his way through after her.

"OK.", said Jenny to the assembled group.

Clifford relaxed and smiled at her.

"On one condition!"

"Go on Jenny."

"No killing! They may be sick bastards what took him, but I'm not having anyone dead. Let the police lock them up and throw away the key. Let them rot."

Ian shared a glance with Clifford, who gave him a slow nod.

"I understand your concern Jenny, but if Lewis's life is in danger at any point we may have to…"

"No killing! Or I go to the police myself and tell them where they are and let *them* sort it."

"We're going to be putting our lives in danger for your son. What do you expect us to do? Give them a harsh telling off while we let them kill…"

"Emily!"

She stood to attention, rolling her lips in, and leaned towards the wall next to her. She could see Jenny was getting anxious.

"No. Jenny is right. It will mean having to change our plan, but we will do it. We will get Lewis out safely, and no-one will be killed."

Clifford stepped past Emily, who had gone red in her cheeks, and took Jenny and Ian by their arms.

"That's my promise to you Jenny, and if I break it, I will drive you to the police station myself and hand myself over."

Jenny nodded.

"You are the parents of our Creator, and what can be more important than family."

Emily pushed past Grant and fast-walked down the corridor as he watched her go.

CHAPTER 39
OUTSIDE AN EXPENSIVE DETACHED HOUSE IN ELEMENT CITY

You're a stupid fool Harvey. Utter idiot! You had spent over half a day parked across from Martin Molloy's apartment block again until you worked it out. Moron! Moron, moron, moron!

You cursed at yourself more than your work colleagues would ever do, and you deserved every second of it. Over half a day wasted, and you almost missed this! Nothing of interest had happened at Martin Molloy's apartment of course. He hadn't gone out. Again. A woman you recognised arrived and was in the building for an hour or so. You remembered her from your research on his Hero team The Pulse, and of course her face had been all over the news for a last few months along with his, Professor Maria Gionchetta. The Black Witch. An emotional affector.

You wondered if she had corporate rates; she could show some of those bastards you worked with what humility felt like.

But that was it. It was as you were sat there, peeling strips of bacon fat from your BLT sandwich, that you suddenly got it. Clifford had told you from the first meeting that your power was knowing the right thing to do. He had asked for your help, knowing your power was knowing the right thing to do and what did you do with that power? Nothing. You sat in your car, watching a fifth floor window, knowing it wasn't the right thing to be doing. Idiot! It was a test.

You thought about it yourself the last time you saw him, it was about trust. You both barely knew each other. He needed your help, brought you into his bosom, made you a part of his Church, but he needed to know if you were willing to embrace your powers, if you knew how to push yourself to do the right thing, even if it meant taking the life of another. That's what you talked about, wasn't it? Because if you weren't, you were of no use to him. If you weren't, you may as well go back to that trading estate, to the plain birch desk, to the meeting room with its stained whiteboard, staring across at the talented people in the engineering firm opposite, wishing you had their craft and ingenuity, their will to know what was right. But you knew what was right, and it wasn't sitting in your car trying to catch a glimpse of the only man in the world who led a less interesting life than yourself. So you dropped the sandwich box in the passenger seat, on top of a copy of The Element Times, and pulled away.

Soon you were parked just up the road from the boarded up Oak and Archer Pub, eyes fixed on the top of the stone stairs that led down to the basement. It was less than fifteen minutes after you arrived before you saw two boys come out, the tall black one and the thin wiry one. The black lad showed the other a piece of paper, snapping it with his finger before shoving it in his front pocket. The two of them set off towards you. You had opened the paper out across the steering wheel and took a slow bite of your sandwich as they passed. You were pretty sure one of them spotted you and glanced in. Probably the black lad, he was a sharp one, you could tell. They obviously deemed you to be of no importance and they walked past, turning right at the top of the road behind you. You waited a minute before turning the car round and following. You just knew they would be going after another target, and you knew they probably wouldn't have a car, (you doubted either of them could drive anyway), not to mention it being too risky to be seen driving back and forth to where they were holding the child. So they must be heading for a bus stop.

As you came to a halt at the junction you saw them disappear up another side street across the road. It led up to the main road through this part of the City where there was a stop either side.

You turned left, away from them, which led to a mini-roundabout on the road. You went right and pulled up in a small car parking bay in front of some houses that gave you a view of both of stops. You knew it, they were waiting at the stop on your side. They both jumped on a number sixteen that arrived a few minutes later and you followed the bus carefully, only having to overtake it once when you got a bit too close just before a stop. You knew the route anyway and were able to keep safely ahead until you saw them get out in the Henton Meadows area. You and the wife had hoped to find a place to live here one day, to bring up your children. Of course, the children never happened, and you never became the hotshot and moneyed man she thought you would become when she married you, so you had to settle for your, still very lovely, 1950s three bed semi, not more than three miles from here.

You had to suppress a smile. The lads looked so out of place in this area as they hurried along, hands in pockets, hunched over with their hoods up. Instantly suspicious. But this didn't feel right for more than one reason. From the reports of their other attacks they seemed to have intimate knowledge of their victim's movements, their daily lives. Much like you, they would have been on stakeouts, following them for days. This looked like they had an address and were about to do a home visit. Very risky. They had no idea what they were heading into. Perhaps they hoped it would be empty and were going to lie in wait until the owners came home? Still dangerous. Parking was easy enough round here, every house had a driveway. You were able to stalk them in your car for several streets as they checked their phones, probably on Google maps, until they stopped outside a very pleasant detached house tucked away in a cul-de-sac. It was off-white from weathering, with dark grey stone cladding around the ground floor and a spacious silver Renault car parked up on a sloped stone chip driveway. The front garden was all grass, surrounded by a tall fir hedge. Those things grew at an astonishing rate, you knew this from personal experience, and this one looked pretty well looked after, apart from a few fronds pushing their way out along its length. It had new windows, including one in the loft. A family house? Going by typical ages of the victims, you doubted they would have any children living there now, but it could probably be a couple with plenty of savings.

The two lads nodded at each other and walked up the driveway. The black lad went round the left side of the car and you saw him quietly open a black metal gate before disappearing round the side of the house to the back garden. The skinny one slowly made his way to the front door, taking his time so that his friend was ready when he made his move. He pressed the doorbell and waited, jittering around nervously on the large flat step. It took a few minutes, but eventually a woman, not much bigger than him, answered the door. She had light greying hair, that you think must have been blonde in her prime, and she was wearing the standard retiree pastel jumper and light beige trousers. She smiled at the strange boy and there was a conversation for a while before she suddenly seemed distracted by something in the house and quickly turned to move away. The boy slipped in and shut the door behind him.

You didn't get involved. Clifford had said you had to keep your distance, and in this case at least, he was more than correct. You were worried though. Although you were more concerned for the two boys. If they were up against two Heroes, no matter how elderly, and they missed something, or got cocky, they would come out of this worse. Sure enough, it wasn't long before you saw a flash of light from the living room. You could only see vague shadows moving around, they had net curtains and the sallow sunlight wasn't at the right angle. You drew down your car window and heard banging, some shouts from inside. Then it fell quiet. And it was quiet for a very long time.

***

As of right now, you have been sitting here for over forty minutes since the last of the noises, with what was left of the sunlight slowly draining away. You hadn't taken your eyes away from the house. You want to get out of the car and investigate, but you remember Clifford's words.

You hope they haven't run out the back. Luckily your patience is rewarded when, in the gloom, you see the tall black lad emerge from the front door. He appears to be limping, clutching his side. His hood is up and he isn't looking around him at all, he seems preoccupied as he hobbles past the car, having to lean on it as he stumbles briefly. Then he's off again, onto the pavement and down the road. You watch him go. You don't follow him. You know where he'll be headed anyway. What's more of interest is what's inside the house. You know what to do. You get out of the car and open the boot. Inside is your work briefcase, but you allow yourself a moment of fake surprise when you open the shopping bag next to it to reveal your earlier purchases: a box of latex gloves, some blue clinical foot coverings and plastic surgical gown, exactly what you needed right now. You remember striking up a conversation with the young Indian girl on the counter at the pharmacists. She seemed quite upset at the thought of you looking after your cancer-ridden wife on your own, changing her bed sore bandages daily, making sure she took her medication and was always comfortable. You allow yourself a chuckle. You were quite convincing Harvey, you didn't overplay it at all.

You slip your new leather gloves on, your first extravagant purchase in many a year, fold the booties, gown and a handful of latex gloves up into a small plastic bag in your pocket to keep fibres off them, and confidently walk across the road to the house.

You glance at the car as you pass, a smeared blood print down the side. The front door is still open. You pull out the booties one at a time and slip them on before walking onto the stone step and crossing the threshold. This feels bold Harvey. Definitely wrong, but you know it's right.

What a delicious feeling. The house smells of lavender pot pourri. You can't abide the stench. That was the one concession the wife made for you, and swapped hers for rose petals instead.

There is also the strong scent of ham and vegetables. It hangs thickly in the air along with... beef stew, strawberries, ah and that one was suet. You haven't smelt that since your mother made pies for you as a child. The decoration is typical 'eighties' flowery papering, red wooden cladding, white painted handrail up the dark blue carpeted stairs, the same carpet under your feet. To your left the door is open into a dining room, you see one end of an oblong wooden table from here. To your right is the living room with puffy flowery sofa and chairs.

Straight ahead past the stairs you see the kitchen, what looks like classic farmhouse oak cupboard doors, flowery cups hanging on a rack, an open door to the dark back garden. Oh, and there is a woman face down at the end of the hallway, her blood violently spattered over the walls. You walk towards her, keeping your feet out of the blackening stains and press a finger into her neck. She's dead. It doesn't shock you. Why should it in fact, what with all this blood? And you've seen plenty of dead bodies on TV, more violently disposed of than this too. You can't help noticing the blood in her hair, clumping it together in dark flat strands they sag heavily onto her scalp and neck. You hear a groan and whip round. That was from the dining room. You see an entrance to it just to the left of the kitchen door, but you don't want to drag any blood with you, so you head back the way you came and go in from the front of the house.

At first you don't see anything untoward and wonder if you've come to the right room. Then you spot the damage on the display unit. The front has been smashed in, glass shattered, a lifetime of trinkets spilling out. You walk around the end of the dining table and see the body of a man, curled up on his knees, between the bottom of the unit and the chairs under the table. You can tell right away it's a body by his misshapen skull, like a bursting balloon frozen in time.

You hear the groaning again. You so hope that isn't the man. You crouch down, peering between the square trunk-like legs of the dining chairs and see the skinny lad lying slumped at the far end of the table against a dresser. You walk round the other side of the table to him. He's in pretty bad shape. Whatever that flash of light was, it tore most of his lower arms off and burned the clothes from his chest, not to mention the skin from half his face. There are fat, swelling blood blisters on most of the exposed flesh that isn't charred, and he appears to be having some trouble getting air. No wonder, slouched so low like that.

You stand up, unfold the gown and slip it on yourself, tying it round your back. You then put your arms under his and lift him up. He screams, which becomes a fit of coughing, as you pull him back to sit straight up against the dresser. The pain has sharpened his senses and he is breathing a bit more easily now. That's good. You did the right thing, even though your medical knowledge is very limited. Another area to work on. You crouch down by him again and smile as he makes eye contact with you.

"Hello there. My name is Harvey. I'm telling you this because I know you will be dead shortly. But before you go, there are some things I really need to know. And if you don't tell me, I will make you wish you were already dead." You are bluffing. You know you are. Although if he doesn't talk, well... it wouldn't be pleasant, but you know what you would have to do. "So, let's start shall we?"

CHAPTER 40
MARTIN'S APARTMENT

Hayley had called moments ago to tell him she had information for him and that she'd be there as soon as she could escape the madness of the Command Centre. True to her word, within the hour she appeared in the empty corner of the apartment next to the TV, the safe zone he kept clear for her, carrying her backpack and a pair of boots.

"I've got the list of people they are tracking. Technical are still trying to trace the origin of the video, not helped by having to deal with YouTube USA and all the legal channels that involves, but these forty-five are in the running." She handed Martin a list of names on a sheet of lined A4 that had been ripped with some gusto from a larger pad.

"Forty-five? Christ, that hardly narrows it down."

"Yeah I know, but everyone is piling in to this one with a lot of pressure from above. Even the PCA are sticking their oar in to, 'advise the investigation', even thought it's technically not their case. So the DCI is looking for any leads he can get right now. Anyone you know on there?"

"I'm supposed to..." Martin stopped when he saw Hayley's face. It would have been a huge risk for her to take down this information and sneak it out of the station and here he was about to be ungrateful.

"I'll check it over and see if I recognise any names. Thanks for getting this."

"No worries boss."

"At least we know your guys aren't any further ahead than we are right now."

"Biscuits?"

"Where they always are..."

"Bostin'." She left the backpack on his sofa and jogged through to the kitchen. A sudden chill wind made her look towards the bedrooms and she spotted the window leaning up against the corridor wall, a folded bed sheet stretched and pinned over the square opening in the wall behind the bed. "You auditioning for DIY disasters? Don't forget I saw how your last flat ended up."

Martin ignored her as she reached up into the cupboard for the biscuit tin.

"Ian pop round for a chat? Tell him where Jenny was yeah?"

Martin gave a non-committal "Mmm.", as he let her work it out for herself.

"Went to that Church didn't she? The one you visited?"

Forty-five names hastily scribbled in large loopy writing that all merged with the lines above and below it. It was like deciphering spaghetti dropped on the floor.

"Christ Hayley, you write like a Spirograph."

"A what now?"

"You know, those spinning things you put a pen in to... no, before you were born. Thanks for making me feel old."

"Don't need me here to feel that Dad."

It took him a second to be certain he wasn't holding the paper upside down, then he started reading.

Hayley crunched her way through two chocolate digestives sandwiched together as she plopped herself into the stool facing him and leant her elbows on the breakfast bar.

"You know, I hope we get these guys. Get Lewis back."

"We will."

"I can't believe I was so close to the guy who slashed Mr Harrison's neck. If I'd have got him, they might not have taken Lewis."

"We can't know that Hayley, don't beat yourself up over it."

"Yeah, but if I could have jumped I would have got him, but if anyone had seen me..." she looked up at him with a biscuit between her lips. "Have you ever been unable to help someone, despite having your powers?" she crunched.

Inna's tormented face came back into Martin's head as did Barry blowing his brains out across the shopping centre floor.

"It... happens. You can't save everyone. We're only human after all."

Hayley nodded, deep in thought.

Suddenly Martin recognised a name from the swirl of the first few lines.

"Jeremy Norfolk?"

"Journalist."

"Yeah, I know, he's left messages on my phone wanting an interview. He's on a watch list?"

"Always seems to get the inside scoop on Hero gossip. Nobody knows his contacts so, yeah, watch list material right there."

"Better be careful who I'm calling then... hang on." Martin went silent long enough for Hayley to get annoyed and jog back over to him.

"Mmm?"

"Is that Fairbrass? What's that... Bodeley...?"

"Bobby. Bobby Fairbrass. You know him?"

"I know the surname from a while back. A long while back. There was a fairly small time Hero with powers called Flashbulb, we crossed paths with a few times ..."

"Crap name."

"Crap name... could create bright flashes of light which he used to blind and disorientate people. Got to know his real identity in the end, Jack was a bit obsessive about that sort of thing. Arnold Fairbrass."

"Well let's have a look then." Hayley delved into the backpack and pulled out her tablet.

Martin stared at the name. "As far as I knew he never registered. Went quiet like me. I guess he just wanted to get back to a normal life."

"Is this him?"

He took the tablet from her and found himself looking at a big grinning face in a yellow and black mask, hair brushed up straight into a flat-top like a cartoon character.

"Yep. Wow, that brings back memories."

Hayley grabbed the tablet back and tapped at the screen for a while before handing it back.

"Aaand this is Bobby."

Martin looked at the picture of the young, dark curly haired guy and the same memories came back.

"Blimey, he's the spitting image of him, ignoring the hair. That's got to be his son. I'm certain. Where's this photo from anyway?"

"He's on a watch list for running an anti-Hero group called 'The Real Heroes'. You think he's graduated up to 'The Hero Killers'?"

"I don't know, but it starts to make sense. Those people they say they killed, how could they have known their natural identities? That information is only on the Register or known by Heroes themselves."

"Yup, that's one very active line of investigation right now. Anyway, no Hero would tell an anti-Hero group those identities would they? Unless they wanted revenge for something?"

"No. And it's too random. I've spent hours trying to work out any connection between the people they killed. Nothing."

"So Bobby is getting this from his dad... maybe he wrote it down somewhere, like in a journal..."

Martin and Hayley shared a look.

"Always a very bad idea..."

"...as we know from experience. Bobby probably finds out accidentally from this that his dad is a Hero, which I bet doesn't go down well, and now he's got a list of Heroes to take out his anger on, in lieu of his father."

She took back the tablet.

"They've got form too, judging by their blog, they do regular protests, meetings, they made videos before, even appeared outside court for, er... your ex-team mate's trial. They really don't like us much."

Martin kept reading to the bottom of the page.

"I don't know any of the other names on that list. I think he's the most promising. And since his dad didn't register it's going to take longer for the police to work out that connection, so we have a head-start. Where do they meet up?"

"Doesn't say anywhere obvious. Hang on, they've got a discussion forum too, I bet it's buried in there somewhere. I'll find it, don't worry." Hayley sat down on the sofa and started swiping and tapping at the screen in silence while Martin went to the kitchen area to fill the kettle.

As the kettle growled into action he stared at the utensil holder, punctured by Ian's claws.

Screw, "not getting involved". This wasn't some drug to him, he didn't relish the fighting and didn't want the attention. This was something he just had to do because it made sense. That was all. Ian wasn't even a friend, he barely knew the guy, but there was a baby boy whose life was at risk and he had information and help from another Hero that could save him, avoiding bloodshed. It was a no-brainer, and he knew he… they could do it. He just needed a strong coffee first, then he would begin his mental preparations for a mission.

CHAPTER 41
ROOMS UNDER THE OAK AND ARCHER PUB

It was quiet and still under the Pub. Rebecca was in the cellar watching over Lewis. She had read him a story to send him to sleep. She was sitting in one of the uncomfortable fold-down chairs from the hall, slid down so her bottom teetered on the edge, legs stretched out, feet resting against the cot. She was thinking about her and Bobby and the baby, while she crossed her arms and dozed in the warmth from the halogen lamp heater. Its orange glow escaped into the main hall where Bobby was still up, scouring the news websites on Carl's stolen laptop for any and all mention of them and Lewis. The official response had been that the law applies equally to all, which he spent a good ten minutes telling them all was bullshit. He had been further incensed to hear INNATE come out and say that the statistics actually showed bias *against* Heroes when it came to sentencing. He had then delivered a rant to anyone who would listen about how they should get longer sentences for similar crimes because they were more dangerous. Right now he had reached a stage of grumbling indignation, quickly skipping over any comments or items he deemed pro-Hero, only briefly cheered up by a small opinion piece in The Mail Online that wondered what the PCA were doing with all their resources while allowing powered criminals to use their powers without immediate arrest. Then he spotted another story on the site about a black guy from a poor neighbourhood in New York who used his powers to stop a bank robbery, only to have the police arrive and beat him unconscious. The story supported the guy's family and the pressure groups wanting the officers charged. "Fucking hypocrites", he cursed to himself.

Carl was sleeping in the corner. He was wrapped up in an old thin double duvet under the blue mottled moonlight falling through the thin windows above him. He hadn't gone home for days. "Family problems", he told the others and they had just nodded. Truth was, he was too scared to go back. He was too scared to leave the Pub too. He was certain that he was being followed wherever he went and was terrified of being arrested because he knew he wouldn't be able to talk his way out of it like Bobby would. Everything would get dumped on him. He would go away for life. He jolted awake as the door swung open. Jed walked in, closed the door shut behind him and spotted Carl and Bobby in the blue and orange gloom.

"Done another one," he said, and limped over to some seats in the corner opposite Bobby, slipping his baseball bat from his sleeve and resting it against the wall. Carl noticed he was shaking.

"What do you mean, 'done another'?" said Bobby, sitting back. "And where's Michael?"

"What do you think I mean," replied Jed, talking out his mobile. "Mikey didn't make it."

Carl noticed the light shining off curls of blood on the back of Jed's hand.

"What do you mean, 'Mikey didn't make it'?"

"That's the risk we take, to take those bastards down. But I got them good for him, made them pay," he said before looking away to his phone. Carl started shaking. This was his fault. Again.

Bobby stood up, calves angrily pushing the chair back as he strode over to him and put his hand over Jed's screen.

"What the fuck do you think you're doing Jed?"

Jed pulled his hands away from him and put his phone back in his pocket.

"Eh?" he said, flexing his arms and clenching his fists.

"What. Are. You. Doing?"

"We're spending too much time sitting around here doing fuck all about them out there. They still need sorting, baby or not, yeah?"

"It is too risky at the moment. I told you, they know we are the same ones who went after those powered bastards Carl picked out for us, so they'll be doubling down on any investigations into that and trying to find any links to where we are. So until we're done here we can't 'do another', yeah?"

Jed squared up to Bobby. He was only an inch or two taller, but with his hood up he stared down on him.

"I didn't sign on for fucking babysitting. I signed on to bury shits like the ones that killed my cousin, and that's what I'm going to keep doing you hear?"

"Not if it's going to get us all killed, or arrested! We can't take any more of them out if we're in prison, can we Jed?"

Jed just stared at him.

"Now, basics yeah? Did you make sure you weren't followed?"

Jed snorted and turned away.

"HEY! I said were you followed mate?"

Jed whipped round to face him.

"I got some names from Carl. We did in a couple who were involved in the deaths of six firemen in that Kirkhill warehouse fire twelve years ago but fucking got away with it like they all do. We did them in as we we're supposed to do, not making YouTube videos with babies telling papers not to use certain words like that's going to change a fucking thing. And no, I wasn't followed!"

Jed made sudden gasping noise, eyes wide, then went limp as three yellow claws emerged from the front of his chest. Bobby took a step back.

"Wrong.", said Ian, throwing Jed to the side and stepping into the light. "Now where's my son."

"Shit! Carl, get him!"

Carl jumped to his feet in response then wondered what on earth he was supposed to do against this guy. Rebecca appeared round the doorway.

"Bobby, what…?"

Bobby pointed at her, arm shaking.

"GO! Take him somewhere safe. GO!"

Rebecca stood shocked on the spot until she saw Ian standing in the room, at which point she stumbled backwards and ran to grab Lewis form his cot.

"You leave my son alone!" Ian started towards the door, only to have Bobby block his path. He was holding his flick knife with both hands.

"How dare you, Savage! How dare you think you have any right to lead a normal life after what you've done. And I know what you've done. You should have spent the rest of your life in jail for your crimes. You shouldn't have been allowed to have a family. Your kind destroys families. That's *all* you do."

Ian looked him up and down.

"Well you're a murderer too. I guess that makes us the same after all." Ian swiped his hand across the gap between them and there was a moment where nothing seemed to have happened.

Carl was standing in the middle of the duvet, frozen to the spot in confusion as both of Bobby's hands, still clutching the knife, dropped off and clattered to the floor.

The next second was full of screaming as Bobby fell to his knees, trying to fumble some way to stop the bleeding with no hands, as his mind slipped into shock. Then he choked, an oblong blue bulge appearing across the side of his neck and face as a second figure emerged from the darkness behind him, fingers pointed at the back of his head. He slipped to the floor. He was dead.

Bobby was dead. It didn't matter what happened now. He couldn't let them get to Rebecca and the baby. Carl grabbed a folded up chair next to him and launched himself towards the two men, bellowing obscenities. The man with spiky hair raised a hand and Carl felt like he had landed face first into a swimming pool.

He suddenly remembered a half-forgotten memory from when he was a child. He had jumped from the ten metre board in a school swimming class to show Bobby that he wasn't afraid. He had been. He was terrified, but he did it for Bobby. Then he panicked as he jumped, landing stomach and face first, knocking himself out. Bobby had saved him from the pool, which gathered him much praise from the teachers. He had been so embarrassed when he came round poolside he started crying. The instructor panicked and got another pupil to call the ambulance while he dithered all around him, Bobby leaned over and whispered in his ear that that was the bravest thing he'd ever seen. His body slammed into the wall then dropped onto the duvet. As he lay on his back, vision fading to nothingness, he could see Bobby's face smiling at him, and he knew he had been brave for him.

***

Rebecca had grabbed Lewis from the cot and ran up the stairs to emerge behind the bar. She took the key from the small hook next to the old delivery rota and was halfway across the room to the door when she heard Bobby scream. She stopped in her tracks, desperately wanting to go and help. Then it went silent. A second later she heard Carl shouting, followed by a noise like a jet engine. There were two thuds then more silence. Tears welled in her eyes. Lewis was all that was left of them both. She had to take care of him. She had to hand him over to the girl next to her. There was nobody next to her. She had to hand him to the girl next to her. A girl with dark hair seemed to materialise out of nowhere, yet it seemed she had always been there.

"Give him to me."

Rebecca started to hand over Lewis, before taking a step back.

"No. No, you're one of them. I don't trust you. What are you going to do with him?" She didn't trust this girl. She trusted this girl completely and was going to give her the baby to look after. He would be safer with her. Rebecca handed over Lewis to the girl, who held the now awake and very puzzled baby to her chest. Then she and the boy were somehow no longer there.

"What... what have I done?" Rebecca had no idea what she had just done. Rebecca had never seen the girl just now. She also didn't know where Lewis had gone. She did know that The Savage had killed her friends and she was going to back downstairs and wait for the police to arrive before telling them that he had killed their friends and she didn't know where Lewis had gone. Rebecca made several slow movements towards the bar. She turned round at one point, but didn't see anyone in the darkness. She shook her head, as if to clear out something, then she went down. When she was gone Emily made herself seen again and looked up at the tall figure of Mark standing next to her.

"Nice one Whisper. Time to go now," she said.

***

"Lewis?"

"It's OK, Emily and Mark have got him upstairs," said Kevin.

"What?"

"See, told you we planned this properly."

Ian nodded, looking down at his bloody claws.

"Been a long time has it?"

"Yeah. I'd thought never again. Promised Jenny too, but she didn't understand this…" he gestured to the bodies on the floor, "…was the plan, to get them down as quick as possible before they have a chance to hurt him. It's how it works, she just wouldn't get it though. Lewis is OK yeah?" He looked at Kevin pleadingly, his claws dripping onto Bobby's corpse.

"He's fine. They have him already. In fact we need to meet them back at the van, now."

"Please… don't tell Jenny about any of this."

"She won't know anything, I promise. We'll get you cleaned up before we get back. You've done well Ian. You need never worry about your son ever again."

As Ian turned round to head back out the door, Kevin pointed his fingers to the back of his neck.

CHAPTER 42
THE CHURCH OF THE NEW GODS

As you walk into Clifford's office, you immediately notice he is very agitated. He is at the far back corner of the room on his mobile, angrily hitting the glass surface with his finger.

"Clifford, I got your message. I wasn't expecting you to call, I had my phone turned off for most of the day."

Clifford turns sharply to look at you. His face is rigid with anxiety. Did you say something wrong when you called him back earlier? He seemed impressed, if confused, with the information you gave him about the kidnappers and the layout of the rooms under the Pub. Was he about to lecture you over, "getting too involved", again? If he was, you were ready to argue your case, emboldened by your information gathering from that skinny youth, who was definitely dead when you left the house.

"What's wrong Clifford?"

Clifford's face melts and he looks at you like a relative returned safely from war. His arms relax and drop to his side. He barely makes the effort to lift his hand to slide the phone onto the desk as he walks towards you, smiling.

"Oh Harvey. Harvey my friend. I…" he ends there, stuck for words.

"Is it the rescue plans for the Child? Has something happened?"

He rests on the edge of the desk.

"Plans are… ongoing. I can't say more than that I'm afraid."

"No need."

"Your information was invaluable to us. Your resourcefulness has astounded even me."

You smile to yourself and raise a finger to him.

"Ah, but I worked out it was a test you see."

"A test?"

"Of course. You needed to test my dedication to the Church, to you, and to see if I was ready to fully engage with my abilities, to believe I truly knew what was the right thing to do."

"Uh-huh. A test. Yes. And you passed with flying colours Harvey." He stands up and walks right up to you. "I can see it in your eyes. I can see you know yourself now. You have come so far in only a few days." He dips his head and shakes it, pausing on the spot, then looks up again, dewy eyed and brings his hands to your cheeks. "I knew, out of everyone, I could trust you."

You feel light-headed. You know Clifford well enough now to know he is a very touchy-feely kind of guy; always grabbing your arm, shaking and holding your hand, a palm behind your shoulder, that sort of thing. As Clifford cups your face in his hands you can't help but feel awkward. This is much more intimate. Personal. True understanding. A bond with another person the like of which you have not had before. It isn't sexual, although it is the most physical contact you have experienced in years, causing your face and groin to tingle involuntarily, much to your private embarrassment. No, this is caring. Clifford truly cares about you deeply, worried about you out there in the world fumbling around with your newly discovered powers.

The tingle fades and is replaced by a warm glow in your chest. You feel lifted. Your spine straightens. Your head tips up. You smile.

"That's because I know what needs to be done. That's what I do."

Clifford smiles like the proudest uncle in the world.

"That is what you do." He lets go of your face and embraces you strongly, patting you solidly on the back. Your arms are trapped under his, your only available movement is to bend them in at the elbows. Your fingers meet in the small of Clifford's back. After a moment he steps away, holding your shoulder. Then his face drops. His eyes tighten. He looks back towards his phone. He lets out a huge sigh as he walks back to the desk, before clutching his forehead in a pincer grip and squeezing tightly.

You instinctively know something is wrong, and instinctively know what to do about it.

"What do you want me to do?"

Clifford looks puzzled. Your power has bamboozled even your mentor.

"Something is wrong Clifford. I can tell, remember? And I know there is something I can do to help fix it. Tell Harvey what it is."

Clifford examines you from foot to eye, one hand frozen mid-air next to his face. Then he relaxes slightly and shrugs.

"Of course. I should know better than to be able to keep anything from you Harvey."

The tenseness reappears.

"But this... this is..." He drops the frozen hand to the desk, his fingers tracing the edge of it as he walks around it to his chair. He puts one hand on the back of the head rest and swivels it towards him. "...this is too much. This is something I can... I can never ask of you." He slowly sits down.

"But of course I can..."

"No!" He holds out a palm to silence you, realises he spoke too violently and pulls it back as if in pain. "I'm sorry. Oh by The Creator himself why am I sown such conflicts?" Clifford turns the chair side-on to the desk, and leans forward, clutching his head in tight fingers. You have never seen him like this. It's like his confidence is being sucked out of him as you watch. Something is tearing him apart from the inside. You can't bear it.

You walk up to the desk, place your hands on it, leaning forward urgently.

"Tell me Clifford!"

"I need... I need you to do something for me Harvey. Something my heart can barely allow me to ask."

"Ask. I will know if it needs to be done."

"But there are some things that should never be asked of another person. Subjects that should never be broached. And I am fearful, for all that you have opened your mind up to the possibilities that your powers give you, that you do not understand. Cannot understand. And you will be horrified by it. By me."

You know straight away that this is another test. The other tasks were nothing in comparison. This is his true test. You can see the pain Clifford is in and understand. You know that whatever you have to do is for the good of the Church, the good of The Creator. Clifford wouldn't ask you otherwise, and he would not be in such pain if it wasn't so important. You can take this pain away. Take this pain into your own hands, swallow it into your soul and do what needs to be done, whatever it is.

"Clifford, I owe you everything. You let me into your Church and showed me who I really am, what I can be. For the first time since I was a teenage boy with the imagination to see my future self as an astronaut or a deep sea explorer, my future is filled with endless possibilities. That crushing feeling of waking up to knowing this day will be exactly the same as all the others, a fifteen minute drive to a desk for eight hours of uninspiring busywork surrounded by people who barely register your existence? It's gone. My... my mind is open to so many things. I feel there is nothing I can't do, if it's for the right reason. You have saved my soul Clifford, and it is time for me to repay that debt."

Clifford spins round in the chair, reaches over the desk and grabs your hands in his, clasping them tightly as he perches on the edge of the chair.

"You are stronger than you know Mr Harvey Morrell. Stronger than me."

"Oh no I…"

"Oh yes!" Clifford's eyes are bright as he stares into yours. "Here am I, full of doubt about the task at hand, questioning what needs to be done and yet you… you are my rock. How can I keep forgetting you were created to understand?" Clifford tenses his lips, takes a deep breath and steels himself. You wait, expectantly. "I am afraid."

"Afraid of what," you think to yourself.

"I am afraid about our plan to save the Creator. I think it is in jeopardy."

"How?"

"I think someone is going to tell the police."

"What? Who?"

He lets go of your hands and sits back. You straighten up, alert and listening intently.

"I only told a select few of the details of the plan, my disciples, and the mother of the Child…"

"You know the mother?"

"I know both parents. The father is… well, no-one knows his whereabouts, you were probably the last person to see him…"

"The Savage."

"The mother, Jenny, she has been staying here. We have all been supporting her, protecting her from the police and the media."

"I didn't know this."

"I apologise for not telling you, but I could not compromise her safety. Not that you would tell anyone, I know this Harvey, but the..."

"...the fewer people who know the better. It makes perfect sense, no apology necessary."

Clifford nods calmly.

"I told her of the plan to rescue her son. I told her the full details. Perhaps I was too trusting, but I felt as the mother of our Creator she deserved to know the risks we were taking and the... possible outcomes for those who had kidnapped Him."

From the start you knew these Hero Killers were a bad bunch, you had read the news reports of their killings, seen the video threatening the Creator's life, and tonight you had just seen for yourself what they were capable of doing. But for some reason it wasn't until just now the full extent of the sickening violence they were capable of became clear. They would kill the Child if they had a chance. That meant the disciples would have to make sure they didn't get that chance, which meant killing them first. Murder. One life for another. But... no less than armed police or Special Forces would do if they had to raid the place. The only life that matters is the one you're saving, anything else is a threat. Black and white. Few things in life were as cut and dried as that. You wish there were more.

"Of course, not everyone is as rational as you Harvey. Not everyone can see things that way".

"She doesn't want the kidnappers to die does she? She thinks they will. The thought has panicked her and you're worried she is going to tell the police."

Clifford looks stunned.

"You know Harvey, I don't know why I remain surprised at you. I know your abilities, yet your clarity of thinking still astounds me."

Your clarity of thinking is already two steps ahead of him. You know what has to be done, and the knowledge twists your guts into knots.

"She needs... she has, she... can't be allowed to tell them."

"And you're already ahead of me. You already know before I have even formed the correct words in my head to try and ask you in the least distressing way I can. I can't believe I could even consider asking this of you, but I don't know of anyone else who I trust to know what to do."

You look down at the desk. One corner of the green leather pad is going white and bulging up. You get the sudden urge to squeeze it down with your thumb. "That needs sorting", you think.

Of course you're only trying to distract yourself from the present. This girl, the mother of the Creator, could threaten the safety of her own son, not to mention the disciples, because of her own lack of comprehension. Lives, the whole mission, the whole purpose of the Church is at risk. There was no decision to be made. The path that needed to be taken was so obvious it almost made you laugh out loud now that you could see it. Time to step up Harvey. In any case, you waited for that young lad to die so you knew he couldn't tell anyone you were there, so this wasn't such a great stretch.

"I just need to know one thing. Where is she?"

CHAPTER 43
OUTSIDE THE OAK AND ARCHER PUB

"It's too quiet."

Martin and Hayley had jumped to a spot behind an off licence on the main road before travelling a few short jumps to get closer to the Pub. They were crouching in the darkness behind the wall of a small garden of a house just across the road from it. They had been eyeing it up for a few minutes.

"Yeah, and I don't see any way in I can jump to."

"Looks like we'll have to do this the hard way then. You go in the front and I'll see where those side steps go."

"Gotcha boss." Hayley jumped away and he saw her appear by the door which she tapped. It swung open. She looked back towards him as he was crossing the street. He made a, "go slow", motion with his hands. She nodded and went inside as he reached the top of the concrete steps. There was a row of railings, behind which was a narrow gap to the wall of the Pub, filled with dirt and refuse. There were three thin windows behind the railings, just below pavement level. The glass was mottled, but he could see a faint orange glow from inside. He crept down the steps as quietly as he could until he reached a door at the bottom. Like the front door, this too was open. He hated going in anywhere blind, especially a place that looked like somebody had been there first. Martin took a deep breath and moved inside.

The door creaked noisily, but there was nobody inside to be startled. He could smell blood in the air. To his left he could see a body slumped on the floor. Further down the same wall was another one, lying on its back on some bedding. There was a third, straight ahead, lit from the orange light coming from a doorway. Lying near it was a pair of severed hands holding a knife. In the middle of the room lay Ian, sprawled out face down on the floor, like a snow-angel.

Martin ran over to him, carefully turning him over. He was still alive, but breathing incredibly shallowly, eyes glazed over, a large purplish bulge across the side of his face above his ear.

"Ian. Ian! Can you hear me?"

His expression didn't change. He made no attempt to move, apart from his lower lip which trembled.

"Ian, what the hell happened?"

"...Church...Church..."

"The New Gods place? What have they got to do with this?"

"...Lewis..."

"They took him. They got here first didn't they?"

"…find…"

"Don't worry, we'll get him back, but we need to get you to a hospital first. Hayl… erm… Jump? Downstairs!"

"…no…" His breathing slowed as he got heavier in Martin's arms.

"Hold on OK? You're going to see him again. I promise you that. If nothing else I promise you that Ian. OK?"

His breathing stopped. Martin slowly drew his arm out from under him before closing his eyelids shut.

"He killed my friends."

Martin jumped up to see a girl, not Hayley, standing in the doorway across from him.

"He killed my friends and I don't know where Lewis has gone."

"He didn't kill anyone!"

Hayley appeared behind the girl and put a hand on her shoulder.

"Boss, I don't think she's right. In the head, that is. There's a cot in the room next door and one of Lewis's toys."

The girl seemed to be in shock. Little wonder, if she had seen what had happened here, thought Martin.

"Who took Lewis?"

"There was nobody here, I don't know what happened."

"There must have been someone else here. You must have seen what happened?"

"I don't know where Lewis has gone."

"I think she's been brain dumped or something. Or we're asking the wrong questions." She turned the girl so that they faced each other. She seemed unsteady on her feet, but locked her eyes to hers.

"Hey, what's your name?"

"Rebecca."

"OK Rebecca, we just want to know if baby Lewis is all right."

"Oh yes, he's safe!" She nodded vigorously. "He's safe."

"Good, good. Who did you give Lewis to?"

"There was nobody else here."

"OK... did you hand him over to someone, to keep safe?"

"Yes, I gave him to her. I trusted her completely. She was never there..."

"Did she have black hair?" asked Martin.

"Yes, but..."

"And they... they came here together?"

"Yes, but... nobody else was here..." Rebecca's face was screwed up, half not-believing the words coming out of her mouth, despite having been told they were true. She slipped past them both and knelt by the handless body, putting one hand on his shoulder, the other on the back of his head, rubbing his curly hair.

"I'm not stupid. I know he wasn't that into me, or too much into his other things to care, I just hoped that one day he would need me again."

The alarm call of sirens approaching caught their ears as Martin stared at Ian's body, finally at peace with itself.

"I'm to stay downstairs and wait for the police to arrive before telling them that he killed my friends and I don't know where Lewis has gone."

"I know where she's gone, and it's a long way from here," whispered Hayley to Martin.

Martin flinched.

"She'll be OK. The police will look after her. We have to go get Lewis back, if they haven't already run off with him."

"The Church place you were talking about?"

"Yeah, you know it?"

"I know some place near enough. Let's go."

CHAPTER 44
NEAR THE RANDALL HOUSE

The street seemed quiet. It was the first time she had been back since going to the Church and it felt strange to be here. It didn't help that it was night time. Everywhere looked different at night. Clifford had told her to sneak back to their house to grab anything they would need as it was their last chance before they were to start a new life far from here. She couldn't get it out of him where they were going, and Emily had gone silent on her for some reason, but Kevin let slip it was in Scotland. She had never left Element City before, so this was going to be a big change, but she had managed to convince herself it was the only way. She had to convince herself, there was no other option. A new life for all of them. But first she had to get some familiar things for Lewis. Clifford had said there would be a friend of his waiting at the house to help her carry whatever she needed and bring them back to the Church. They had to avoid being spotted by neighbours and any police that might be looking for her since Ian broke out. She would be the first person he would go to as far as they were concerned and would already be panicking that she wasn't to be found at her house or at her mum's.

And she wasn't to contact her mum, however much she wanted to. She was just up the road from here. Jenny had gone to her for help after Ian was arrested. She hugged her, made her a cuppa, said she could stay with her for as long as she needed to. Then the conversation changed to Jenny getting Lewis back on her own and moving in with her permanently, that Ian had made his own mistakes and that he should be punished for it, that he wasn't the right role model for Lewis to be growing up around. Then the argument, when her mum couldn't believe Jenny wasn't as horrified as she was that Ian had attacked that Eleanor woman. Jenny telling her he hadn't attacked her, he went to talk to her.

"By destroying her office?" asked her mum.

Then it finally came out that she had never approved of Ian, no matter how polite he was to her, no matter how much he could prove he had changed.

"They never change, not their type," she said. She said he wasn't right for her, never knew what she saw in him, needed to forget about him and instead concentrate on Lewis. As if saying that somehow cancelled out every horrible thing she had just said about Ian. That was when Jenny left in tears and crossed the City to get to the Church, the only place she had left to go.

But now her mum was just up the road. She so wanted to go, wake her up, tell her she didn't need her anyway and that she had new friends who actually cared about the three of them, and then storm off. But she also wanted to go, wake her up, tell her she loved her and just wanted her blessing for the three of them, as they went off to live a new life together. But she didn't. Instead she stood in the dark gap between street lights at the top of the small rise in the road, looking down towards her house.

She did as Clifford had asked her, she looked around for people sitting in cars. They would be police officers, watching the place for either of them to come back. She saw them. A car that was far too expensive for the area parked across the road, halfway between her and the house. She saw two silhouettes in the front. They were talking, one holding a cup of something that was steaming up the windscreen. She slowly walked forward, keeping an eye on them, before ducking down a path, almost colliding with the concrete bollard in the middle of it. She followed it round and down the back of her row of houses, being careful not to get caught up in the overgrown brambles reaching out for her, or tripping over discarded toys and rubbish hidden in the blackness. Clifford's friend must be waiting for her round the back somewhere. She thought she found the gate, but the hook felt different. This was the house of her neighbour but one. She would get confused even in the day, as the backs of the houses all looked so similar. She kept going.

She thought of the things she would need. Mostly stuff for Lewis, but then even with two of them to carry it they couldn't take much. It really was going to be a fresh start. Her foot embedded itself in a black bag filled with something that clanged loudly then clattered as it scraped away across the path. She stopped dead and listened. There was no noise. No lights came on. No-one came out. She realised she was holding her breath and gasped out. She was shaking. She had to do this quickly. Get the stuff and go. She stepped over the bag and jogged down to her gate. She lifted the latch and slipped through with no further noises. The back of the house was dark. No sign of anyone. She pulled the keys out of her pocket, feeling for the right one. She found it and was soon inside the kitchen, closing the door quietly, making sure the lock didn't snap loudly when it shut. She stood there for a moment. The familiar smell was comforting, but she felt scared to be here.

"Hello?" she whispered.

Silence.

"It's Jenny. Is there anyone here?" She was answered by creaking floorboards from the living room and then a bald figure wearing glasses came out into the hallway, the orange street light through the front door glass creating a glowing outline around him.

"Hello Jenny, my name is Harvey. Clifford sent me to take care of you."

CHAPTER 45
THE CHURCH OF THE NEW GODS

Clifford had been pacing up and down the aisles for over half an hour when the dark blue van finally pulled up outside. He opened the front door to see his disciples spilling out of the vehicle. Mark slowly stepped out of the rear doors, holding onto a laptop, while Claire jumped out of the driver's seat to reveal Emily sitting in the middle, a bundle in her arms.

Kevin, who had been sat on the far side of Emily, stopped Mark closing the rear doors and climbed inside, emerging moments later with pieces of a cot under his arm. Emily carefully climbed out, trying not to disturb the boy in her arms. They were all looking around nervously as they approached the door, but the street was asleep.

"We got him," said Claire, as she came through the door past Clifford.

"That's great news."

Emily had called to Mark and they came inside together, she cradling the boy, him clutching the laptop for dear life. Kevin came in last with the cot.

"Thought this might come in handy. Also got you a bonus. That computer Mark's got? I think we figured out how they knew where to find those old Heroes."

He closed the door behind him and Clifford drew back to the space by the windows and looked at them all. To his relief they were all uninjured, and looked incredibly relieved to be back.

"So how did it go?"

"The plan worked perfectly," said Kevin. "Everything is done."

"Excellent work Kevin. Excellent work all of you. You have no idea how proud I am of you tonight."

Emily stayed by the door, holding Lewis tightly.

"We found Him. After so many years of searching, we... you and I... are the ones that found the Creator. Just as I knew He would return."

Grant and Richie appeared from upstairs and approached the group, stepping around piles of boxes arranged next to the benches.

"We did it?"

"Oh yes Grant, we did it. Can't you feel it?" he stretched his hand out towards Emily. Grant stared at the ball of blankets. After a moment, a tear ran from his eye.

"It's like nothing I've ever sensed before. He... he exists. Not... not that I thought He didn't, mind! It's just... I never thought I would..."

Clifford came over to him and put a hand on his shoulder as he started to blink, sniffing back the tears.

"Allow yourself to be overcome. I would expect nothing less in His presence. He has come here to save us after all."

Grant wiped his cheeks as they all turned to look at Emily.

"May I?" said Clifford.

Emily hesitated.

"What about Jenny, isn't she..."

"She is no longer a part of our Church. Please, the Child..." He held out his arms. Her face relaxed and she handed him over. Lewis was still asleep, the rocking motion of the van having sent him into a deep slumber.

Clifford drew his fingers across the boy's forehead and smiled. This was it. All the trials, accusations, running, convincing, spreadsheets, waiting, the endless waiting, it was all over. They had found Him and He was young enough to be moulded into the person He needed to become. Clifford stepped back from the group, holding the boy close to him, pulling down the edge of the towels so they could all see his face.

"My disciples. We have a huge responsibility ahead of us. The Creator Child, his name is Lewis, is our child now. We are his parents. For He is the hope inside each one of us for the future of this world. And we will hold that hope, and Him, close to our hearts and nourish them. But do not underestimate the work we have ahead, for this is only the beginning of His journey, and we are going to be with Him for every step of it, learning from Him, as He learns from us. Everyone, prepare to leave to our sanctuary."

They all nodded and headed off towards the stairs. Emily stepped forward to take Lewis, but Clifford held Him back.

"I will look after Him. Gather your things Emily. It's time for the second part of our lives together."

Emily smiled and looked at the boy as he scrunched up his face.

"You really mean that Clifford?"

"With all my heart girl. We have found Him. There is nothing we can't do now."

She beamed, went on tip-toes, gave him a peck on the cheek and ran off to join the others. The hall started to echo with scrapes and bangs from the bedrooms above as Clifford slowly walked with the baby to his office.

"It's time Creator. It's finally time."

CHAPTER 46
MORRELL RESIDENCE

You have surprisingly little to take with you. The few people you know closely enough to have visited their houses seem to have accumulated van loads of books, DVDs and CDs, trinkets, papers, hobby stuff, clothes and other knick-knacks during their passage through life. Your only personal items include a few favourite causal shirts and trousers, a very comfortable pair of soft leather shoes you wear in the summer, some family photographs in a small blue, felt covered album, an old pack of playing cards your uncle bought you as a present for your tenth birthday, a silver-plated folding razor and your briefcase. As you fold your clothes into the small suitcase you retrieved from the top of the wardrobe, your wife comes in, having heard the noise of you taking it down. She asks what you are doing and before you have any chance of replying says she hopes you're not being sent to the Brighton office again, since the last time you went she had to change a week's worth of plans, food in the fridge was spoiled and you got no recompense for the extra work, and this time it is even shorter notice.

It was eight years ago you had to go to the Brighton office for a week. They needed a point of contact down there who was familiar with the policy procedures while they updated the database. You enjoyed the change and the challenge, and having the responsibility, although it did seem that your boss was reluctant to send you. But with two others off work with holiday and illness, you were the only choice. On your return he seemed stunned that everything had gone fine. The next time the Brighton office needed help he sent Alex. You only found out about it after he had already gone down there. You think that was the first time you fantasised about killing them both.

As you place the final pair of trousers in the case you tell her the marriage is over, you then walk past her into the bathroom to gather some toiletries. She doesn't follow you immediately, no doubt trying to take in the strange words that just came out of your mouth. An opinion? From Harvey? My goodness yes, that would take her some time to process. You smile at the thought.

Eventually she comes into the hallway outside, doesn't come into the bathroom itself, and asks you what you mean by, "the marriage is over". Her voice seems to be shaking. Of course such a sudden change is going to be a shock, but it really shouldn't be that much of a surprise, and it really was the most favourable outcome. You repeat to her that the marriage is over, that there has been nothing between the two of you for decades and that it would be perverse to try and drag each other through another day of this mutual misery.

She says nothing as you place your toothbrush into a small travel bag, along with the other items you picked up, and walk past her again, back into the bedroom. She slowly follows you and stands by the doorway. She just asks, "Why?" So you tell her. You tell her you know you were never good enough for her in any way. Everything you attempted to do was wrong, or not enough, or too much, or too soon, too late, the wrong kind, too expensive, too cheap, over-thought, not enough thought. You tell her that for years you had driven yourself to distraction trying to please her, trying to get something, "just right", for her. But in the end you realised it was all wasted effort, because you would never get anything, "right", because you were always going to be Harvey Morrell. You were the wrong *person*, so no matter what you did and how you did it, it would always be wrong to her.

As you put the soft leather shoes into a small bag and wrap them up, you tell her that you eventually gave up trying and simply accepted all the things she was saying of you, worthless, useless, stupid, inconsiderate, a selfish idiot. And you believed her. As you pick up the photo album, stroking the velvet cover so the fibres all ran the right way, you explain that over the past couple of weeks you came to realise that she was wrong. You say that you used to hate her deeply for the things she said to you, (which, on reflection, were true), and that you hadn't understood how someone could be so cruel.

But it's only now you have realised that she wasn't angry with you, she was angry with herself, for marrying the wrong man. You place the photo album at the top of the suitcase, above the wrapped up shoes. You take the silver folding razor, still in its plastic presentation case, and slip it into the toiletries bag before zipping it up and placing it on top of the album. She is very quiet. So you tell her the simple, unavoidable fact, you don't need her any more, so she could stop being angry.

She looked suddenly shocked enough to cry, as if this was a surprise to her too. You tell her she is now free to be happy again, as you remember her when you first met. You apologise that it has taken you so long to come to this realisation and, without telling her all the details, you say it has only happened now because you have found your true purpose in life. It is something you have always known deep down, but it took someone special to show you the truth about yourself.

She instantly snaps at you about another woman, but you cut her off. You tell her that while that would give her someone to be angry at, some off-screen vixen who has stolen her husband, it was hardly going to be likely given her husband's age and general attractiveness. You are self-aware enough not to be one of those late middle-aged men who goes around smiling at younger women in the street, thinking that he's a magnet for the female sex, even though it's nothing but his own ego. There was no one else you tell her. There never was, and there most likely never will be. You have too much work to do.

You repeat that you don't need her, but make sure that she understands that she doesn't need you either. You pick up the pack of cards from the bed. The cardboard packet is worn, velvety along the edges and corners, a bit of give in it allowing the cards to rattle around more than they should. You mostly play patience games with them, when you find a quiet moment. You tell her you know you were never her first choice to begin with. You know that Muriel Harding grabbed Brad Lumpy, the son of an American airman, from underneath her, the year before you got married. You knew he was a successful businessman now and that they had three kids. Still together, so there must have been something in it after all. But you tell her she can't keep thinking of it, as it has brought her nothing but disappointment, trying to compare you to him all these years. You have brought her nothing but disappointment. So that was it. You slip the pack of cards into your inside pocket, just behind your diary. The pocket feels fat and heavy against your chest.

She says she didn't know you knew about Brad. Well, we all have secrets don't we. As you zip up the suitcase you tell her you think the two of you could have been friendly enough acquaintances under different circumstances, but marriage was the wrong decision. You wouldn't say the last twenty nine years had been wasted, but you could both have certainly used them better.

So now was a chance for a fresh start for her, as well as for you. You tell her that you will pass on a new address as soon as you have one, so you can exchange divorce documents. You say you may have provided everything while you were together, but you are happy to go with whatever she wanted now, you have no need of material possessions anyway. You lift the suitcase with one hand, before bending down to pick up your briefcase, sat at the bottom of the bed next to you.

For the first time since you came home, you turn and look at her. Goodness, time has definitely passed you both by.

You think back to the wedding day. You had more hair, thinner glasses and were actually quite trim, by no means athletic, but you took regular walks and ate healthily. She was slim, curly blonde hair, smiling, but with an inscrutable sadness in her eyes. Now the sadness has acid etched itself into the lines across her face, the rolls of skin hidden under loose clothing, the fake curls, (a fact you didn't realise until after you were married, the naive young man you were), now hanging long, all the bounce gone out of them. This is the best thing for her too. You wish you had done it sooner. You say goodbye and walk out of the bedroom and down the stairs.

You drop the house keys on the small, white shelf under the hallway mirror. You separated them from your car key fob earlier, to make this part of the process go smoother. Then you leave the house and don't look back, but you know she is standing there watching you. As you put the suitcase into the boot of your car, you realise that telling her the truth felt better than plunging a knife in her back would have been. More purposeful. Yes, you're glad you went for the second option.

CHAPTER 47
SOMEWHERE NEAR THE CHURCH
OF THE NEW GODS

Martin and Hayley had appeared on the pavement outside the new developments, right outside their front windows, causing Hayley to yelp and re-jump a few metres further down the road, near a pathway that disappeared round the back of them. As they ran down the path she explained that she hadn't been in this area for a while. Unless she kept her internal map fresh in her mind her, "beacon", for locations started to wander by a few metres here and there. Also, she wasn't sure whether the new flats had any outward facing CCTV. It was a bit out of the City Centre for her knowledge.

Martin told her not to worry. He was more worried about bumping into any of the disciples patrolling the area. From what Clifford had told him, they didn't like to be seen around, in case the Council got wind they were living there, but now they had the child, security was going to be their main concern. Until they moved him, which he hoped they hadn't done already.

The foot and cycle path led straight down the side of the flats before splitting right and left. They went right, behind the flats, hidden on both sides by overhanging bushes and trees. There were a few street lamps along here, hastily stuck up after a number of attacks in this patch of undeveloped land, but their dim orange light didn't have much effect through the undergrowth. When the bushes on their right gave way to a tall red brick wall, Martin knew they were at the back of the Church.

"Boost!"

Martin put his back to the wall and lifted Hayley up by one foot. She could see the light on in the rear room. Four huge glass windows, a desk, some shelves, a cot, Lewis. Clifford suddenly appeared into view from behind a section of wall. He seemed to be talking to himself, quite animated. Maybe he was on the phone? She couldn't make it out, but she could definitely see the floor and made a quick mental map of the objects and distances before tapping Martin on the head to let her down.

"I see Lewis. Clifford is with him, but no-one else."

"They must be clearing out to leave. At least that's what I'd be doing. Too dangerous to stay now they have the baby. OK, give me time to get round the front. I'll create a diversion to give you the chance to grab him and get the hell…"

They heard a woman's cry, something about, "bloody things", and they saw a silhouette further down the path angrily swatting at overhanging bits of bush. They pressed themselves into areas of darkness and waited for her to pass by. Instead she slowed down as she passed the narrow path heading up the side of the hall. She peered down there for some time, before pulling a roughly folded map from her black jacket pocket and studying it carefully. Once satisfied, she put the map back, then walked closer towards Martin and Hayley. She stood gazing up at the top of the wall, then at eye level, pressing a hand against the red bricks, as if hoping they would disappear.

"Oh, you'd think there would be a back gate," she said to herself.

Martin could just make out Hayley shrugging at him. This woman wasn't leaving.

He tilted his head towards her and Hayley jumped as he came out of the shadows. By the time he was standing in front of the now, very startled, woman, Hayley was already behind her, blocking her way when she instinctively wheeled around to run.

"Can I help you?" asked Hayley.

"Oh God. On no. You're from the Church aren't you? I... I'm..." She took a deep breath and quickly straightened herself, not greatly increasing her small height. "I'm here for the boy. Lewis. I know you have him. I'm here to take him back into Care. I worked out it was you, you know, which means the police will too. So best hand him to me before they get involved, it will be safer for everyone, especially the child."

Martin narrowed his eyes and shared a puzzled look with Hayley.

"Who are you, exactly?" he asked.

She turned to face him.

"The name's Eleanor Cheadham. I'm a Senior Child Protection Officer with Element City Council. I was assigned to look after Lewis before he was kidnapped, and I'm going to get him back, whatever you people do to me."

Hayley was shaking her head and Martin just nodded.

"It's OK, we're not from the Church," she said.

Eleanor looked back and forth between them, slightly confused.

"You're... what?"

They moved next to each other to save Eleanor twisting her neck.

The woman was dressed in black jogging pants, gloves, beanie hat and trainers and had a blue fleece top zipped up to under her chin. It wouldn't have surprised either of them if she had pulled a crowbar from up her sleeve. Her large framed glasses and the wisps of auburn hair poking out from under her hat were the only two hints that she wasn't a professional burglar. Those, and the fact she hadn't the slim build required to squeeze through half-open windows, or to scale drainpipes.

"She's right. We have no affiliation with that place. We're here to get Lewis back. I'm a friend of his father, Ian Randall."

Eleanor seemed to both relax and tense at the same time.

"Oh, my goodness. You know him? Why on earth did he break out of prison? He won't see the boy again in his lifetime..." She looked at them suspiciously. "...

unless you're going to hand Lewis back to him. Is that your intent?"

Martin sighed. Of course, she wouldn't know about Ian yet. That would only be on the news tomorrow.

"No. The boy needs to be in your care."

"But maybe under some better security, you know?" said Hayley.

Eleanor nodded.

"That was the worst moment of my life, when I heard what had happened. I was determined to put things right, but all I heard was, 'let the police handle it'. What would they do? There are Secure Care Centres that are not public knowledge. I know exactly where to take him. My car is parked on the road down there," she pointed back down the pathway.

Martin gestured at the wall.

"So what was your plan then? Did you think you would just be able to walk in there and pick him up?"

Eleanor looked behind her, up at the top of the wall.

"I really don't know what I was thinking. Thought I might sneak in, distract them somehow." She turned back to look at them. "I'm desperate. I'm certain he's in there..."

"Oh yeah, he is alright," said Hayley.

"...I didn't know what else to do."

"OK, I think we've got a new plan," said Martin. "My partner here was going to drop him off at the police station, which as I'm sure you will appreciate carried some risk to her. Not to mention it would have left me to deal with a bunch of pretty pissed off Heroes on my own. If we can get the child to you, can you get him to one of these secure places quickly?"

Eleanor nodded.

"Name it."

Eleanor stared at Hayley, hiding behind her black Venetian eye mask.

"The secure place you're going to take him."

"Well I hardly think I can trust…"

"Same here Mrs."

Eleanor paused for a moment.

"The Coppham Centre, near Spalding."

Hayley nodded.

"Yep, she's legit boss. We're good to go."

"OK, Eleanor, we need you to stay right here. Do NOT move until she comes back with Lewis."

"Got it."

"Better take a quick peek again, see if the coast is clear."

Martin gave Hayley another boost up as Eleanor stepped back to observe.

"Oh crap."

Martin looked up into Hayley's stomach.

"What? What's…"

"Bastard!" She jumped without warning, leaving Martin half crouched, hands out as if checking for rain. He pointed at Eleanor.

"Stay!"

Martin sprinted round the corner into the alleyway. Eleanor could hear his footsteps pounding on the rough tarmac into the distance. Then she was alone.

"Well, that was unexpected," she said to herself.

CHAPTER 48
THE CHURCH OF THE NEW GODS

Clifford closed the door and listened with closed eyes for a moment to the excitement outside. There were footsteps running up and down the stairs, cupboards being flung open and emptied, shouting about who takes what and in which vehicle. When Clifford opened his eyes, he had one hand pressed against the wood of the door and a smile on his face. He turned to the cot that Kevin had set up in the middle of the room to see Lewis standing, hands grasping the bars and looking at him. The laptop was open and powered up on the desk.

"My…" he laughed to himself, "..my God. Because that is what you are. You are here before me, I…" Clifford let go of the door and brought his hand to cover his mouth. "I am overwhelmed." It took a while before he could compose himself, to stop the thoughts swirling around in his head. He walked over to the cot as Lewis stared up at him, his little legs occasionally twisting as he kept himself upright. "You are more beautiful than I imagined. Oh dear, can I say that? Am I allowed to? I find I am unsure of myself before you. I find myself doubting my own words. I guess I would have been much the same had I met you when you were last with us." Lewis got tired of standing and sat down cross-legged.

Sweat formed between the lines in Clifford's forehead, a shrill whine entered his voice.

"I have been trying to ease your passage into this world for years. The research I have done into powered children and their parents, into which types of powers give rise to which powers in their offspring, what level of power, age of manifestation. I tried to find similar classifications to your original parents, tried to birth you several times with types as closely matched as I could find, but... but you don't fit any pattern I had looked at. The son of a physically mutated power and a non-powered mother. What kind of combination is that? Is it random? After all my studies? Were you eluding me, or simply not ready to be born?"

Lewis tugged at his pyjama legs, rolling the material between his fingers.

Clifford broke into a smile and rubbed the tension from his face.

"But you're here now. You have finally made your way to me, my Creator." He stepped over the cot and held his hands in the air above Lewis. "I... I can almost feel your power around you. The very atoms in my body stir at your presence. I am truly blessed my Creator. Blessed. I..."

Clifford slid to his knees as his body suddenly shook with tears. He looked away, wiping his eyes on his sleeve, before looking into the cot. "I am sorry you have to see me this way, but I have waited for so long to meet you. I have been through so much. Sacrificed so much. You… you would not wish to know the things I have done in your name so that this moment could come to pass. But it has. And you are here now. You will grow to learn your true place in the world with my help. We are all ready for you. We have prepared for this for years."

He glanced away. His hands, his forearms resting on the sides of the cot, were trembling. He rubbed his thumb against his fingers to try to make them stop as his breathing quickened.

"But I need to be strong for you. I… I am ashamed to admit that I am weak. I need your blessing to be able to carry you through this world. It is for you I ask this, not for me." He shuffled closer to the cot, straightening up from his knees, leaning further in to hold Lewis by his sides. Clifford spoke weakly. "I need power." Tears weaved their way down his face, dropping off his chin, soaking into the blanket. "I need to have power. To look after you. All my life I knew I should have it. My sister was taken from us because she was blessed. I was tested, and… nothing. Blank. Empty. USELESS!"

Lewis stared at him with large eyes.

"Useless." Clifford hastily pushed up the boy's t-shirt before pressing his hands on either side of his belly. "But you can make me useful. You are my Creator. You control the very atoms themselves, make anything, CHANGE anything. Change me! Make me strong so I can serve you as I KNOW I CAN. I want to. Please." His voice shook.

Lewis was looking down at the man's hands on him, confused.

"Come on! MAKE ME BETTER! I am nothing without you! I've spent years searching for you, sacrificed so much. At the very least you can give me this? Bless me!"

Lewis stared at him with a tiny frown.

"Why can't you? Why won't you? What have I done wrong for you? BLESS ME! BLESS ME YOU STUPID CHILD!". He lifted the boy in the air, shaking him like a broken radio.

"You can go fuck yourself."

Clifford gaped in shock, holding the now crying boy at arms length before twisting his head to the side in time to see Hayley's fist split his nose open. He let go of Lewis to clutch at his face. Hayley dived to catch the boy, and quickly rolled to her feet before grabbing a blanket from the cot and wrapping him up. Clifford was staggering backwards, bent over forward, blood pouring from between his fingers.

"No! NO! He's mine! I need Him!"

"He owes you nothing." Then they were gone.

***

Eleanor nearly screamed when Hayley suddenly appeared inches from her, a burst of air whipping at her clothes.

"Damn it! We told you not to move, I almost jumped inside you there!"

Eleanor started to shake with the shock.

"I'm sorry, I didn't know."

"Look, take him."

The night gloom, combined with the pale light from the lamps along the path, made it hard to see anything at first, but then she caught the glint from his eyes as Hayley held forward a crying boy wrapped in a blanket. Eleanor quickly took hold of him. One of his arms came free and wrapped itself around her bosom as she pressed her cheek against the top of his head.

"OK, get to your car and get out of here quick. There are going to be some serious powers coming after him in a very short time. We'll hold them off as long as we can while you get him to safety."

"I promise." She looked around into the dark behind Hayley. "Where's the other one?"

"Holding them off, now go!"

Eleanor quickly nodded and with one arm under his bottom and the other forearm pressed against his back, hand cradling his head to her chest, she scampered back down the way she came with Lewis. Hayley watched until she couldn't see or hear her any more. Then there was shouting and the noise of something breaking from inside the Church.

"You've started without me?"

***

Clifford howled and fell to his knees, blood streaming down inside his sleeves, curling out from between his fingers and spattering across the floorboards where it quickly soaked in. The door flung open and Grant ran towards him. He spotted the empty cot and the blood and Clifford on the floor and had trouble putting together a scenario to explain it all.

"Cliff?"

He said nothing. He was on his knees, one hand on his face, layered with blood, the other on the floor to steady himself as he shook, trapped somewhere between rage and fear. Grant reached the cot and looked inside. He didn't know why, he could see it was empty from the doorway.

"Cliff? What the fuck hap..."

"SHE TOOK IT! Some teleporting bitch took it. HIM. Took The Creator for herself. Find Him! We can't lose Him, not now."

"Got it." Grant ran back to the doorway where Emily and Kevin had appeared.

"Oh God, Clifford!" She went to run to help him but Grant stopped her.

"The Creator is gone, a Hero took Him, teleporter. I need you to split into twos and scour the streets around the Church. I'll get in touch with my Council contact, just in case He reappears at an assessment centre. She can't have jumped far and there are limited places she can go. Get to it!"

"But if she's a teleporter she could be anywhere in the City, or beyond!"

The other disciples were already in the corridor behind them and started to split into groups.

"But if she isn't, if she's nearby, then we need to start looking! Come on guys, we haven't got time to squabble, let's go."

"I'll save you the trouble."

They all went silent and moved to the sides of the corridor. Near the front of the hall by the table stood a large figure wearing a black leather jacket, dark trousers and a balaclava. Grant's eyes widened.

"Oh no," he turned to see Clifford on his feet and walking towards the door. "No! Stay in there. Too dangerous. We'll deal," he shut the door on Clifford as Kevin stepped forward.

"I've got the boy," said the figure.

Kevin walked faster as Claire and Richie formed behind him. Emily ghosted and followed at the back. They reached the end of the partition wall and stopped as they entered the hall.

"Give Him back to us."

The figure didn't move.

"He's not yours to have."

"Yours neither. What makes you think you know what's in the best interests of The Creator? Do you worship Him?"

"I only know what's in the best interests of a ten month old boy, and that doesn't include being passed around like a trophy."

The air started to ripple around Kevin's hands.

"How dare you speak about Him like that!"

"How dare you treat him like that! He's only a child."

"Give him back to us now,." said Claire.

"If you want him, you'll have to go through me first."

"My pleasure," said Kevin, smirking. He clapped his hands together in front of him, blasting a shockwave down the length of the aisle. It tore posters and picture frames from the walls and pillars before it hit the table display and ripped it into chunks of wood that rattled off the walls like bingo balls in a tombola.

"Damn it!"

Martin had ducked to the side behind a bench with plenty of time to spare, having seen that coming a mile off. That Kevin might have a powerful blast on him but he made it very obvious when he was about to use it. There was no time to get cocky though. He scurried along the back of the seat, bent over, and hoped that Hayley was still with him.

"There he is!"

Bright flashes burst in the side of his eyes and he was lifted off the floor as a series of lines of energy tore through the air around him. He landed against the outer wall under a window, several smashed benches falling from the air on top of him.

"We've got him now," he heard one of them say.

"Not yet you haven't," he thought to himself as he spread his arms, grabbed the back of one of the benches and launched it horizontally towards the voices and footsteps. There were shouts and a scream and the air trembled in his ears as Kevin reacted instinctively, sending random bursts of shockwaves into the hall in front of him. They tore like tornadoes through the bench, ripping it into pieces, spraying wood dust everywhere. One wave cracked through a pillar, another hit high above Martin as he flung himself low to the ground, erasing a curved line of glass from the window. Bits of bench collided with the walls, one catching Claire on her leg, knocking her over.

"Mine!" said Richie, grabbing another bench by one end and, lifting it high above him, before running with it down the central aisle towards Martin. He swung it down hard. Martin had only just got to his knees as he saw the dark wooden line bear down on him. He pressed his two fists together and held them over his head as the long bench crashed and split over him. Grabbing the broken end he stood up, stepped back enough to get his foot up and into the raw end of splintered wood and kicked hard away from him. The other end buried itself in Richie's stomach and sent him flying backwards, slamming into the base of the stage. Then the lights went out and everyone was confused.

"Hey, you didn't think it was going to be this easy did you?"

CHAPTER 49
THE CHURCH OF THE NEW GODS

You had been waiting for the noise of fighting to die down before you went in, when you saw a girl appear out of nowhere by the corner wall and smash a power junction box to pieces with a mallet. Funny how the more unusual things you see, the more normal they become. You've learned to expect strange things to happen around you, now your eyes have been opened. You have noticed things have been strained here, falling apart even. Clifford was overly emotional earlier, very unlike him. Was he losing control? Unsure of himself? You weren't. You could see the risk and knew Jenny had to be killed to protect the mission. It was obvious from the moment it came from Clifford's lips. You see things. That's what you do. That's your power. Clifford just had to trust you to get things done right.

Then there was this. You tidy one mess up and you return to find another. Who was this girl? Who else was she with? Why were Heroes attacking the Church anyway? Unless they were villains, wanting the Child for themselves. In which case, how did they know He was here?

Somebody has slipped up somewhere and you know it wasn't you. You get out of your car and walk over to the front door. It's open. You can see broken wood and glass on the floor inside. You can't avoid it, but then no-one is going to hear it above the shouts and noises of destruction. And even if they did they are all occupied with the unwanted visitors. You crunch over the floor and move quickly to the side wall behind the pillars. It's very dark, only some vague street light coming through the windows. You see odd curves of movement in the hall. Fast. You hear a punch. That must have hurt. The legs of a bench scrape across the floor as someone falls against it. You are almost blinded by flashes of light, peculiar arcs of ragged energy that sweep the length of the hall. A scream. But you know you're safe. You quickly walk down the side of the hall, ignoring the noises to your left.

There is a crash and a shout as a large man and several pieces of wood slide across your view. You stop dead in your tracks as he hits the wall on your right. You hear the sound of bricks moving. He scampers to his feet before launching himself past the pillars and out of your view again, never even noticing you were there. You can't help but smile to yourself, then hurry to the safety of the corridor down the side of the stage. You hear people above you, people shouting, someone on the stairs trying to see something. You slip past and reach Clifford's office. You open the door and are surprised to see lights on. There is a battery powered lantern sitting on his desk and a new laptop is next to it running off its own power, the screen giving out a cool blue glow. A cot sits empty in the centre of the room. Clifford is running between his desk and the bookshelves, gathering up papers and books, stacking them in piles, stuffing them into three different sized backpacks, one on his chair, one on the desk, a larger one, that looks like it could be used for a month long camping trip, sits on the floor and keeps tipping over.

He grabs the front end of a magazine storage holder and pulls. It rips, sending thin magazines sprawling across the floor. He curses out loud, scooping them into his arms like fallen babies.

Suddenly he senses the door is open, probably from the louder noises outside, and looks up at you.

"Harvey! Christ, thank the Creator. Close the door. Close it." He waves his arms frantically and you shut the door behind you. "Help me with this!"

You are concerned. You go over and pick up a few of the magazines before putting them on a neat pile on the desk. You see a bloody sheet from the cot on the desk. Then you see blood caking Clifford's face, slowly tricking from his nose.

"What happened Clifford?"

"They took Him! They took the Child away from me. We have to find Him." He stops moving and points at you. "You need to find Him. While we have them distracted out there you need to find Him for us."

He goes back to sorting papers into backpacks. He runs back over to the shelves, cursing out loud, he can't find something.

"Why are you leaving?"

"It's not safe here any more. They know where we are. Those... bastards out there have brought everyone's eyes onto us now. We have to move on. Have to find the Child and move on." He talks to himself more than he talks to you, leafing through plastic folders with stickers on. Things are falling apart. This is no time to run.

"No Clifford, we have to stay here and finish what we started."

"What? What the hell are you talking about? We're DONE here! Go find the Child. The teleporter took Him, she can't be far."

"You keep sending me away to do this and that Clifford, but I am needed here right now. We need to stay here and carry on our work. I know this."

"You don't know anything! Can't you see what's happening?" Clifford shakes a handful of folders at you, "We're exposed now, we have to hide, to get somewhere safe."

"No, that's not the right thing to do right now. I know what needs to be done Clifford. That's my power, remember? I understand things."

Clifford suddenly starts laughing. You think he's cracking up under the pressure.

"You have no fucking power you stupid, dull little man. Grant told me the moment you came in the door. You have nothing, unless you count gullibility as a power. I only told you that because I knew you needed to hear something meaningful and I needed someone to do the shit for me that I couldn't have any of my lot seen doing," he thumbed through the wall to the fight next door.

Now you know he's lost it. He stares at you, puffy eyes glowing orange from the lantern light, brown blood smeared across his chin and cheeks, a bright shining raw cut of flesh curling down the front of his nose.

"You're nothing. You're a powerless freak like me. If The Creator himself wants nothing to do with me, then He's not going to give a waste of space like you any powers."

"I have powers. You told me I..."

"You're NOTHING I tell you! Half of a man who never could. That's all you are, as useless as I am! Now if you're not going to find the Child you can fuck off and leave us all alone. Go on!" He turns away from you and grabs two more boxes of papers from the bottom shelf.

Of course you have powers. You always have, you just never understood them. Either this is another sort of test or Clifford can't be relied upon to complete the mission any more. You watch him for a moment, waiting for the big reveal, but no. He's lost it. You know what must be done. As he tries to jam a poorly gathered armful of periodicals into the larger backpack on the floor you take the koala bear letter opener from the pen jar and with a thrust, jam it into his back. It goes deep. He doesn't scream. He must be too shocked to. He just wails quietly and collapses to the floor, rolling onto his back, one arm twisted under him to clutch at the pain. As he does so, you kneel over him and punch the letter opener up under his left ribcage. He starts to cry out but it is cut off as you pull it out.

You feel warmth trickling over your hand and soaking into your suit sleeve. You'll need to burn that. As you stand up you see his body relax and his head rolls to the side a bit. You are sorry for having to do this, but you know what needs to be done, even if Clifford doesn't. Didn't. You take the sheet off the desk and try to wipe as much of the blood off as you can before wrapping the letter opener in it. You'll need to burn that too.

The glow of the laptop screen entrances you. It feels like something important. You walk round and sit in Clifford's chair. You push your finger across the track pad, (how you hate those things), and slowly piece together what you see. Some type of database of names and addresses. Next to some of them are aliases. Powered aliases. Most are blank. You see the database name overlaid on the Government crest: "Innate Powers Register: Element City Sub-Set - CONFIDENTIAL". A warm feeling hits you. It starts in your stomach then rises up through your chest. It almost suffocates you, chokes you, but then it hits your head and you smile. This is it. This is what you need to do. It's like Clifford said, sometimes people are useful, sometimes they are not, and sometimes they get in the way of people trying to do good things. Like those ones fighting the disciples next door.

None of those people are useful, they are all just in the way. You just need someone who is prepared to do the things others aren't. Something crashes against the wall opposite and one of the bookshelves, now top-heavy with all the magazines emptied from the bottom, topples over, crashing onto the cot and smashing it to pieces. Well. That's that then. You close the laptop and tuck it under your arm. You are going to leave this room and walk out the same way you came in and nobody will notice you, because that's how it's meant to be. And besides, you have a lot of work to do.

CHAPTER 50
THE CHURCH OF THE NEW GODS

The scream cut through all the fighting and shouting, putting everyone to a halt where they stood. Martin had one foot up on a bench, holding Robbie by his T-shirt, about to deliver another blow to his face while Claire was readying an energy blast at him as she hid behind a pillar.

Hayley had leapt on Kevin's back, one hand over his eyes, the other fending off his arms as he tried to aim behind him and deliver a concentrated shockwave to her face, or any part of her at all.

Grant couldn't see much in the darkness, cursing his failing eyesight, and was hiding at the side of the stage, keeping his head down to avoid the flying pieces of furniture. Mark was crouched down, squatting in the corner by the front window, hands over his ears. It was too loud to concentrate to whisper to anyone and he was glad the noise suddenly stopped. Emily was the one who had screamed and came running through from the office to witness the frozen diorama of chaos. She could barely get the words out of her choking throat.

"Clifford's dead!"

Hayley jumped next to Martin as he and Robbie shared a confused look.

"It wasn't me. Or her. We've both been in here fighting you." He let go of the boy as everyone took cautious steps away from each other.

"You can't mean, 'dead', Emily?"

"There's blood everywhere..."

"Well, I broke his nose earlier, but I didn't think that would..."

"No, he's been stabbed. He's gone." Emily slumped onto a nearby seat, shaking with tears.

"Yeah, that wasn't me," Hayley shook her head firmly.

Martin and Hayley watched as it dawned on each of the people in the semi-darkness in front of them that their leader, their mentor, was gone. The fight was over. Everything had been superseded by this.

Kevin suddenly bolted round the side of the stage. They heard a quiet, "Oh God", from round the corner and one-by-one they followed him, in various states of hurrying, depending on how much they actually wanted to believe what they were about to witness was true. Martin whipped round as a shoe scuffing on the floor alerted him to Mark still being in the hall. The tall, gaunt figure slowly walked behind the pillars towards the side of the stage. He kept glancing over at the two of them nervously. Just before he went out of sight he turned round and stared at them both, before saying in a deep voice: "This is no place for you now," and disappearing into the darkness.

All they could hear were mixed sobs echoing from the room behind the stage.

"Doesn't look like they're going to be chasing after us, or Lewis, any time soon. I think we should go now."

Hayley nodded, and in a flash of crimson they were outside on the path at the back of the building. They looked around, but it was quiet.

"I hope she got him to safety," said Hayley.

"Yeah, me too."

They surveyed the damage to their costumes and tentatively stretched out the parts of their bodies that hurt as they processed the unexpected end to the fight.

"Hey boss, how did she work out Lewis was here anyway?"

In the rush to rescue the boy, neither of them had had much time for spare thoughts.

"Dunno. She didn't say."

Everything seemed suddenly much quieter.

"We didn't ask."

CHAPTER 51
ST ANNE'S HOSPITAL, ELEMENT CITY

"Carl Morrison?"

Carl lazily turned his head from the rain-smeared window towards the door. His face was mostly covered in bandages. Any exposed skin was swollen and bruised either from the attack or from one of the two operations he'd had since. He clocked the two plain-clothed men were police straight away and turned back, preferring the window view. The tall officer turned, said something to a uniformed officer standing outside who nodded, and closed the door behind them.

He motioned his colleague to sit the on other side of the bed. As they sat down, Carl looked up at the ceiling.

"My name is DCI Forrester and this is DI Burns. The doctors tell me you've recovered enough to speak to us, which is good news, as we thought we might lose you for a while. We need to ask you a few questions about baby Lewis."

Carl said nothing, just swallowed against a dry throat, the motion tugging the tender, healing skin across his chest, making him wince.

"Let us refresh your mind and get you up to speed on what you've missed while you've been asleep, then we can start going through the details, OK?"

Carl sighed but said nothing.

"You guys, The Real Heroes or Hero Killers, however you prefer to be known, were keeping him at the Oak & Archer. You were attacked and he was taken. Remember that?"

Carl swallowed again.

"Two of your friends were killed, Jed Morgan and Bobby Fairbrass. Did you see who did that?"

Carl nodded.

"Savage."

"Ian Randall, yes. We found him there."

"You did?"

"He was dead," said DI Burns.

"He wasn't..." Carl shook his head.

"So I'm guessing that happened after you were knocked unconscious."

"But how..."

"There were other people there, people with powers. Someone who could create vibrations in the air, enough to send you flying backwards, and to kill Bobby and Ian Randall. Someone who interfered with Rebecca Kirk's memories, made her think Ian Randall killed you all, and possibly a third person, a girl, we're really not sure on that one as Rebecca has been... difficult to get information out of. We had hoped you could fill in some blanks for us, and for her"

Carl turned to look at a cup of water at head height on the bedside table. He couldn't reach over with his left arm as it was strapped up in oily organic bandages and throbbed in pain, keeping time with his heartbeat. His right arm was too stiff, stitches too tight to let him bend at the angle needed to grab it. Forrester spotted his dilemma, picked up the cup and held it to his lips for him, letting him drink until he dropped his head back into the pillows, breathing hard with the effort.

"I want to see her. Why won't you let me see her?"

"She's receiving treatment," said DI Burns, "at a psycho-psychiatry unit. She's had a breakdown, something to do with having her memories altered during a traumatic event?"

DCI Forrester nodded.

"Yeah, something like that anyhow. I don't know about that stuff myself. What I do know is those bastards fucked her up Carl. They took the boy and messed Rebecca up in the head. If you can remember anything about what they looked like, anything they said, you have to tell us."

Carl let his head sink back into the pillow as a tear ran from his eye. He had spent every moment since he awoke four days ago trying to remember all the details of what happened. It started off fine. He was in the basement of the Pub with Bobby and Rebecca. Then he realised he couldn't see Lewis and started feeling panicky. Then everything was pitch black, pure emptiness of thought, into which random flashes of horrific things flung themselves, claws poking out of a chest, Bobby screaming, The Savage emerging from the shadows, a pair of twitching hands bouncing on the old floorboards, the panic of wondering if Lewis was safe, the feeling of air being rammed down his throat, choking, choking...

"I can't. I just remember The Savage. He cut Bobby's hands off! I don't remember anyone else. You've not found Lewis?"

"No, he's still missing."

The panic returned.

"He was a good kid. I think... I think Jed was going to do something to him. I wasn't going to let him. I couldn't let him hurt the boy. I looked after him. Me and Rebecca. We made sure he was OK."

"We know, Rebecca was able to tell us that much. Please Carl, we know the doctor's have said you're suffering from amnesia, and you've been out for weeks while they fixed you up, but anything at all - doesn't have to be something you've seen, could be a sound, a smell - anything that could help find these people."

Carl started shaking gently as both eyes watered.

"This is all my fault. Oh God..."

Forrester and Burns shared a look as Burns shrugged.

"This is my fault. The names, the baby. Bobby would never have done any of this if it hadn't been for me. I just wanted to impress him. Show him I could be useful..."

"The names?"

Carl looked at Forrester.

"The people we battered the shit out of. Killed. I gave them the names."

Burns made a, "sucking in air", face in Forrester's peripheral vision.

"Look Carl, we know about the people your group attacked. You never got involved physically though, did you? You were the lookout, the distraction. We've seen all the CCTV footage and the reports. Like you say, you were just trying to impress Bobby, we get it. As for the names... we'll come to that later. All that matters right now is the boy."

"He's right Carl. What you did to those people, taking Lewis from the Assessment Centre, they're not important at..."

"I didn't."

The men paused.

"Didn't what?"

"Take Lewis. From that Centre."

The officers paused again.

"Well... we don't have to worry about that yet..."

Carl could sense the change in their body language.

"I'm telling you, I never stole him! I found him."

"Found him?" said DI Burns, screwing up his face. "Where, in a skip? No no, you took him from his room. The Boyden Bridge Secure Assessment Centre, remember? Don't tell me you've forgotten that. You got in through the fire escape..."

Forrester made a move with his hand to stop Burns talking.

"No, I found him at my nans! Mum left him there while she went to work."

It was DCI Forrester's turn to screw his face up in confusion.

"I thought Mum must be looking after him. Temporarily you know. She works with those types of kids. That's how I found them all you see, she's got part of the Hero Register list thing on her laptop. Taped the password to the bottom in case she forgot it, stupid cow..."

"Your mother..." Forrester pulled out a notepad and quickly flicked through the pages, "...we've had some trouble trying to figure out who she is, you have no next of kin details anywhere. You don't live with her...?"

"Don't want anything to do with her."

"Look, what's her name for a start Carl?"

"Bitch took back her maiden name when she split with dad. Doesn't call herself Morrison. It's Cheadham, Eleanor Cheadham."

EPILOGUE
A6 AUTOROUTE DU SOLEIL, PARIS TO LYON, NR. JUNCTION 24

The sun blanched the concrete road a pale orange, the white lane lines cutting through it like strips of ice. Balls of collected, dry grass spun into the air in the vortex of the passing car, before settling gently back in the gutter. All the windows were open, a glorious cooling wind rushing through the interior. Eleanor's thin blouse top fluttered around her upper arms, the sun shining off her sunglasses. She kept glancing out across the fields of two-feet high green plants laid out in neat rows across to the hills and down to the red-roofed houses ahead of her. Were they grapes? Runner beans? She couldn't tell at this distance, but she smiled anyway at the thought of a nice white wine at a sunny table outside some small bar hidden away on a back street. Lewis was quiet in the back, staring out the window, having an amazing adventure. He pointed at the fields and made a noise. Eleanor checked on him in the rear view mirror. He was fine. She sighed, realising the wine would have to wait. After all, she had a new responsibility now.

"This is going to be our new home Lewis. You'll like it here. I used to come here as a child myself, but I've not been back for many years."

He was watching her in the mirror intently.

"My mum used to bring us here, she loved it too. She can't remember it now of course. Can't remember much our mum." She looked back out at the road. It was clear. She passed a road sign indicating "1km" to the next junction. "Must remember the right junction now. I have this part planned out at least!"

Lewis was looking at the fields again.

"Sorry about leaving you with her while I went to work. She may be senile but I knew she wouldn't hurt you. But then you went missing, and oh... I didn't know what to do. I was beside myself with worry because I knew what Carl's friends were into. *He'd* never have hurt you, no no, no matter how much he hated *me* he wouldn't have done a thing to you. Those others in that video though..."

Eleanor shook her head to clear out the horrible imaginings.

"And then I watched as your father and those strange Church people took you from that pub. Well, your father never came out. I fear the worst for him I'm afraid. And Carl..."

She went silent, listening to the sound of the car on the tarmac.

"No, he made his bed... so he has to lie in it. Nothing more I can do for him now."

Lewis made "buh" sounds with his mouth and carefully inspected bunny's ear.

"You see Lewis, none of them really cared about you, about what you needed. It was all about them; what they needed you *for.*"

She passed what looked like a small industrial park, then moved into the middle lane to miss the junction as an overpass whipped by.

"No, no, I knew from the moment I saw you, that I was the only one who could look after you. There was no Care Team, no foster family, no Church that knew what to do with you. Only me. I know how to bring you up right, and that's what I'm going to do."

She stayed in the middle lane, following the signs for Lyon. The fields here were dry, baked in the sun, outlined by dark green shrubs and trees. The motorway split again and the trees made a loud rushing noise as they closed in on the road. A blue sign said, "Lyon 155". Eleanor sighed peacefully.

"Only Auntie Eleanor knows what's right for you dear. That's why I'm the best at what I do."

***

ABOUT THE AUTHOR

Thank you for reading KILLING GODS!

If you could leave a review on your favourite ebook website that would be fantastic, or you can contact me via Facebook, Twitter or email (see below).

This book took me about the same length of time to write as POWERLESS despite being 25k words shorter. It was a harder one to write, even though I had all the events and character arcs planned out beforehand. I think it was because there were more characters involved and I had to make sure they all got similar amounts of time to be meaningful to the story and not just background clutter. There were a couple of chapters I ended up not writing as they wouldn't have furthered the story in any meaningful way. I also had to alter the order of a few of them and do a spot of re-writing after researching UK law, specifically what would happen to Charles. Originally I had Martin and Maria having to give evidence in court and talking about the aftermath of it, but if you admit to a crime there is no jury trial, just usually a single sentencing hearing then you're taken straight off to jail.

This story was originally going to appear later in the series, but I changed the order when it became clear to me that this story fitted into the overall arc better as the second book. POWERLESS was about guilt and powerlessness, about the choice of whether to hide away or to act. So this book had to be about self-belief. Martin has only just come back into Heroics after hiding away for years. He doesn't believe in himself yet, he's conflicted about what he should do. I needed a story where he came to realise that he had to make a choice about where he was going from here on in.

Of course, all the other characters are tied to their beliefs as well. Clifford preaches as if he is powered, but when it becomes clear he isn't, and asks Lewis to give him powers, we see he believes he should be a Hero too, like his sister. Whether it's guilt at being normal or selfishness for his own personal gain, I guess we'll never know now. Bobby believes Heroes are so dangerous he is willing to kill them to make his point (well, at least older ones less likely to fight back successfully). Eleanor believes herself to be the best at her job, in fact her self-belief is so firm she *knows* she is the only person who can help Lewis. On the opposite end of the scale, Harvey has no self-belief at all, no sense of self-worth, just a lack of empathy bordering on psychopathy kept in check by the bullying of his wife and co-workers. When Clifford decides to take advantage of his desire to believe he can be more than he is, he has no idea what he is unleashing.

At least I hope that was all obvious enough from what I wrote? All comments, and your own thoughts welcome.

So, onto writing the third book now, and believe me, it's going to be a good one :)

Tony.

My Mailing List
   www.eepurl.com/biiEr1
My blog
   www.hungryblackbird.com
Facebook
   www.facebook.com/TonyCooperAuthor
Twitter
   @_tonycooper
Email
   tonycooperauthor@gmail.com
Amazon
   amazon.com/author/tonycooper
Smashwords
   www.smashwords.com/profile/view/TonyCooper
Goodreads
   www.goodreads.com/user/show/7234993

OTHER TITLES

POWERLESS
The first book in the 'Powerless' series

When the best friend of a retired superhero is killed by another power, Martin must drag himself out of his self-imposed isolation to find out who is responsible. In doing so he finds himself digging up a past he would rather forget, risking exposing the secret of why the team split up and destroying all their lives in the process.

KILLING GODS
The second book in the 'Powerless' series

When the baby son of a physically mutated eighties villain goes missing from protective care, he goes on a rampage to try and find him.

In his way stand a Child Protection Officer following her heart above her duty, a violent anti-hero group desperate for media attention, a seemingly benevolent hero-worshipping cult and Martin and Hayley struggling to work out who they can trust.

THE RESURRECTION TREE AND OTHER STORIES
A collection of nine short stories about life, death and consequences.

A mix of creepy, disturbing contemporary fantasy and science fiction stories in one book.

HIGGS & SOAP: GALAXY DELIVERY
A galactic romp featuring killer cyborgs, sneak thieves and undeclared goods.

It was supposed to be a simple, straightforward job: transport a data card from one solar system to another and get paid. But it turns out that the data on the card makes it the most valuable item in the galaxy. With highly trained killers and thieves after it, the only people standing in their way are Higgs and Soap, and they really, really don't want to die.

Made in the USA
Charleston, SC
06 January 2016